Dark Echo

By
Sharleen Johnson

ISBN **1590885511**
First Published by Wings ePress
February 2006

Cover art by my son, the photographer,
Michael Wooten
www.MemphisWootens.com

Author 's website
www.sharleenjohnson.com

Prologue
April 13, 1959
Oxford, Mississippi

Even with his back to her, he could feel the heated anger boiling from his wife as she stood in the doorway of their tiny kitchen.

"Salvatore? I found these cuttings from the newspapers in your underwear drawer. What's the meaning?" She spoke in English but with a heavy lyrical accent.

"Nothing you would understand, woman," he responded without looking at her. "Put my things back where you found them."

"I'll do nothing of the sort. I want an explanation. You have every article on all those poor little children who were murdered. Why?"

Salvatore Varossa erupted from the kitchen chair so swiftly it tipped over backwards with a loud clatter against the linoleum floor. One large bony hand clamped cruelly around his wife's neck, while the other tightened into a menacing fist held aloft. Shocked by his outburst, she dropped all the papers and began clawing at his painful grip.

"Why? Why you ask?" He lapsed into his native Italian tongue, his voice low and gravely. "Ester, it's something you could never understand. It's a chore I must do. The voice of God is loud, strong and very clear. I must obey His will." His chin trembled as he experienced a fleeting moment of weakness, but his resolve quickly firmed again. "And...it's because a man likes to keep trophies of his exploits, that's why."

When he released his handhold on her neck, she fell to the floor sobbing. "You? You killed all those innocent little children?"

"There is no innocence in this world. Evil begets evil."

From the corner of one eye, he could see his ten-year-old daughter, Catherine, dart behind the sofa. That his streak of violence had recently grown more pronounced was known by every member of his family, even the cat. Catherine was a simple-minded child probably born of someone else's weak seed, certainly not his own. All the children Ester had borne for him had died in their infancy...except this one.

While his wife huddled in the corner, Salvatore kneeled onto the floor and painstakingly, almost lovingly, picked up each of the newspaper articles, read them aloud, one-by-one, then folded them and placed them in an envelope. But, it was the report in today's paper that upset him more than his wife's untimely discovery. He ransacked the kitchen drawers to find the scissors and carefully cut the item from the newspaper and reread it several times, once out loud.

Desperate to find the killer, the City Police of Oxford announced today that they have sought the advice of a self-professed psychic, Rainy Skies, Native-American wife of noted cotton exporter Jonathan Wingate. Rainy Skies, descendant of several generations of Chickasaw tribal shaman, is said to have the unique power to see faces and feel emotions when touching objects that have belonged to or been touched by the killer or his victims. Pressed by angry citizens, local police have reached a point where they are willing to try anything, even the supernatural, to bring this heinous killer to justice. Mrs. Rainy Skies Wingate, who spoke from her home at 703 Azalea Lane, has graciously accepted the invitation to meet with the detectives tomorrow morning.

Salvatore carefully folded the item and placed it in the envelope. He tucked in his shirttail, spit on his fingers and slicked his thick black hair away from his face. His mind raced at a furious pace searching for a solution. There seemed to be only one. He climbed the narrow stairs to the bedroom he shared with his wife and opened the top drawer of his dresser. First, he hid the envelope beneath his socks, then found his prized hunting knife, kept safely stowed in its scabbard. He removed the blade from its sheath. Little beads of blood sprang from his thumb as he tested the sharpness. *Buono.*

He whistled softly as he strolled out of the house and down the street. It was almost too warm for a light jacket, but the breast pocket was the perfect hiding place. The fingers of his right hand traced the pattern of his weapon concealed beneath the fabric. Empowerment calmed him and tamped down his rage into a manageable emotion.

Chapter One
August, Present day
Memphis, Tennessee

The black cast iron skillet slipped from her hand and crashed to the floor, spilling the yellow crumbles of scrambled eggs across the red brick-patterned linoleum floor. The blinding pain in her chest was overwhelming, sucking the breath from her lungs as the burning sensations spiked down her left arm. Bathed in suffocating terror, she folded to the floor, hit her knees, then pitched forward onto her face. She was afraid of dying, and yet somehow managed to yank on the phone cord and drag the instrument within reach. Nine-one-one. The frightening wait for help. Lights, voices, oxygen, needles. The rocky ride in the ambulance. Sirens. White-coated people rushed around, barking harsh commands, asking stupid questions, but they couldn't halt the excruciating pain, or stop her from dying, from slipping away from this world into another without the solace of a comforting hand. Her whispered call for help emerged as a piercing scream—

—a noise so chilling it tore Dannah Wingate from sleep. Gasping for air, she bolted upright and tried to moderate the chaotic thumping of her heart by breathing deeply, slowly. In. Out. In. Out. Soggy curls clung to her forehead and neck as she tried to shake the nightmarish dream from her sleep-shrouded mind. Convulsive tremors wrenched her slender frame as she crawled from the tangled bed covers and sat on the edge of her bed. The small electric clock glowed a green 11:45pm. It seemed she had fought the dream throughout the entire night, when in truth, she had only been in bed for thirty minutes.

In spite of the air conditioning, her thin cotton nightgown was plastered damply to her body, portraying a voluptuous image in the remote glow of the August moon spilling through the bedroom window, but there was no one to enjoy the view. Dannah lived alone.

For the past few weeks she had been plagued by unpredictable dreams and random thoughts of death and occasionally violence and the ordeal was both frightening and exhausting. The recurring images sometimes came as night dreams—like tonight—while others came spontaneously, materializing without provocation; but they were so striking, with realism so detailed, they made her feel as though the terrifying events were happening to her. Tonight's dream was more genuine and more detailed and explicit than any previously experienced. The heat from the stove was still vivid in her mind, the weight of the skillet in her hand, the piercing agony in her chest as well as the sharp pain in her joints when she fell to the floor.

Dannah shuddered as her imagination sent an unpleasant tingle grinding down her spine. She massaged the phantom pain in her knees. Even when she was awake, her thoughts were being monopolized by a strangely persistent pull to do something, to go somewhere, but she didn't know what or where.

After shuffling barefoot down the carpeted stairs to the fridge and pouring a glass of milk, she sat down at her kitchen table piled high with computer printouts; photocopies of old court documents and penciled sketches of family trees. Tracing her ancestry had been her hobby for many years. In fact, she was often accused of exhibiting obsessive-compulsive behavior on the subject. She had successfully traced her maternal line. Unfortunately, her mother, Della Taylor, had been an only child begotten of an only child, which meant that Dannah had no aunts, uncles or cousins. Other than one paternal aunt she'd never met, Dannah had been unable to locate a single living relative on either side of her genealogical tree, creating an abysmal sense of isolation.

This must be akin to what Chinese families experience with their rule of one child per family. No brothers or sisters, no aunts and uncles.

The young woman took another swallow of the cold milk then glanced at the huge twelve-month appointment calendar affixed to the fridge door with magnets. She had marked a big red "X" on July tenth. That was the date she had her first dream. It was nearly as frightening as the one which awakened her tonight. That one also involved her own death, but in a far different scenario. In the July dream, she was lying in bed—her surroundings comfortable and familiar—and died more peacefully and without pain or fear. She distinctly remembered a woman's hand reaching out to her from a bright white, but opaque mist. Faces were maddeningly out of sight.

"Foolishness. This is all pure foolishness," she argued with herself.

She needed to cleanse her mind of these disturbing images so she could concentrate on her writing. In the past, she was doggedly persistent chasing after the truth and exposing local corruption with her own unique brand of "go-get-'em" journalism, but lately, because of too little sleep, she was more consumed by lethargy than dedication. Truthfully, her exhaustion extended bone deep.

The inauspicious creditor-wolf would be banging down the door if her inspirations and creativity dried up. Trying to make a living at freelance writing wasn't easy. If all else failed, she could always go back to her old job at the newspaper, but punching a time clock would be a last resort. Although she enjoyed the freedom of being self-employed, she honestly missed the camaraderie of her co-workers.

Dannah finished the milk and as she turned off the kitchen light to return to bed, the shrill ring of the phone exploded into the midnight silence. As she placed the receiver to her ear, her hand trembled slightly with the worry over who would call at such a late hour. "Hello?"

"This is St. Francis Hospital. Are you Dannah Wingate?"

"Yes, I am." Her heart beat stuttered, then escalated.

"Your father, Coleman Wingate, has just been admitted to the Cardiac ICU through the ER. He's had a heart attack."

"Oh my God. Is he okay? Is he alive?"

"Yes, he's in critical, but stable condition. He's asking for you and we think you should come as quickly as possible."

"I'm on my way."

***

The streets of Memphis, Tennessee, were always busy.

The hustle and bustle of her citizens never ceased, even in the dead of night, and especially on Poplar Avenue, just east of the interchange with I-240.

She was ushered into the hushed atmosphere of the cardiac intensive-care unit. Tiny, glass-faced rooms were arranged in a semicircle around the hub of the nurses' station with banks of black-screen monitors alive with dancing icons, jagged lines and ever-changing numbers.

"Wingate is in room four. Right now, he's stable and breathing on his own."

"Daddy?" she whispered softly as she approached his bed.

When Coleman Wingate opened his dark brown eyes, the beeps on his heart monitor quickened. "That my girl?"

"Yes, it's me, Daddy. You okay?"

"Don't reckon I am."

"What happened?" she asked and gently combed her fingers through his thick salt-and-pepper hair.

"I was fixin' me a late night snack—scrambled eggs an' toast—then the pain hit an' I fell. I managed to call 911. By then, I didn't have the strength to call ya."

"Oh, Daddy, you're going to have to listen to me. You can't continue living alone. What would have happened if you couldn't get to the phone?"

He grasped her wrist with surprising strength and pulled her close. The tendons in his neck tightened as his head came away from the pillow. "Listen hard, girl. Ya need to go see your aunt Gova Wingate down in Oxford, Miss'ippi." He paused to suck in a labored breath of air. "She's at 703 Azalea Lane. Phone: 555-1234. She knows, she'll tell ya all about it."

"All about what?"

"You know. Them dreams ya told me about. An' them other things that's been happenin' to ya. I hope it ain't a'ready too late. I was hopin' ya wouldn't get burdened with 'em, but, but, you're next in line." Tears began to spill from his eyes. "Gova knows." He sank back onto the bed, as if the effort to speak had left him totally exhausted.

"Hush, Daddy, hush. Save your strength. We can talk

about this when you're feeling better."

"No, no. Time's runnin' out fer me."

When the beeps began to race in erratic fashion, one of the nurses swept in. "You're upsetting your father, my dear. You have to leave."

"But-but, he was upsetting himself," Dannah protested. "I can calm him down, then I'll just sit in the corner and be quiet. He'll be more comfortable with me here."

"No, I'm sorry. Rules are rules. Visiting hours are posted on the door. You can come back at eight tomorrow morning."

Dannah squeezed her father's hand and kissed his pale, cold cheek. "The nurses say I have to leave and let you rest. I love you, Daddy. Concentrate on getting well. Get a good night's sleep and I'll see you first thing in the morning. We'll talk more about Aunt Gova then." He reached for her hand again, as though reluctant to let her go. When she whispered "I love you," a second time, he managed to respond with a weak, half-smile.

The trip back to her apartment was less hurried as she tried to plan for her father's rehabilitation. He would have to sell his little house in the eastern suburbs and move into an assisted-care facility. There was a nice place just two blocks from where she lived in the midtown Garden District. It would make it easy for her to visit him on a daily basis. Riding her bicycle that distance would give her some much-needed fresh air and exercise. Together, she and her father would turn this bad situation into something good.

Dannah was barely in the door of her apartment when the second devastating phone call came.

Chapter Two
Tuesday following Labor Day
Memphis, Tennessee

The combined hum of voices, ringing phones and the clatter of computer keys greeted Dannah as she stepped from the elevator at the offices of the Memphis Commercial Appeal newspaper where she used to work before launching her career as a freelance writer. A couple of former co-workers called her name and waved an enthusiastic greeting. Truthfully, she missed the tension-filled excitement of working against a daily deadline. She especially loved the challenge of tracking down statements from reluctant city officials and firing questions that made them squirm in their seats. She had been a damned good reporter and had even faced real, physical danger when investigating price-padding in the road-repair division of city government.

Since Pete Jordan's door was ajar, she poked her head into his office. "Have you got a minute?"

"Always got time for my favorite girl. How you holding up?" Pete snuffed out his cigarette, rose from his chair and strode across the carpeted floor.

As they embraced, a jolt of perception unexpectedly coursed through Dannah's mind like rolling thunder. A full and certain awareness of a chronic illness dispersing through his chest sprang clearly to life in her consciousness—

—a black gooey substance creeping inexorably over red and ravaged flesh. Long tentacles of disease, like those on a giant squid, were reaching into tiny crevices seeking to consume and destroy what little healthy tissue remained—

Dannah jerked free of contact as if she'd been jabbed with an electric cattle prod, but Pete didn't seem to notice her recoil. She stammered, "Oh, oh, I'm holding up okay, I guess." Pete, her former boss, was like a surrogate father to her, always there to pick her up when she was down. After the second massive heart attack claimed the life of her father, she had frantically called Pete. The two of them sat up all night talking and drinking coffee at Denny's near the airport. He helped her make the funeral arrangements and stood by her side as the casket was lowered into the ground next to her mother.

Pete wrapped one arm around her shoulders and ushered her to a chair. "Been a helluva bad time for you, hasn't it, hon? Sit down and talk awhile."

The smile she attempted had a wistful shading.

"Been almost a month since your dad died," Pete continued. "You need to keep your mind occupied, start working again and stop moping around like a Gloomy Gus. I've got a new assignment you might like. It's this serial killer business. In case you haven't read the morning paper, there was another one over the Labor Day weekend. That's the sixth. It's got the whole city on its ear."

"Pete, I don't have any connections with the Memphis Police Department. They're tighter than clams on this subject."

"No, no, I was thinking of a sideline story about how those psychological profilers do their work. You know what I mean— white male, a loner, someone who hated his mother. I hear those profiler guys can get really immersed in their work. Almost spooky."

"Sounds interesting, but I'm just not ready yet."

"What happened to the story about the 'Cornbread Mafia' you were working on."

"I got derailed. I needed to go to the Gulf Coast for a few weeks to investigate their attempts to infiltrate casino gambling there. I just couldn't leave Daddy that long. Although I could definitely use the money, my concentration is shot to hell." This time she managed to tweak out a half-smile. "I guess that's a gross understatement. I've spent the last year caring for him and trying to talk him into moving into a retirement community where he wouldn't be alone so much of the time."

"That's all behind you, honey. You should get out more, start living again. You're young and beautiful."

"You're prejudiced."

"Well...maybe." He winked and paused. "You're not dating anyone, are you?"

"No, I'm totally unattached. To be truthful, I've been so busy with Daddy that I haven't had time to even think about dating since I broke up with Philip last year."

"Why not join the gang this afternoon at the Rendezvous for a round of drinks and a few laughs? Remember all the fun we used to have when you worked here?"

"Yes, and it sounds tempting, but I don't think so."

"We hired a new sports-writer guy you might like." He dished out another sly wink. "He's good-looking and he's single."

"Not right now, Pete. It takes a lot of energy to go through that testing, getting-to-know-you, small-talk stage. I'm not up to it. Maybe, in a couple of months. There are too many loose ends to tie up."

"For crying out loud. What's eating you, Dannah? It's not like you to mope around like this. You're usually the peppiest one of the bunch. Always up for something new."

Dannah nervously twisted the strap on her purse, stared at the design on the carpeting for a few seconds, then met his gaze directly. "I've got to talk to somebody. I'm about to come apart at the seams."

"Tell me, what's cooking? I'm always here for you, hon."

"Well, yes, I know that." Dannah scooted to the edge of the chair, uncomfortable revealing—even to Pete—the strange phenomenon that seemed to defy description. Having knowledge of occurrences happening elsewhere and unseen was abnormal. The unsettling emotions were beginning to consume her and had begun to adversely affect her work. "Let me back up to a conversation I had with Daddy two weeks before he died." Pete sat on the corner of his desk giving her his undivided attention. "You see, I told him I was having some strange dreams, sort of like...well, like visions about people, their thoughts and what's happening to them. Maybe you could call it a perception, an insight. I see these things playing out in my mind—almost like a video tape. I don't know how else to describe it." Dannah's hands jerked around nervously as she spoke. "When I told him about it, he got all serious and quiet and said, 'I wondered when it would come to you.'"

"Visions? Dreams? What the hell does that mean? You're hearing voices or something? Having visions about the future? That's crazy talk."

"No, not voices and not the future. Images—like pictures without words. Night dreams, and occasionally during the day. Like when I shake hands with someone, I get slapped in the face with these images."

"You're not going psycho on me, are you? Going over the edge?"

Dannah half expected this negative overreaction from him, but tried to ignore Pete's deep frown of fatherly concern. "No, no, nothing like that. It's difficult to put into ordinary words."

"Maybe you should go see a head doctor. They got medicines now to keep your mind going in the right direction. You know, you've been under a helluva lot of pressure lately, burying your dad. Maybe things are out of whack up here." He tapped the side of his head.

"I'm not whacko, at least I don't think so."

"Maybe you've gotten all hormonal. My wife goes bonkers almost every month."

Dannah rolled her eyes in exasperation. "Pete, please hear me out. Then, on the night Daddy died, he said something else really weird."

"Like what?" Pete prodded.

"He said, 'I was hoping you wouldn't be burdened with them, but you're next in line.'"

"Burdened with what?"

"I don't know, unless he was talking about the visions."

"Damn, Dannah. Do you think he meant you're the next relative in line to have the visions?"

"I guess so. Geez, I don't know." She threw up her hands in a helpless gesture.

"Is this some secret Wingate family curse? Your grandmother, your aunt? Or, was this on your mother's side? Did she have them?"

"I don't know. Mother died of cancer when I was young. Daddy never had any contact with relatives on either side of the family. That's what has me so puzzled, so upset. I can't understand why he made such a heroic effort to speak if it wasn't important. He also told me to go see my Aunt Gova Wingate down in Mississippi. He said, 'She'll tell you all about it. She knows.'"

"She knows you're next in line?" Pete continued to prod.

"I'm not sure. As far as I know, Daddy hasn't spoken to her in years."

"Maybe your old man was off his rocker at the end. Maybe he was getting dementia or that Alzheimer's thing."

"No, he was completely sane and rational." Up until today, Dannah had thought it might be best to withhold the information about her foretelling vision of her father's heart attack, but now she was rethinking that decision. Maybe confiding in Pete would be a mistake, but she needed to tell someone because carrying the burden alone was becoming too much to bear. "Pete, it's almost like, well, like…." Dannah stood up and walked over to the window. "Let me give you an example. On the night Daddy had his heart attack, I dreamed that I was having the heart attack. I dreamed I was standing in front of the cook stove, holding the black cast iron skillet and was fixing scrambled eggs when the pain hit. I even remember falling, then pulling the phone to the floor to call 911. When I woke up and went downstairs to the kitchen, the hospital called to tell me Daddy had been admitted with a heart attack. And, when I went to his house after he died, to get some clothes to bury him in, well, well…." She blinked furiously to stop the threat of tears before turning around to face him. "The skillet and the eggs were lying on the floor just like my dream. So was the phone." Dannah wisely refrained from telling him that she ran from the house screaming and hadn't been back since, and that she purchased the clothing for him to wear in his grave.

Pete's eyes widened with disbelief. "Jesus, Dannah. Are you telling me you simply woke up one morning and all of a sudden you're a, a. What's that word? Psychic?"

"Yeah, I guess that's a good word." Dannah combined a shrug with a nod. "July tenth to be exact."

"Jesus! You even know the date? I thought most psychics were born with the power."

"I don't know about these things. I don't even know if 'psychic' is the correct description." Again, she gestured helplessly.

"Neither do I. Go check it out at the library. Wait. I know. Let's go to the dog track over in Arkansas and try out your new talent. Maybe you can predict the winners."

"Pete, I can't predict the future and I don't think you're taking this seriously. I'm not joking."

"I'm not joking either. I'm dead serious. Have you got any idea how much help you could be to the police on this serial killer investigation? They have the killer's DNA from the semen in his rape victims, but no match and no idea what the guy looks like. No fingerprints, no eye witnesses or anything. For God's sake, he's killed six young women. Yes, they were prostitutes, society's castoffs, but that doesn't mean they deserved to be brutally murdered."

"Pete, I have absolutely no control over these things. I don't know what triggers them, or when they're going to happen. They come to me out of the blue—like when I touch something or someone. And even then it doesn't seem to work on every one or every time."

"If you held this killer's DNA in your hand, you might get a vision of the bastard. It's worth a try."

Dannah shook her head. "No, no. I need some time to understand what's going on, learn to control it. Besides, I'm not in the mood to be ridiculed by the Memphis Police Department, or anyone else for that matter. I refuse to become a sideshow freak."

"Okay, okay," Pete huffed. "What about this Gova Wingate? What do you think she knows?"

"I'm not sure, but there's only one way to find out. I'm going to visit the woman today. I tried to call her right after Daddy died, but the phone number he gave me has been disconnected. She lives down in Oxford, Mississippi. It's not too far. Maybe she can tell me in person what she knows," Dannah stated with an air of new confidence.

"Call me as soon you get back, hon." He handed her a business card. "I got a new cell phone number. Call me any time day or night."

"Thanks, I will."

"Promise?" He stood up and grasped both of her hands. His craggy features continued to be marked by concern.

"I promise." Dannah assured him.

"You got me real worried. After you get this 'thing' figured out, we need to get with some of the detectives working on this serial killer case. Maybe you can be of help. Those guys are getting desperate."

"I don't know, Pete. I think it's too soon. I honestly don't know what I'm capable of doing...if anything substantive." Dannah turned to leave then halted and looked back at her dear old friend with a distracted frown. "You know, Pete, you really should quit smoking. It's doing terrible things to your lungs." She knew he was waiting politely until she left his office before lighting up.

"Yeah, yeah. You sound like my wife. One of these days I'll quit."

Pete's hacking cough reverberated down the hall as she headed for the bank of elevators.

***

Dannah felt better as she emerged from the building into the steamy September heat. Unloading her burden on poor unsuspecting Pete had been a cathartic experience. Maybe after talking with her aunt, she could put the matter of her dreams to rest once and for all, she thought as she headed for her car.

Her father's death had forced her to take stock of her situation. The personal portion of her life seemed to be bogged down by a long string of disappointments. She'd made some poor decisions when it came to choosing men. She and Philip Henderson had lived together for over a year. Her fetish for neatness earned her the degrading title of "grandma." His favorite insult was to call her "Daddy's girl." Phil either couldn't understand her dedication to her father, or was jealous of the time she spent with him. Sundays were their special time together. Dannah would accompany her dad to the early church service, they'd have a leisurely brunch, then she'd take him grocery shopping. Her dad had given up driving two years earlier. Phil always slept till noon on the weekends anyway, so why did he make such an issue over the few hours she devoted to her dad?

Their unrest had been fermenting for a long time prior to their predictable breakup. During those last few months, there were no sparks, no passion. Their scheduled sexual encounters were nothing more than perfunctory performances: spaghetti on Monday, sex on Tuesday, bowling on Wednesday. More often than not, the episodes left her wanting more than Philip was capable of giving. Eventually, he moved out. When the end finally came, she was relieved it was over, but resentful that she'd wasted so much time on a dead-end relationship. And another twelve months had slipped into eternity since their breakup.

Without contradiction, Dannah was both quiet and quick to laugh. Her droll sense of humor, however, was lost on many of her friends who claimed her jokes left them more puzzled than amused. Now that Philip was gone, she cherished her solitude—at least that's what she told everyone. But there was a private part of her longing for love and a permanent commitment. She tried to ignore those vague cravings for permanence, but when faced with saying the life-altering "yes" word to Philip, she backed away from him. She managed to traverse the dangerous twenties, when the potent urge to procreate was at the pinnacle of its power. Now that she was thirty, the ploy of attributing her feelings to the monthly rush of hormones was a thin excuse and she knew it. Her biological clock was definitely ticking.

Chapter Three
Tuesday following Labor Day
Oxford, Mississippi

The deep-throated purr of a powerful engine never failed to excite her. Her brand new red Corvette hugged the road as she exited the southbound lane of Interstate 55 and merged into traffic on the broad thoroughfare leading east into Oxford. The force of speed pushing her deep into the leather bucket seat was exhilarating. The pressure she applied to the accelerator forced the RPM's to jump to four thousand, and the car responded with a delightful surge. Her favorite CD filled the interior of the vehicle with music; however, her enjoyment was short-lived when she saw the flashing blue lights of a highway patrol car in her rear view mirror.

"Geez," she muttered under her breath. "These small-town cops are a pain in the butt." She pulled over, fumbled in her purse for her driver's license, proof of insurance and press card and—trying to appear unflustered—handed them out the window when the burly black police officer approached.

"Miss Dannah Wingate," he said after reading the name on her license. "Do you know how fast you were driving?"

"I was going a wee bit over the speed limit." She was not the eyelash-batting type and maintained a neutral expression.

"I clocked you on the radar at seventy-seven. The speed limit is fifty-five on this road. These sporty cars can get outta hand, can't they? How much horse power you got?"

"I'm not sure. Two-sixty, I think?"

"Where you headed in such a hurry?"

"To visit a relative, Miss Gova Wingate. She's celebrating her birthday this week," she lied with an endearing smile. Maybe a little idle chatter will make him forget the ticket.

His eyes were hidden behind his mirrored sunglasses as he shuffled through the papers she handed him. "A press card. You a reporter from Memphis?" he asked.

"Yes, freelance, but my hobby is genealogy." More idle

chatter.

The police man pushed his hat back a few inches and looked askance at her. "You collect rocks?"

"Genealogy, not geology. Roots," she drawled. "Not rocks."

The officer remained stone-faced as he wrote out her ticket. Dannah occupied herself by lowering the convertible top.

"That'll be eighty-five dollars, ma'am. You can pay me in cash or add five bucks and I'll take a credit card."

Miffed, Dannah thumbed through her collection of plastic money, then asked, "Where's Azalea Lane?"

"That's where all them old houses are. Take the Lamar exit, turn left, then go down to the light and turn right."

"Thank you," she muttered in an attempt to be civil.

"Thank you, ma'am. Our local government appreciates your kind donation."

***

Oxford was like any typical college town with rows of unattractive concrete apartment buildings. One entire street was devoted to pizza parlors, hamburger joints, coin-operated laundries, and an assortment of book stores, plus one artsy movie house. Construction equipment was everywhere, rearranging the red Mississippi clay to make room for expansion.

On the east side, Oxford was the picture of a sleepy country town filled with old homes on picturesque tree-lined streets. The atmosphere was quieter, cooler, and a pleasant contrast to the frenetic pace in Memphis. The clock tower spiraling above the courthouse was the tallest structure in the center of what was once a thriving farm community. These days the university brought in more money than cotton. Local society, which in olden times revolved around wealthy plantation owners, now encompassed an eclectic group of college professors.

As Dannah turned onto Azalea Lane, she admired the neighborhood's warm look of permanence. Dogwood trees, ringed by azalea bushes, ranked single file down the grassy median in the center of the street. By their solid appearance, the houses seemed to be boasting of being there for the last hundred years and daring to remain for another hundred years to come. Some were large and stately, some were smaller "painted ladies," but nearly all of the dwellings had been lovingly restored down to every little Victorian turret, acorn finial and dentil, creating the experience of having stepped out of a nineteenth-century fairy tale.

The Wingate home exuded a magnetic charm all its own, and in spite of its noble state of decay, Dannah fell instantly in love. It was the second house from the corner and the only one on the block not yet restored. She drove onto the crumbling concrete driveway, passed a metal fence with a muted haze of rust. Although the grass had been recently mowed, the house was obviously empty. The thought that she might have arrived too late to meet her aunt created the threat of tears. They weren't for the woman she had never met and didn't know, but from the fear that the elusive family secret might have been taken to the grave by both brother and sister. Her father rarely spoke of his younger sibling. Could it be that the old woman died without any next of kin to inform her father?

"I hope it ain't a'ready too late." Her father said those words on his deathbed. Although she pressed hard and often, she couldn't get him to divulge the history of the Wingate family. It was a source of occasional conflict between them. His oft-repeated statement was, "You're better off not knowin.'"

"Wow," she muttered as she emerged from her car. "It's huge." Compared to her father's old post-World War II bungalow where she grew up, this appeared palatial. The house stood out as the largest among its neighbors and the only one made entirely of red brick. There was a Queen Anne style turret on the left side, rising past three stories to a sharp pointed roof with a slender lightning rod reaching into the sunny, cloud-free sky. Two of the third-floor windows she could see from the front were boarded from inside the house. The roof was metal with a soft patina of age. Two red brick chimneys reached for the sky.

The oak planks on the front porch squeaked beneath her slight weight. The plaque next to the front entry stated "The Wingate House 1880."

Dannah opened the screen, tried the door and found it locked. Opaque curtains covered the turret windows, and drawn shades covered the others, preventing her from seeing inside.

She tried to envision her father as a youngster in short pants playing on the porch and in the yard of this stately old house, but the image wouldn't materialize. In the visage of him most prominent in her memory, he always seemed too serious and much older than his calendar years. The spreading branches of an aging magnolia tree on the west side of the dwelling offered welcome shade from the hot afternoon sun. The ground beneath its gently curving boughs was littered with large brown leaves and cones filled with bright red seeds.

In spite of the growing list of needed repairs, Dannah visualized the house as it could be, not as it was in the harsh light of reality. Enchantment with the graceful style of the edifice colored her assessment of its age, state of neglect and the high cost of restoration. She decided to investigate the rear of the house to look for any signs of life and walked around the residence making mental notes of her observations along the way. Air conditioning units were hanging precariously from several of the windows. At the far back of the property, she saw a freestanding ramshackle garage completely enveloped by the large green tentacles of a pervasive wisteria vine. Heavy seed pods, remnants of the purple springtime flowers, hung like tattered Christmas ornaments from its weighted branches. Peeping through the dirt of one small windowpane, she saw a sedan of undetermined vintage resting low on rotted tires. The tall wood plank fence extended across the rear property line was also in need of repair.

A porch stretched halfway across the back of the house with torn bits of screening wafting gently in the hot, late summer breeze. A rusting metal lawn chair silently surveyed three empty bird feeders. An assortment of decorative flower pots, once lovingly tended, were lined around the flagstone patio, their plantings dried up and dead.

After making a full circle, Dannah returned to the front and surveyed the two nearest neighbors. "Hmmm, there's a vehicle in the driveway next door," she muttered to herself as she crossed the yard. "Maybe there's someone home who can tell me what happened to Aunt Gova."

Next door, a similar plaque hanging above the doorbell announced it was the Dunhill House, built in 1876. She lifted her hand to ring the bell and halted abruptly when she heard a loud, angry male voice coming from deep inside the dwelling.

"Dammit, I'm not a maverick. I'm a serious and methodical researcher and resent the hell out of your accusation." There was a short pause. "If the campus grapevine told you I was at Chucalissa, then it must be true. You seem to lend a great deal of credence to gossip. Look, if you were so damned anxious to claim the dig site, why weren't you there in June? It could have been a joint effort if you'd get off your dead ass and get out in the field. It's dog-eat-dog in the world of research. You know that. You can't continue to live off old glory. Your findings from twenty years ago were good at the time, but now they're obsolete."

Dannah could only hear one side of the conversation.

"Dammit, Baxter," the voice continued; then there was another lengthy pause. "I don't have to take that kind of verbal abuse from you or anyone else. I don't give a damn if you are the department head." Another pause. "Why did I choose Chucalissa? My reasons had nothing to do with you." Another moment of silence. "The discovery you made twenty years ago is ancient history and, I might add, wrong. You're just eaten up with jealousy, that's your problem. You made the decision not to join me or the other research teams, so you're going to have to live with it. What was unearthed this year is my discovery. You can work the dig site next summer with your own group of grad students. Who knows? You might find something to upstage me. I've been invited to join the University of Virginia next year at the newly discovered fort at Jamestown."

During another pause, a dog started barking and prevented any further eavesdropping. When the large animal rushed at the screen door, Dannah pushed against it in case it was unlatched and hurriedly rang the bell.

"Gunner, come," boomed the angry voice. "Baxter, I don't have time to argue about this right now. I've got to make a rush trip out of town for a couple of days." There was another pause. "No, I'm not after your job. You can't believe everything you hear over the campus grapevine. No, I'm not ready to make a formal announcement. When I do, it will be made through the President of the University. You can join me on the podium if you like." Another pause. "Yes, I've already told him. I've got to go. I'll talk to you next Monday morning before I go public." The slam of the phone into the cradle could be heard throughout the house.

Within a few seconds, the owner of both the voice and the dog appeared at the door. "Yes?" he asked.

"H-hello," Dannah stammered. As the man stepped onto the porch, her gaze traveled from his exceptionally long, lean torso upward into his scowling face, rising a foot taller than the top of her own head. His shoulders were slightly sloping, his chest broad, tapering into a narrow waist. Although slender, his male presence was large, authoritative and dominated the small porch. The logo of the University of Mississippi was emblazoned in navy blue across the front of his gray tee shirt. There was also a small caricature of an old Southern Colonel waving a tiny clenched fist. The man, about her own age, was wearing tattered denim shorts and leather sandals. His features were heavily tanned, his brown hair was damp, curly and maybe a bit too long. It had been streaked by the sun and was tousled into strands of red and gold. He smelled like he'd just stepped from the shower—clean and sort of woodsy. In the heavy shade of the covered entrance, she couldn't see into his tightly squinted eyes. However, he was extremely handsome, albeit rumpled. Her interest dwelled on his body longer than was proper.

"Is there something I can do for you?" he asked, frowning slightly. "I'm in a bit of a hurry to leave town."

"I-I," she stammered and ran her fingers through her wind-blown hair. As Dannah inched away from him, she was aware of the man's own evaluating glance raking over her body. *Tit-for-tat,* she thought. Admiring a well-shaped figure wasn't limited to either sex.

"If you're selling something, little lady, I'll buy a dozen." A hint of a smile fought to replace his previous ill humor.

She finally composed herself and responded to his friendly repartee. "No, I'm not selling anything. I'm Dannah Wingate." She pointed to the house next door. "I'm trying to locate my aunt, Miss Gova Wingate."

"I'm Jason Dunhill. Sorry, but you're a little late. Your aunt died a couple of months ago," he stated bluntly. "Had a stroke a year ago—I think it was May. Left her paralyzed on one side. Been in the Sunny Care Nursing Home since then," he said in a mellow, baritone voice. His manner of speech was softened by his slow, southern drawl. When the large, black Doberman Pincher began to nuzzle the visitor, his owner gave him a quick verbal command. "Gunner, come up and sit." The dog was quick to obey, silently circling behind his owner and sitting at his left side with a look of quiet anticipation in his big, adoring black eyes.

"Oh, I didn't know. I had no idea she'd passed away. I never met her. She was my father's younger sister, but, but they weren't very close." Dannah rattled on, pressed by the usual urge to apologize for Coleman's lack of interest in his only kin. "I guess that explains why her phone was disconnected. Of course, I was hoping to talk to my aunt in person and learn about the Wingate family, but...but, maybe she left a diary or some personal papers. I'm interested in genealogy, you know, family history. According to court land records, Gova lived in the same house all her life and her parents and grandparents lived there before that."

"That's true, and I imagine you'll find the attic full of family skeletons. The entire neighborhood is old and some say every house on Azalea Lane has its own resident ghost."

"Skeletons? Ghosts?" She tipped her head up and met his gaze straight on searching for some hidden bit of laughter, but saw none.

"It's a shame you didn't get to meet your aunt. She was a rare old bird. Unfailingly in a good mood. Every kid on the block—including me—loved her home-baked brownies. Say, if you want inside the house, there's a key hidden in the electrical box on the back porch. I watch over the place whenever I'm in town. In fact, I mowed the grass this morning." His line of sight drifted over her shoulder to her shining new red Corvette and his brows arched appreciatively.

Although tempered by sadness, she smiled timidly. "No, I don't think I'll engage in trespassing. Do you happen to know who's been handling my aunt's affairs?"

"Sure. First Union Bank. Oh wait. I just remembered something. They called me last Friday asking if I knew the whereabouts of Miss Wingate's next of kin. I didn't know she had any relatives. No one ever visited her. Say, I have their business card if you'd like to call."

"Thanks. Maybe they'll let me inside the place legally to look for old photos and such."

"Come in, you can use my phone." He opened the old-fashioned screen door with a grandiose gesture. Even the dog politely waited for her to enter first.

"Thanks again." As Dannah stepped into the cool interior of the old house, she had to dodge a dusty, battered suitcase parked in the entry hall.

"There's a wall phone in the kitchen. The manager's business card is on top of the phone book," he said, pointing down a narrow hallway which ran parallel to the staircase. "Go through the dining room. Help yourself."

A few moments later as Dannah hung up the phone, she heard the dog bark again, followed by two male voices engaged in a heated argument. The sounds filtered through a closed door between the den and kitchen. She hesitated and waited, afraid to interrupt.

"Professor Dunhill, I can't believe you flunked me again."

"Sorry, Mister Henning, but you didn't earn a passing grade."

"Yeah, but you told me if I went on the eight-week expedition you'd pass me."

"Yes, I said I'd pass you if you were an active participant. Sitting on your bunk all day playing video games on your laptop computer doesn't qualify you as an active participant."

Dannah heard the temporary silence before the young man came up with a rebuttal. "That freakin' F you gave me is all that stands in the way of me gettin' my degree. My dad is in a rage over this. I thought I did okay on that final exam."

"You thought wrong. You were totally unprepared for the topic. The answers you gave were ludicrous."

"Trick questions. That's all you freakin' professors think about."

"It appears we have a bit of a personality conflict, Mister Henning. I suggest you take another course under a different teacher. You have plenty of time to take a make-up class between now and graduation next spring."

"I was supposed to graduate last spring."

"I strongly suggest that you go see Professor Baxter. He's the department head. I know for a fact he's in his office right now. I just talked to him on the phone. He'll see about arranging everything for you."

"Maybe you don't realize how much money my parents donate to this University, especially the Anthropology Department."

"Whoa. Wait a minute. Are you threatening me, Mister Henning? You know, you can get permanently expelled for that." Jason's voice remained level, but strained. "Besides, Gunner might take offense."

"You'll be surprised what money can buy."

After a litany of muttered profanity, the front screen door slammed and silence settled in. Dannah retraced her steps to the front of the house and peered furtively into the living room. It exhibited most of the earmarks of a masculine owner—no pictures, no lacy pillows or vases of flowers. There was nothing fluffy or feminine to reveal the presence of a woman in his life. Not even a pretense of Victorian decor to match the old house's elegant interior wood trim. The high-ceilinged room was dominated by a big comfortable sofa, two gigantic leather recliners and a large-screen television. Heavy brass lamps overpowered the two small end tables, while the long, book-cluttered coffee table bore scars of rough usage. Through a pair of French doors, Dannah could see the clutter of a den turned into an office and Dunhill was hurriedly rearranging the papers on his desk.

She tapped on the glass door with her fingernails to

announce her presence. "Is it safe to come out?"

"Oh damn, sorry about the ruckus. This just hasn't been my day. Lawrence Henning, The Third, unfortunately did not inherit his father's intelligence. He's a poor excuse for a student. Been a thorn in my side for the last year. I think he's on something—you know, like drugs. Always has a spaced-out glaze in his eyes. This is the first time a student has come to my house to threaten me. It was an unsettling experience when he sparred at me with his clenched fists."

"I can imagine so," she said and offered him a sympathetic smile while recalling a couple of frightening threats she had received when she was a reporter.

"I could have 'decked' him, but didn't think that would be proper behavior for a teacher."

"Guess what? I have an appointment tomorrow morning at ten at the First Union Bank. Said they'd been searching for me. Something about my aunt's estate."

"Maybe they want you to pay her burial expenses," he stated without looking at her, becoming preoccupied with sorting through a stack of papers.

"Whoa! I hope not. I don't need another unexpected expense right now. I buried my dad last month."

Her exclamation caused Jason to glance up momentarily. "Yeah, I buried both of my folks three years ago. Twenty car pile up on a foggy freeway."

"Double whammy," Dannah commented as she nervously shifted her weight from one foot to the other. "Tomorrow I'll find out what they have in mind. I planned on driving back home to Memphis tonight," she rambled. "Didn't bring anything for an overnight stay. Guess I'll have to find a motel and buy a change of clothes."

Jason stared at her for a long moment, his distracted gaze became contemplative and burrowed into her. "Say, I've got a proposition for you that might help solve both our problems."

"Proposition? Wh-what sort of pr-proposition?" Fear caused Dannah's heart to sink. She maintained a tight grasp on the purse strap as she cast a hurried glance over her shoulder searching for the quickest pathway to the exit, and prepared to take flight.

"I've got to drive to Athens, Georgia tonight to pick up four artifacts I've had radiocarbon dated. Didn't want to risk them getting lost in the mail. I took them over last week. Now they're ready. My buddy pushed them through the queue. You can bunk in my house in return for feeding Gunner and letting him out a couple of times a day. I usually take him with me, but this is a rush trip and I don't have time to mess with him. Besides, it's way too hot to leave him in the car."

"Well, I don't know. I, I...." she continued to stammer as she wavered.

He shrugged, turned away and called to his dog. "Gunner, go get your leash. It's off to the boarding kennel for you, buddy."

"Wa-wait a minute. If you're going out of town, I guess there'd be no harm in—"

"Miss Wingate? What did you say your first name was?"

"Dannah. D-A-N-N-A-H."

"Dannah, I'm not the neighborhood pervert. Truthfully, I'm a hardworking college professor with a great deal on my mind." He slouched against the tall door frame between the living room and his office, silently signaling fatigue with the deep slant of his shoulders. He massaged his temples with his fingertips as if trying to thwart a threatening headache. "I've been working day and night gathering information for a paper I'm writing for a scientific journal and need the certified reports on the ages of the artifacts I unearthed at the Chucalissa Indian site just south of Memphis. I've got to get my article, along with these pictures and certificates of authenticity, in the mail by the end of the week to make the November issue." He pointed to some glossy photos scattered across his desk. "This is what I found there during this summer's dig and this is what my article is about." Jason glanced at his watch. "It's already three and I've got an eight-hour drive ahead of me. My problem is...I need someone to look after my dog until I get back, and your problem is that you need a place to stay for a couple of nights. Okay?"

Dannah could relate to his writing against a deadline, having experienced the same pressures herself when she worked for the newspaper. However, she continued to falter. His scowling intensity was a little frightening. Then, for the first time, Dannah saw the vivid blue honesty shining in his eyes as he looked at her directly. Sunlight reflecting through the windows lightened her initial fear. "You don't even know me." She finally spoke.

"True, but since you're related to old Miss Gova, you must be trustworthy."

"Thanks, I like to think I am, but maybe you better tell me about your dog before I commit." Her gaze sought the object of their conversation who had obediently returned to his master with his leash clamped in his mouth.

"I call him Gunner—short for his German name of Gunther-Von-something-or-other. Too hard to pronounce," Jason explained. "He's got a pedigree a mile long."

"I don't care about his pedigree, I only want to know if he's friendly. He's awfully big."

Jason smiled. "Sure. Dobermans got a bad rap a few years ago, but nowadays the breed is very stable emotionally. He's a gentle giant unless asked to be otherwise. His bloodline is German—not backyard breeder. He's three years old and still acts like a pup, but he minds really well. In fact, he's obedience trained—knows all the basic commands of heel, sit, come, stay, plus a few more I've taught him. Just say his name and give him a command. Sometimes I feel like he's reading my mind. I'm downright amazed at what he understands." He absentmindedly reached down and stroked his dog, who responded by leaning into his master's leg. The dog stared at him with unabashed adoration in his eyes. "You staying here at my place tonight will save both of us a few bucks."

Dannah slowly nodded her head as her fear subsided, replaced by the pressing need for financial practicality. Next month's mortgage, car payment and credit-card bill loomed largely like insurmountable objects. She hadn't written a single paragraph, much less an entire article, in the last four months. Her bank account was shrinking. "You know, you're absolutely right. I could stand to save a little money. Got a ninety-dollar speeding ticket coming down here today."

"Nice set of wheels."

"Corvette."

She shrugged guiltily, but managed a shy smile. "Impulse buy. I had this childish image of the top down, the wind blowing through my hair and six speakers blaring out my favorite songs."

"Nothing wrong with that," he responded with a soft chuckle.

"Yeah, well, now the old proverbial wolf is knocking on my door." She extended her hand. "It's a deal." As he swallowed her tiny hand in his warm, firm grasp, a hazy vision drifted into her consciousness of...of.... She squeezed her eyes closed to brace for an unpleasant image, but absolutely nothing materialized. Her eyes popped open and a genuine smile parted her lips.

Well, this was a pleasant surprise. Someone she couldn't read. All of a sudden, she felt better—a lot better.

"Great. It'll save you at least fifty bucks and save me about the same. He gets charged the 'big-dog-rate.'" Jason's broad, congenial smile exposed an even row of straight white teeth and softened his sun-bronzed features. He took her on a tour of his house, showed her the guest bedroom, location of bath towels and dog food, then they returned to his office. "I've been out of town for eight weeks on an archeological dig with my graduate students."

"Your house is so clean. Even smells fresh—sort of lemony."

"Very clever of you to notice. Professional house-cleaning service. I splurge once a year and get it cleaned from top to bottom by an entire platoon of energetic young ladies." When he grinned, humor erupted from his vibrant blue eyes. "I have absolutely no domestic talents. I did get to the grocery store and filled the fridge. There is coffee, milk, bread, cold cereal, orange juice, eggs, lunch meat, canned foods, beer—you know, basic stuff like that. Help yourself. Just don't touch anything in here. My office may look like a mess to you, but I know where everything is," he explained as he slipped a nylon dust cover over the huge top-of-the-line flat screen monitor and ergonomic keyboard. After placing another cover over the tower, he made a halfhearted attempt to neaten the stacks of papers. "Other than that, make yourself at home." With arms folded across his chest, Jason leaned against the door frame and watched as Dannah glanced around; checking the titles of the books and magazines strewn on chairs and end tables. There was also a locked gun cabinet containing one shotgun and two hunting rifles.

"Have you been written up in the National Geographic?" she asked, pointing to some pictures on the wall.

"My dig site was—a couple of years ago up in Alaska. Some of the University funding comes from that august society."

She couldn't help being impressed. In her eyes, neither a man nor woman should be judged by a title, occupation or salary, only by his or her excellence—or lack of it—in their chosen field of endeavor. This guy was stacking up quite favorably in more ways than one and was probably a lot more intelligent than the sportswriter guy Pete Jordan had tried to foist on her. The opposite wall was lined with floor-to-ceiling shelves; heavily weighted by golf trophies, stacks of textbooks, trade magazines, shards of pottery and crude tools.

"What are these things?"

"Artifacts. Bones are bones, everything else is an artifact," he stated in what was obviously his teacher mode. "This is a Clovis point and this is an atlatl." He demonstrated the implement by loading a spear and launching it through the French doors where it landed softly on the living room carpet.

Dannah picked up another item which she quickly replaced. "Geez. Are these human bones?"

"They're plaster casts of fossilized bones of ancient Native Americans, descendants of early man who traversed the Aleutian land bridge during the last ice age." He paused and glanced at his watch. "As much as I'd like to continue your education in physical anthropology, I've got to go." He hurriedly scratched a few numbers on a scrap of paper. "This is for my cell phone. Let me know if you have any problems. Gunner's a good dog. He minds."

"We'll be okay. I won't bother anything." She dug a business card out of her purse and handed it to him. "It's got my mobile number on it as well. Maybe the bank officer will let me in the house to look for genealogy materials. Whatever, I'll wait for you to get back before I leave to go back to Memphis. I'll take good care of your dog. I promise." She followed him out the door as he headed for his car.

"Oh, you'll need these." He tossed her a ring with two keys. "To the front and back doors. Thanks, see you tomorrow night. I'm going to drive straight through to Athens and bunk with my buddy, Randy. In the morning, I'll pick up the bones, the pottery shard, the certificates of verification and come right back home. Don't hesitate to call me, and I'll call you if I'm detained by traffic."

"You don't have to rush, I'll look after everything."

"Thanks. It takes a load off my mind." He pointed a finger at his dog. "Gunner, you have to stay home. Mind your manners and mind Miss Dannah. She's a nice lady and she's the boss while I'm gone."

The dog's alert black eyes traveled between the two people as if he fully comprehended every word uttered by his master.

As Jason opened the car door, he stopped abruptly and swung around quickly. He grasped Dannah's empty left hand and squeezed. As his thumb stroked the flesh across her knuckles, warm sensations spread through her body. They were fuzzy feelings, ill-defined, yet comfortable, as though they had been intimate friends for a very long time. No distinct image materialized, but the perception imprinted on her mind was of blue skies. Their gazes locked for several awkward and silent seconds. Their connection was as alive as the trees above them with their leaves fluttering in the late afternoon breeze.

"The...my dog, huh, Gunner," he stuttered. "He means a great deal to me."

Dannah smiled and pulled her hand free from his grasp. "Don't worry. I'll take good care of him."

"Thanks."

After the dust-covered Ford Explorer disappeared around the corner, she looked down at the sleek, well-muscled black Doberman Pinscher—built lean and powerful, much like his owner. He was a beautiful specimen of his breed, with a glossy coat, regal bearing and expressive eyes. "I guess it's you and me, Gunner. Come on, we'll go for a nice long walk through the neighborhood, then I'll measure out your dinner." She led him back inside the house. "We'll get along okay. Now, where's your leash?"

He woofed softly in agreement, picked up the six-foot leather lead he had dropped earlier and wagged his stubby tail.

Chapter Four
Tuesday following Labor Day
University campus, Oxford, MS

Where could he be going? William Baxter seethed silently. He ran his fingers through his thick white hair as he hung up the phone after his verbal altercation with Dunhill. He slouched his bulk deeper into his creaky chair, lit another cigarette and launched into a spasm of coughing. So, the gossip he heard through the campus grapevine was true. Dunhill had made some sort of significant discovery during the summer dig at Chucalissa. When he was younger, he had done the research that dated the civilization at 1100AD. He didn't think there was anything else to be uncovered there.

Why did Dunhill chose that particular site?

The discovery you made twenty years ago is ancient history...and I might add...wrong.

Wrong. The word echoed inside his head.

Two other groups from his department had returned from their own digs at other locations and had found nothing noteworthy. Dunhill was this season's star.

He's probably preparing an article for publication in a scientific journal. That's the usual routine. An announcement with the University President in attendance. Fame. New research grants. An invitation from the University of Virginia. He'll probably get a promotion. Damned maverick.

If Baxter was forced out of his job as Department Head, then retirement was his only option. He didn't have the energy to go back to the daily grind of teaching. Managing the paperwork for more than forty separate classes, their students and teachers, was enough load for him to carry. He certainly didn't have the drive or strength to spend eight weeks in the broiling summer sun working with a dental pick and a tooth brush. Not to mention the pain in his low back and arthritic knee.

His life had gone to hell in a hand-basket since his wife died six years ago. She was the glue that held him together.

Whenever she called him Billy, it brought a smile to his craggy features. Without her sweet, gentle prodding, he had lost all ambition and the will to live. There was nothing quite so pathetic as a childless widower. He had no one. Not a single living relative. His father had abandoned his mother when Baxter was only four years old. Disappeared and never heard from again. Growing up and getting an education had been lonely and tough.

You can work the dig site next summer... There might not be a next summer.

His recent trip to the doctor had not gone well. A small needle biopsy was performed last week on a suspicious lump in his lung. Now he was scheduled for surgery and chemotherapy.

He was making a distracted attempt to straighten his desk when there was a knock on the outer door. He heard a male voice exchange words with Martha, his secretary. As she walked into his office, he wondered what sort of scholastic emergency he would be forced to deal with this late in the day. Baxter prided himself on being readily available to all of the sociology and anthropology students and, for lack of anything else to do, came into the office even during the slow summer months.

"There's a young man to see you," the secretary announced. "Larry Henning."

"Send him in. Why don't you go on home, Martha? There's nothing else pressing to be done. We've got two more weeks until the rush of registration." Baxter shook hands with the young man, then settled in his chair and listened patiently to Mister Henning's gripes against Jason Dunhill.

"I need to resolve this situation in the shortest amount of time, Professor Baxter," Larry insisted. "I was supposed to graduate in June, but Professor Dunhill gave me a failing grade for the semester. I need that credit. At his suggestion, I spent the summer at the dig site, but he gave me another failing grade. I don't want to spend another year here at the University just to take one class."

"I can make arrangements for you to take the final exam a second time. I'll give you a reading list and a couple of weeks to study. How does that sound?"

The young man smiled broadly. "Better. Much better. I'm certain it will make my Dad loosen the old purse strings."

"Larry, what say you and I go have dinner and a couple of beers? My treat. You don't mind indulging a lonely old man, do you?"

With his mood improved, Larry agreed. "Sure, Professor Baxter. I never turn down free food and free beer."

"You know, Professor Dunhill is a thorn in my side as well."

"Yeah, he's a real asshole in my book."

If Bill Baxter was going down for the full count, he had no intention of going alone.

Chapter Five
Later Tuesday evening

After taking care of Gunner, Dannah drove around town until she found a discount store, bought a few toilet articles, a pair of pajamas, some underwear, a couple changes of clothes—tee shirts, jeans and a pair of sneakers—and an inexpensive suitcase to pack them in. Life seldom caught her this unprepared, but never in her wildest dreams did she think she would be spending the night in Oxford, Mississippi. She rolled her eyes as she tossed her credit card on the counter.

I'll worry about paying for everything next month. Whatever made me think I just had to have that new convertible?

She needed to get a firm grip on her emotions, get some uninterrupted sleep and start writing again. Hopefully she could get control of her finances. Maybe she would learn something in Gova's house that might explain her father's bizarre statements about her being "next in line." She wanted to get answers to her questions, then put the entire matter to rest once and for all.

Throughout all her many internal musings, Dannah found it odd that she could not even think the word "psychic," much less say it, or apply the definition to herself. "Perceptive" seemed far less frightening. Then again, she tried to rationalize; maybe they were nothing more than coincidental incidents brought on by stress.

Later, she fixed a sandwich, settled in the living room and plugged in her laptop—she never went anywhere without it. Her computer signaled that there was a wireless internet connection available, so she logged on. Unfortunately, her mind was as blank as her screen. It was painfully obvious that she wasn't ready to tackle a new assignment, no matter how intriguing the twisted minds of serial killers and their profilers might be. Right now, she was wrestling with the convolutions in her own mind.

It was interesting that she'd had no perception of anything—either sinister or otherwise—when shaking hands with Jason Dunhill. Could it be possible that a person must be experiencing a hidden illness, like the problem with Pete Jordan's lungs, or some other sort of exceptionally strong emotion before she could read them? Jason seemed to be an extremely concentrated individual. She could see the intensity in his eyes, but his passion was apparently directed toward his research project, not at seducing strange women. There was also the possibility that her perceptions didn't work on strangers. It was something to think about. Lately, she had used many ploys to avoid shaking hands with strangers, fearful of having one of those godawful images. But tomorrow at the bank, she would test her new theory on the banker.

After sending an email to Pete Jordan and making a lackluster attempt to search the Internet for information on profilers, she finally turned off her computer and scooted on to the floor to visit with the dog. He had been sitting in front of her with a toy clamped in his mouth and hope shining in his big black eyes. "Okay, boy, I'll play a game with you."

After thirty minutes of rough housing, Dannah decided it was time to take Gunner outside for his nightly "constitutional." She leaned against the railing on the back porch and stared into the ebony sky. Stars seemed so much brighter here than in Memphis. Probably the wash of big-city lights overpowered their distant glimmer. The peaceful sounds of the night invaded her senses, imbuing her with contentment. Gunner attended to his duties with speed and efficiency, then dashed back into the house.

Although desperate for a good night's sleep, she was reluctant to pursue it, afraid of dreaming. "Maybe nightmares don't travel out-of-town," she mused as she turned off the kitchen lights and plunged the entire house into total darkness. She remembered a table with a lamp in the entry hall and stumbled through the dining room, holding onto Gunner's collar with one hand, feeling her way along the wall with the other. The bulb offered a glowing circle of tranquility. Light—even forty watts—possessed the magical power to dispel fear. She decided to leave it burning all night.

After pulling in two shuddering breaths of air, she squinted up the staircase. Her hand was on the railing as she stood on the bottom step, looking up at the gaping black hole at the top. The stairs loomed above her like the last door on death row, leading into the notorious room from which no prisoner emerged alive. She had gone to the Brushy Mountain State Prison once, and the place was not nearly so frightening as the dark passage rising before her. Cool air seemed to flow like water down the steps.

With a determined stride, she ascended. The wood grumbled underfoot, adding to the "thump-flop" of her heart and an entire cacophony of a thousand other real and imagined sounds assaulting her senses. Gunner bounded up the stairs ahead of her, his docked tail wagging, his toenails clicking against the bare wood. He was light on his feet, dancing effortlessly up each step. He had a fuzzy squeaky toy in his mouth, and his eyes were sparkling with both intelligence and devilment. The loud creak of the stairs bolstered her spirits. In her warped thinking, at least no one could sneak up on her in the dead of night. She tested the discordant squeaks, noting that if you placed your weight next to the wall, the risers and treads remained quiet.

On the second floor, she frantically batted the walls searching for the light switch. Two overhead fixtures flooded the long hallway with their meager, but cheery glow. It was ludicrous for her to be afraid. There was nothing in the house to fear. She was letting her imagination play games with her mind after all that talk about ghosts and skeletons in the closet.

She started singing… *"Bye, bye Miss American Pie. Drove the Chevy to the levee, but the levee was dry. Found some good old boys drinking whiskey and rye, singing this'll be the day that…I…die.* Maybe I better find a song with happier lyrics." As her crystal voice filled the silence, her state of mind improved. *"How much is that doggy in the window? The one with the waggly tail?"*

The bathroom was nice. The large tile shower, appeared as if it had been remodeled within the last few years. Gunner shadowed her every step, even sat on the bath rug while she showered and continued to sing. *"Born in the USA, born in the USA. Eeek!"* Gunner poked his nose around the shower curtain and peeked in. "You scared me. What? Your owner doesn't sing in the shower?" she asked, as if expecting an answer. She flicked some water droplets in his face and he snorted in response. Never having owned a pet of any kind, she was a little surprised at how much companionship the dog offered. There was also a bit of reassuring comfort in performing the mundane tasks of brushing her teeth and creaming her face. She carefully hung up the good clothes she had been wearing along with her new purchases, happy to see that the steam from the shower diminished wrinkles and that new smell.

"It's not going to be easy to sleep in a strange bed, in a strange house, and in a strange city," she muttered as she slipped into her new pajamas. It was eleven when she finally climbed between the musty-smelling sheets, hoping for a dreamless night. After an hour of tossing and turning, she rose from the tangled covers. She couldn't quiet the ramblings of her mind, wondering why on earth her aunt's banker wanted to see her, as well as what she was going to do about her strained financial situation. And last, but certainly not the least of her worries, was her odd new abilities.

She peered out the window at the Wingate House, shrouded in filtered moonlight and mist. It appeared ominous, maybe even a little sinister, with its darkened windows and shadowed, steep-roofed dormers. Jason's house had central air conditioning and several other modern improvements, including new, vinyl storm windows. She twisted the lock and raised the glass several inches. The daytime heat had given way to cool nighttime breezes. The slick leaves of the huge magnolia tree clicked and rattled beneath the gentle wind. Cicadas whined their songs of seduction, sliding up and down the musical scale in melodic counterpoint.

After shopping, she closed the convertible top and pulled her car behind the Wingate House, hoping to keep it out of harm's way. The space between the houses was much narrower than current practices. Even though the two driveways were side by side, there was only twenty feet or possibly less between the two structures. "The houses were built in the 1800s, long before the invention of the automobile. Hmmm, I guess a horse and buggy weren't very wide." The sound of her own voice invading the quiet startled her.

A bit of movement caught her attention. The curtain in one of the second-story windows on the east side of the Wingate House seemed to flutter in the breeze. "No, that's impossible." During the daylight when she had walked around the house, it appeared that all the windows were tightly closed with their shades drawn. She closed the casement and searched for the dog.

"Gunner, where are you? Come on, boy. You can get in bed with me."

The large dog lumbered into the guest bedroom with his stubby tail wagging, the tag on his chain collar jingling slightly. He jumped onto the bed and lay down beside her. He settled in the crook of her arm with his head resting on her shoulder. His tongue snaked out and placed a wet kiss on her cheek. There was both comfort and reassurance in his warmth and size. Another breathing body, another beating heart, something very much alive.

"I guess I'm a dog owner in the making," she muttered softly, smiled into the darkness and hunkered down beneath the covers.

***

Something jolted her awake. For an instant, Dannah forgot where she was and thought she might be dreaming again. She fought confusion to force her sleepy brain into sharp focus. Gunner's growling hastened her trip back to reality. During the night, she had rolled onto her side and slung her arm over the dog's shoulders. Had she startled him? Was he going to bite her? The rule was never show your fear, but she could feel the rumble in his ribcage and his muscles tighten as if readying himself to pounce. In the blanched stream of moonlight shining in the window, she watched as the dog raised his head, then twisted his ears from side to side searching for the source of the alien noise. His upper lip twitched slightly, revealing his large gleaming teeth. Fear of the dog was quickly replaced by another sort of fear when the shattering of glass resounded through the house and brought a louder grumble. Dannah sat upright in bed, holding her breath and straining to sort out the sounds. Gunner sat up as well and looked at her, waiting for a command, as if asking for permission to do something.

Was someone breaking into the house? Was Jason coming home early?

There was no clock in this seldom-used bedroom. Dannah rolled out of bed, clung tightly to Gunner's chain collar and tiptoed through the door leading into the hallway. All four upstairs rooms opened onto the center hall—three bedrooms and a bath. The stairwell was a straight descent into the main floor entry hall and out the front door. There was no turret in this house as she had seen in Gova's home. She had seen a phone beside the bed in the master bedroom, but before calling the police, maybe she should call Jason Dunhill. After all, the police would ask questions she couldn't answer and might think she was the intruder. Unfortunately, she had left her laptop computer on the coffee table in the living room, her open brief case on the sofa, while her handbag with the numbers and her cell phone was lying on the hall table next to the lamp.

What a dumb thing to do. What if my phone starts ringing?

She stood on the top step shivering from fear, not from the cold. Whoever the burglar was, he wasn't worried about discovery. The fragments of broken glass crunched under each footfall, while ancient floorboards squeaked beneath the weight of a heavy person. The noise announced the path as he walked through the kitchen and entered Jason's office. The intruder turned on a small desk lamp, the pale and distant reflection angling through the French doors into the living room and from there, leaked into the entry hall as a gray shadow.

Voices.

Ohmygod, there's more than one person in the house.

The voices became louder. Angrier. More distinct.

"We're going to set him up," a vaguely familiar voice stated.

"I don't understand," someone countered.

The words spoken by yet another voice were much lower and with a deeper resonance.

Good grief. Are there three?

The conversation stopped, she heard the sound of a

computer being turned on. Fear curled around her heart as her toes curled over the edge of cool wood of the top step. If she and Gunner tried going down the stairs, the squeaking treads would alert whoever had come into the house. There was no way she and the dog could get out the front door unnoticed. Gunner continued to grumble softly. Whoever the noisy intruders might be, they must know that the owner of the house was out of town. They weren't being particularly quiet as they talked, and as drawers grated open and banged closed.

"We gotta hide the wire," the whiney voice said.

"Use his stapler."

What if they're armed—a knife, a gun, maybe even a baseball bat. If she turned the dog loose and he tried to attack the burglars, the dog might be seriously injured or possibly even killed. *Great dog sitter, I am.* She remembered the obedience commands that Jason had used and hoarsely whispered in his perked ear, "Gunner. Sit. Stay. Quiet." Surprisingly, he quickly obeyed. Lordy, what an amazing animal! He yawned several times, an indication of uncertainty, not of fatigue. He possessed an impressive array of teeth.

Good grief. More glass being broken. Could it be Jason's gun cabinet.

Terror blossomed as she sat on the second floor landing and continued to hang on to Gunner's collar. When he growled again, she tapped his muzzle sharply accompanied by a muffled command of "Quiet." Again, he obeyed, although reluctantly. She would rethink her judgment that cats make better companions than dogs. Given the same set of circumstances, most cats would be hiding under the bed. His eyes were like a sentry's, peering into the darkness, ever watchful. He was on guard, tense and ready to react if given a command.

Dannah and Gunner stayed huddled at the top of the stairwell. She had no awareness of time other than its painfully slow passage juxtaposed against the rapid pounding of her heart. Occasionally, she heard deeply muttered commands and responses in a higher-pitched, younger-sounding voice. Footsteps retreated, then returned. She heard bits and pieces of their conversation.

"There's an upstairs."

"He's a bachelor. He doesn't have any jewelry."

"What a haul this is."

"You're the computer expert. Will this wipe out all his data?"

"This'll do it. He's got a CD-burner. He might have everything backed up on disk. Let's take all his disks an' burner as well. We can probably get fifty bucks for this. That'll buy ten nickel bags."

The response from the third individual was buried in a spasm of coughing.

"We're no dummies at this. We know how to remove serial numbers."

The noises grew louder as the footsteps entered the living room. Dannah, still hanging on to Gunner's collar, stood up and as her bare foot moved backwards, she stepped on one of Gunner's forgotten toys. The wheezy noise seemed to drag on forever as the air moved in and out of the hamburger-shaped item. She flattened herself against the wall in the darkened upstairs hallway, barely daring to breathe. Her pounding heart rushed the blood through her veins and, at the moment, she could hear little else other than the roar in her ears. Terror had taken on a life of its own and had gripped her by the throat. Panic tasted like bile rising from her stomach. If they came up the stairs, she would be left with no alternative but to send Gunner after them. Frantically, she scanned her memory for some sort of weapon, but could only think of the toilet brush she had seen leaning against the bathroom wall. Its pink plastic handle wouldn't offer much protection.

Finally, the intruders left the way they had entered, through the back door. Dannah raced to the front bedroom window, pulling Gunner with her. The glow from the street light silhouetted a stockily built, almost barrel-shaped man as he emerged from between the two houses. His short, bushy hair was illuminated by the light of the moon as well. Both hands were full. He was carrying what appeared to be a large briefcase. His other hand clutched a stack of papers to his chest. He hurried past the Wingate House with the uneven gait of an older person with aching joints. A few moments later, she heard an engine spring to life, then saw the blur of a passing car. A light-colored, four-door sedan. That's all she could make out.

"The others must have left in a different direction," she reasoned, her voice slicing into the silence.

It was two-thirty when she found her cell phone, sat down on the bottom step in the entry hall and called Jason Dunhill's mobile number. He was slow to answer with a slurred, "Yeah? This is Dunhill."

"Jason, this is Dannah Wingate. You know, your dog sitter. I'm sorry to bother you this late, but something terrible has happened."

His voice cleared. "Terrible? What? Tell me."

"Someone just broke into your house. Two, possibly three men."

"Three?"

"I think so. Knocked out one of the glass panes in the kitchen door, then got into your computer. Maybe they stole your data, erased it or planted a virus."

"My, my data? Were you hurt? Attacked? Is Gunner okay?" Hysteria crept into his voice.

"No, no, yes. We're both fine."

"Have you called the police?"

"No, I was afraid. I didn't know how I could explain what I'm doing in your house."

Dannah could hear him take a deep breath before speaking again.

"I guess that's logical. We can call the cops after I get home. Did you get a good look at them?"

"No, Gunner and I stayed hidden upstairs. But when they left, I looked out the front bedroom window and saw one of them walking down your driveway. I think he had pale hair—white or maybe blond. Sort of messy. Heavy-set, walked with a limp, like maybe he a bad knee or some type of injury. Cigarette in his mouth. Bad cough. Drove a light-colored, four-door sedan, nothing flashy. Could it have been that disgruntled student?"

"No. Henning is slender, has dark hair, and drives a 'Vette

his daddy bought him. Much older than yours. The dual pipes are loud. Dammit, I'll bet it was Bill Baxter—the rotten bastard. He's the department head."

"Surely a fellow professor wouldn't do such a thing. Maybe it was a group of students. The one I saw was big enough to be a football player."

"No, no. Baxter is the number one candidate. Dannah, are you all right?"

"Scared out of my wits, that's all."

"Why didn't you send Gunner after him?"

"To be honest, I was too terrified. I thought one of them might have a weapon of some sort. I couldn't bear the thought of telling you that I let your dog get hurt or killed."

"Thanks. You're the perfect dog sitter. Gunner means more to me than my computer or anything else in the house for that matter."

"Although I heard several voices, I only saw one person leave."

"Do you think someone is still in the house?"

"Wouldn't Gunner know if he was?"

"Probably. Just to be on the safe side, say, 'Gunner, search the house.'"

Dannah did as she was told and the dog bolted forward.

"Is anything missing?" Jason continued.

"I'll look. I haven't been in your den yet." Curiosity finally outweighed her fear. With her cell phone clamped between her ear and shoulder, she walked through the living room, flicking on lights as she progressed, and then through the broad opening for the French doors and into Jason's den. The overhead light flooded the room. The aroma of cigarette smoke hung in the room. "I can't tell. They left your computer turned on. Oh Jason. The error message says you've been invaded by a virus."

"Ooh, Jesus H. Christ. Everything is probably ruined. Turn it off. Force quit if you have to."

"I don't know how. I'm a Mac-person, not a PC."

"Just pull the plug."

Dannah got down on the floor and found the outlet.

"Done," she said when she returned. "You know, Jason, the most prominent odor I'm getting is tobacco."

"Baxter smokes like a chimney."

"I think he was carrying a very large briefcase."

"Oh shit, no! I left my laptop sitting on the corner of my desk. It was in its own fitted case."

"It's not there now. Those photos that were lying here—they're gone as well."

"Luckily, I still have the negatives."

"Jason, I also noticed that your three rifles are gone. The glass is broken on the front." There was a groan, then a long pause. "Should I call the police now?" she asked.

"No, better wait until I can see what else is missing before we do that. I'll probably have to fill out a stolen property report for the insurance company."

"Do you know who could have done this?"

"Yeah, I've got a pretty good idea who's responsible. I don't think he's a computer whiz—his knowledge is zeroed in on anthropology and nothing else. He lives, eats and breathes it, but from behind his desk, when he should be out in the field sweating and digging like the rest of us. He hasn't made a significant new discovery in almost twenty years. But, that's another story. I'll pick up my artifacts first thing in the morning and then drive straight home."

"Take your time. I'm all right. Honest."

"Is my camera on the counter in the kitchen, or was that stolen as well?"

Still barefooted, she gingerly tiptoed around the broken glass. "No, it's here. It was hiding behind a loaf of bread."

"If you don't mind, would you please take some pictures of the damage done to the door and my desk? And hey, there's a loaded pistol on the top shelf of my bedroom closet. It's in one of those leather zippered bags. Lay it by your bed just in case. Okay?"

"Okay. Here comes Gunner. He must have finished the search. By the way, your dog is terrific."

"Thanks. He's my best friend. See you tomorrow."

Dannah punched the end button on her cell phone, picked

up the camera and studied its various buttons. After completing the task, she sagged into the office-style chair behind Jason's cluttered desk. Her behind had barely made contact with the leather-upholstered seat when a frightening vision slammed into her consciousness—

—of illness. Serious illness. Loneliness. Hopelessness. The color red. A large, hard piece of living tissue was slowly pulsating and expanding inside the chest, crowding discolored lungs and a sluggishly beating heart. Fear. Resignation.—

She sprang from the chair and the vision immediately vanished, melting into a colorless vapor. She turned around and stared at the seemingly innocent chair. Intuition told her that somehow she was in the mind of the intruder. Maybe he's sick, just like Pete Jordan. Maybe he has lung cancer or some other related illness. "Geez, don't tell me I can diagnose disease." Slowly, she lowered herself down into the chair a second time. Her fingers curled around the arm rests and she tried to keep fear at bay as the scattered images began to flow into her mind once again. Random, disconnected images—

—of anger. Venomous anger. Loneliness. Greed. Loneliness. Jealousy. Loneliness. Storm clouds roiling in a blackened sky. A boiling caldron of bitter emotions. Plan. Blame. Murder—

"Murder?" Her eyes popped open.

Gunner's front paws were in her lap and he was licking her face, concern radiating from his liquid black eyes. Dannah blinked furiously and lifted herself from the chair. Apparently, she was out-of-touch with reality for several seconds when having these strong psychic episodes.

"Thanks for caring," she said with a smile and stroked the dog's head and neck. "Come on, Gunner, let me put on some shoes and I'll clean up the glass in the kitchen." As she walked back through the living room, Dannah suddenly realized that her laptop computer was also gone. "Dammit. That's another twelve-hundred bucks in the red." The words of a golden oldie song sprang to mind... *another day older and deeper in debt.*

Dannah cleaned the broken glass from the linoleum floor,

but saved the fragments. The screen on the door had been sliced with a sharp knife to get at the hook-and-eye that secured it. While watching Gunner tend to his "constitutional" in the back yard, she noticed that he was sniffing at an object lying in the grass and went to investigate. "Well, look at this. What a great detective you are, Gunner. You found an empty cigarette package." She wrapped it in a piece of paper towel and placed it on the kitchen counter to give to the police. She didn't remember seeing it earlier in the day. In fact, the grass in both back yards had been freshly mowed. "Maybe the investigators can get some fingerprints." Since a glass pane in the back door was broken and locking it would be fruitless, she slid a kitchen chair into position and tipped the ladder back under the doorknob. "You have my permission to bark your brains out if someone tries to enter again tonight."

Dannah and Gunner mounted the stairs to the second floor. Even though she had no experience in handling weapons, Dannah found the gun, took it into her bedroom and removed it from its case. She liked the heavy, solid feel of it. Maybe someday she would take some lessons at a gun range. Woman and dog climbed into bed, but neither was able to sleep for quite a while.

Athens, Georgia

Getting any more sleep would also be impossible for Jason Dunhill.

"Dammit," he muttered tiredly as he rolled out of the narrow twin bed, scratched his stubbled chin and lumbered into the bathroom. A strict work ethic had been drummed into Jason's head as he was growing up. In the academic world, it's "find and gloat," "publish or perish." Well, he had done the "finding," and by the end of the month, he would have accomplished the "publishing." "Perishing" was out of the question. He wasn't into the "gloat" portion of that equation, but the campus gossip grapevine had spread the information like wildfire. There had been seven graduate students with him on the dig—two women and five men. The blame lay with one of them. But, truthfully, he couldn't fault his students. Being excited over a new find was normal behavior for any anthropologist.

Hell, I'm excited.

Through a great deal of persistence and a little bit of luck, he had found one of the earliest human bones at the Chucalissa Mississippi River Indian Settlement. The radiocarbon-dating process had been done by the laboratories at the University of Georgia in Athens. His friend and former classmate, Randy Carter, had called him the previous Friday and the findings were in. Nine hundred AD. That's three hundred years earlier than any bones previously found at this location. Pottery shards and remnants of an ancient cooking fire found on the same level as the bone all came in with the same date.

Jason's conversation with the University President was satisfying and he promised to arrange a press conference for late Monday afternoon. Also, once his findings were published in a prestigious scientific journal and the news spread, it would mean additional grants for the University, and grants were what keep the research going and what attracts more students.

Money. It's all a matter of the Almighty Dollar.

Baxter had been one of the first researchers at the Chucalissa site back in the early eighties and, through the University, had done all the previous work, wrote a book, and had been published in several scientific journals. The site had been abandoned by researchers for many years because of Baxter's claim that he had reached the very first settlers. These days the compound was nothing more than a curiosity for tourists. It was run by a group of local Native Americans who sold their handcrafted wares.

Then, Jason received an intriguing phone call from friend and former classmate, Dave Brookman, who was a professor at the University of Arkansas. It was his suggestion to use ground-penetrating radar on the site to see if there were any earlier inhabitants. Bingo. Dave was not an anthropologist or archaeologist, but it was his idea to try this new technology in a different way. It would be shared glory, but glory nonetheless.

He was horrified that his combination houseguest and dog sitter had been subjected to such a frightening ordeal. Surprisingly, she had kept a cool head. He barely knew the woman, but still felt responsible for her safety while she was under his roof.

An image sprang to mind of the slightly built young woman dressed in light tan slacks and red silk blouse. His preoccupation with this research project had prevented him from examining her with his usual lusty male point-of-view. Even though he considered himself "off" women in general after his last romantic fiasco, Dannah's portraiture was still striking in his memory. Yes, he was preoccupied, but certainly not immune to the pure joy of checking out a beautiful woman. She was small, but extremely shapely. She had short curly hair so black it seemed to swallow the light. Her sparkling dark brown eyes were rimmed in thick chocolate lashes. There was an odd quality to her eyes, an inner depth that instantly reminded him of old Miss Gova. Even when Dannah's aunt had grown old, her eyes remained young and vibrant. Dannah possessed a genuine sincerity about her demeanor, which had caused him to make his impromptu invitation. Now look what happened? His good intentions for both of them to save a little money had gone straight to hell.

White hair? Bad cough. Four-door sedan? Baxter. It had to be Baxter. Is his professional jealousy that intense? He must be scared to death that I found something to negate his previous work. His name will be relegated to a footnote in the history books.

He was the only one who knew he was going out of town. That is, the only person with an agenda, or an ax to grind. Of course, Henning had tripped over his luggage when he came to air his gripe about the failing grade, but that spaced-out kid couldn't add two plus two and come up with four. Besides, he has dark hair, not light and has a slight build. Baxter is heavy set, has white hair, a bum knee and drives a beat up, beige colored Toyota Camry. The paint had oxidized from lack of care.

"Well, I'll deal with Baxter when I get home," Jason muttered, then got a drink of water and crawled back into bed. It was four-fifteen—one-hour time difference between Mississippi and Georgia. He could get another few hours' sleep; however, anger had the adrenaline pumping through his veins at a furious pace. He tried to concentrate on the steady hum of the air conditioning system, but nothing worked. The vision of the shy, petite, black-haired woman also roamed unwittingly inside his thoughts. He spent the remainder of the night tossing and turning.

Chapter Six
Wednesday morning

As Dannah Wingate entered the First Union Bank in downtown Oxford, Mississippi, the huge sign out front quietly announced it was ten in the morning and the temperature was already a blistering eighty-five degrees. It would be another typical hot, humid day in the Deep South of the Mississippi Delta. With a cutting sense of apprehension, she allowed herself to be led into the private office of the bank manager, Andrew Mahoney, who introduced himself.

"And this is Patsy Smith, a local realtor." He nodded toward a middle-aged woman. "She works closely with our bank to maintain, rent or sell properties handled by our Trust Department. She's been looking after the Wingate House since Miss Gova has been hospitalized."

Dannah shook hands with both people and was once again pleased by the lack of annoying visions.

"I'm terribly sorry we hadn't been in touch with you sooner," Mahoney announced after he motioned Dannah to a chair. "Most of the old files are stored away in the basement. Didn't want to tackle that, so we were preparing to enlist the aid of a private detective to locate you."

"I'm not hard to find. I'm a writer and have a web page. Google or any search engine could have found me in a few seconds."

He chuckled nervously. "Unfortunately, I haven't found the on-ramp to the technology super highway—too old to change my ways. I let my staff handle the computers." His slow, southern drawl was similar to Jason's and was probably indicative of this part of Mississippi. "I've been appointed executor of Miss Gova Wingate's Last Will and Testament. Maybe you'd like to talk to her lawyer and see a copy of the document. She named you as her sole beneficiary, but failed to list your address or even the city where you lived."

The news sucked the breath from her lungs. Words fell out

of her mouth in a confused stammer. "She, she what? But, how could that be?"

"I know, she was only sixty-two, but she had a great many health problems—the stroke, partial paralysis, high blood pressure, overweight, brittle bones, arthritis, diabetes, you name it, she had it. Didn't like doctors. Her health declined rapidly after she retired. However, according to the autopsy, she died of a heart attack."

Dannah's own heart stumbled over a couple of beats as she tried to grapple with this shocking turn of events. "No, no. I mean, how could she name me in her will? I never even met the woman."

"She told her lawyer that you are her only living heir. You are the last Wingate," he stated decisively. "She had a keen interest in genealogy."

"Genealogy?" she asked, hopefully arching a brow.

"You know, searching for your ancestors. She was also president of the local historical society several years ago and was very active in saving some of the old historical buildings around town. She had a picture of you as a little girl. I take it your father was Miss Gova's older brother."

"Yes, but they had very little contact with each other. I, I never really understood why."

Mahoney paused politely for her response, then continued. "Your aunt was known to be a bit eccentric. She taught high school until her health made her retire early. I don't know that she had many friends. She died about eleven at night, on July tenth."

"Ju-July tenth?" Dannah gasped and placed her right hand over her heart as if the external pressure could slow its frantic pace. What a wild chain of events over the past two months. Her first dream about death came on that very night and foretold a peaceful passage, without pain or fear. The full realization finally hit that her first vision, which had come on the tenth of July, must have been a depiction of the death of her aunt.

"According to the nursing-home staff, she died peacefully in her sleep," Mahoney continued. "What a character. Always talking about crazy things like ghosts and visions. Swore up until the day she died that her house on Azalea Lane was haunted. She kept the folks at the Sunny Care Nursing home both amazed and amused with her ability to read minds. It was downright scary at times. Remember 'Black Thursday' back in the eighties? Miss Gova came marching into the bank the Monday before the stock market crashed and moved all her investments into safer havens. She wouldn't invest in tech stocks—said it was a passing fancy—so she weathered the last crash as well. Yes, yes, she was a most remarkable woman with astounding intuition. I should have listened to her ravings. I'd be a rich retiree, sitting somewhere on a riverbank with a cold beer and a fishing pole."

Dannah was dumbfounded and tried desperately to assimilate the man's jumble of words. A sudden wave of frosty air blew across her body, chilling her to the bone. Her absentminded glance searched the room for the offending air conditioner or vent, but saw none. Profound loneliness wrapped her in its iron grip, gnawing away at her fragile peace of mind. Of all the hundreds of ancestors who preceded her, all the uncounted people who lived, loved and died...it ended with her. The Wingate family name had come to a screeching halt. Tears formed on her lower eyelids, then spilled over and flowed down her cheeks.

Auntie, there was so much I would like to say to you, so many questions to ask, and so much to be learned from the wisdom of your years.

"Ma'am? Are you all right?" Concerned by her tears, the bank manager handed her a box of tissues.

"It seems so unfair that I never got to know her." Dannah paused to blow her nose.

"Life has it's peculiar twists. Do you have a husband or any children?" Mahoney asked.

"No—no, I'm single."

"Apparently your aunt had been writing an entry in her journal when she fell asleep, then died."

The flow of Dannah's tears halted abruptly. "A journal?" she asked.

"More like a notebook. It has your name on the front page. It's just a little bit of scribbling. Impossible to read. Both of her hands were crippled by arthritis as well as the usual after-effects of a stroke. Patsy has the journal plus Miss Gova's other personal effects in a box at her real estate office."

"Maybe I can decipher it."

"Miss Wingate, we've prepared a financial statement for you. Once you've gotten over the shock of your loss, please arrange for an appointment to go over the entire estate. Miss Gova's attorney will want to be in attendance. There's the matter of probating the will. There are also tax forms to be filled out, applications and such to change the name on the title to the house, your new checking accounts and investments—"

"Checking accounts? Investments?" In dazed amazement, Dannah studied the computer-generated financial sheet handed to her. There was a little over five hundred thousand dollars invested in various mutual funds and bonds and another hundred thousand-plus in cash. Certainly enough to live comfortably without totally depleting the principal. This money would now offer her a pleasant relief from the constant push and worry to write and sell. It was like manna floating down from Heaven. This lovely windfall was coming just in the nick of time. "Good grief. Where did all this money come from?"

"Gova inherited old family wealth, plus she worked thirty years as a school teacher and lived frugally."

"That's strange. If Gova inherited this so-called 'old family wealth,' I wonder why my father never received any of it? They were brother and sister."

"Oh, but he could have when he turned twenty-one. The parents' will ordered the trust fund to be split between the two children, but he never touched a penny of it. Even signed a waiver. This bank managed the fund until Miss Gova reached twenty-one, then it was all turned over to her. She could have handled the fund very well on her own, but preferred to let the bank do most of the work. I've been in charge of her affairs for the last twenty years, and there were two other managers before me. It's strange that you never met her, because she talked about you all the time. She also paid the University of Tennessee for your entire college education. I wrote the checks myself. A hefty sum, I might add."

Dannah's mouth gaped open. "She, she what? But, but Daddy said...I mean, he told me it was scholarship money."

"Obviously, your father lied to you. Can't imagine why."

"Neither can I."

"Is he still living?"

"No, he died about a month ago." Dannah shook her head as she wrestled with this new information. It was too much to absorb, especially coming on the heels of last night's terrifying experience. Her mind felt emotionally battered. Finally, after a long silence, she handed the financial statement back to the banker.

"Keep it, I have another copy."

"This is quite a lot of money," she commented as she folded the paper and tucked it in her handbag.

"A certain amount of responsibility comes with money."

"You're right. I do accept the responsibility," Dannah stated with firmness as she pulled herself erect. "And I will certainly think everything through and carefully weigh all my options before doing anything hasty."

"Miss Gova had already given me proof of her relationship to you." He shuffled a few papers. "Let's see...her parents' marriage license, her birth certificate and your father's birth certificate. Of course, I'll need verification of your identity: your birth certificate, driver's license, social security number and such." Mahoney stood up, signaling the end of their meeting. "So, what are you going to do first?"

Dannah stood up as well and pressed the wrinkles from her trousers. "I guess the first thing I'm going to do is move into the Wingate House until I decide what to do with it." Dannah watched as Smith and Mahoney traded nervous glances.

Miss Smith, who had been quiet up til now, stated, "Ma'am, I don't think that's possible."

"It's going to have to be possible. I'll be moving in tomorrow or tonight if the utilities are turned on."

"Yes, there's electricity and water, but, I don't know what else you'll find." The realtor continued with her argument.

"According to my neighbor, you were supposed to be maintaining the house and grounds."

"Well, yes, but—"

"Have you been receiving payment for that chore?"

"Well, no, I mean, not me personally, but yes, a maintenance company sends a man to go through the house once a month to check for leaks, bugs or any other problems. I can give you his name and phone number."

"By all means, I want to have a talk with them. The house has only been empty for a year. How bad can it be? A little bit of dust, a few cobwebs. I can make do."

"I don't know when it was last remodeled—forties, fifties."

"The roof appears to be new," Dannah added.

"Yes, but Miss Gova would never allow anyone inside the house to do any modernization. It doesn't even have central air conditioning. The plumbing is outdated, the wiring is a disaster. It's a wonder the place hasn't burned down. Heaven knows, the repairs could cost more than the house is worth."

Dannah quickly reeled in her indignation. "I've seen the house and I don't share your pessimism. Besides, I'll be the one to make the final decision."

The skeptical agent shook her head. "You can stop by my office now and pick up a box of Miss Gova's personal belongings and the keys. You can also make arrangements for the phone to be turned on. But, don't say I didn't warn you."

"Warn me about what?" Dannah snapped back, expecting to hear more nonsense about skeletons-in-the-closet and ghosts.

The realtor's expressionless eyes met Dannah's without blinking. "The deplorable condition. What else?"

As Dannah turned to leave, the realtor made one more comment.

"Miss Wingate, let me make myself perfectly clear. I personally haven't been inside the house since your aunt had the stroke over a year ago last May and went into the nursing home. Then Mister Mahoney and I only made a quick tour of the main floor. I'm certain that Andrew will agree that 703 Azalea Lane is not the friendliest dwelling we've ever been in. At first, our professional opinions were that the house should be rented out during her rehabilitation, but after assessing the poor condition of the property, we changed our minds. Besides, the owner refused to consider it. Please understand that I'm not a superstitious person, but there's something rather sinister and foreboding about the place. Can't quite put my finger on it, but it felt very real to me."

Dannah's gaze traveled between the two people as she attempted to interpret the meaning of Miss Smith's odd declaration. "I guess I'll just have to see for myself, won't I?"

Chapter Seven
Wednesday afternoon

Dannah spent over an hour talking with both the local phone company and Patsy Smith at her real estate office. There were so many details to be taken care of: termite protection, real estate taxes, utilities, home owner's insurance, maintenance, et cetera, et cetera.

It was mid-afternoon when she finally piloted her car onto the crumbling concrete driveway. With keys in hand, she got out of her vehicle and studied the Wingate House in a new light. Thanks to an aunt she never met, this little piece of history now belonged to her. The surprising and unexpected relief for her declining financial situation caused her quiet, but real excitement. Her future was looking much brighter.

The elegant structure appeared strong, sturdy and defiant, and certainly not as deplorable as described by the realtor. The determination to save it, to bring it back to its original vitality, burned brightly in her heart. There was no one and nothing to hold her in Memphis. Her father was dead, her best girlfriend had recently moved to Atlanta to take a new job, and she had broken up with her boyfriend the previous year. The one nice thing about being a freelance writer—she could plug in her computer and do it anywhere.

"I'll bet the University has a great library for research," she stated with another burst of enthusiasm. "I might even go back to school for my Master's Degree in journalism."

Before entering the house, she went next door to get Gunner. He greeted her enthusiastically as she filled his dish with kibble and gave him a fresh bowl of water. She finally led him outdoors for his "constitutional," put Jason's mail on his kitchen table, then brought Gunner home with her.

"Home." She announced the word aloud and enjoyed the sound of it. "You know something, Gunner? This can be my home, my first real home   not like a rented apartment that belongs to someone else." The sign over the doorbell was probably done by some local Preservation Society for every house on the street, she silently mused. She forced the key into the rusty lock, wincing as the tumblers groaned, scraped and finally turned. The hinges squealed in protest as the door reluctantly opened.

Cautiously, she and Gunner entered the gloomy atmosphere and found stale air, dust and shrouded furniture. It looked like a scene from a Stephen King novel, complete with cobwebs gracefully decorating the crystal pendants of the chandelier. Although it was still daylight, she searched for a switch to see if the power was on. Dimmed by a healthy layer of dust, the bulbs in the two wall sconces cast their jaundiced glow into the entry hall.

"A giant can of WD-40 and a couple dozen high watt light bulbs—they'll be the first items on my shopping list."

Her attention was drawn to the lovely inlaid design of the wood floor in the turret. Its beauty could not be dimmed even by dust. A stairway was located behind the turret. The amount of elaborately carved wood trim was awesome. Interior decorators say that every home has a personality, and she was anxious to learn what the Wingate House would reveal to her. Certainly nothing sinister or foreboding.

As Dannah entered the parlor to the right of the front hall, the ambiance transported her into another era, with its high ceilings and elegant crown molding. The ceiling was inlaid with carved wood and the walls were painted a rich, dark shade of red. What had these rooms witnessed? Tragedy? Joy? Children laughing? She still had a problem envisioning her father as a little boy in suspenders and knickers running through the front door, the screen slamming behind him. She yanked the faded covers from the stiff formal furniture. The uninviting sofa, with its two matching chairs was raised on four curved legs and revealed threadbare upholstery.

A glass curio cabinet tucked into the far left corner was the next item to draw her gaze. It was filled with a ragtag assortment of ceramic figurines, along with one intricately beaded item which appeared to be Indian jewelry. She opened the glass door to examine it more closely. Bits of black onyx and turquoise stones were stitched to a leather band about an inch wide and several inches in length with two long strings, probably to tie it in place. Bracelet, necklace, or headband—she had no idea what it was. Dannah gave in to the undeniable urge to touch it. As her fingertips skimmed the beads, an icy puff of air tugged at the curls twining at her neck. She jerked her hand away, fearing a vision. An involuntary shiver darted down her spine, forcing her casual glance to skim the room to see if a door or window was open.

"The weather is still hot, you dummy." She reached for Gunner, who stayed glued to her left side, and stroked his muscular neck. Sensing her unease, he leaned into her leg and snorted softly.

The glazed brick fireplace now contained gas logs, and hanging above the mantel was an oil painting of a handsome couple and two small children. "Goodness, that looks like Daddy," she exclaimed aloud. The mother was definitely Native American. "Whoa! What a shock. Daddy never told me that anyone of our ancestors was Indian." But then, her father always stubbornly refused to even give her the names of his parents—a nagging bone of contention between father and daughter. The woman was wearing traditional Indian clothing, and the band from the curio cabinet was around her left wrist, another beaded band was around her long, elegant neck, and a third adorned her hair. "She's beautiful," Dannah muttered. "Absolutely stunning."

There was a remarkable resemblance between herself and the Indian woman, whose eyes, hair and facial bones were strikingly familiar. Something in the tilt of the young woman's determined chin made Dannah smile. Her own mirrored reflection often revealed the same lofty defiance.

A collection of very old sepia daguerreotypes was scattered across a lovely oak mantle. "Gunner, why did people always look so somber when they had their pictures made in those days? Hmmm? As if a show of humor and happiness was to be avoided at all cost." Other photos were of her father and his sister, Gova, when they were young. It was difficult to drag her attention away from the painting of her mesmerizing grandmother. However, branches of the magnolia tree swaying in the breeze scratched against the window glass and lured her eyes away from the photos and painting.

An upright, antique grandfather clock occupied the space between two west-facing windows. Dannah glanced at her watch, opened the glass door, and set the hands on three-ten. When she gave the pendulum a push, it made only two sluggish swings then stopped. "No wonder it won't work," she commented. "One of the three counterweights is missing." Her wandering glance scanned the room for the misplaced item, but couldn't find it.

The cozy little den, located behind a pair of glass-paned French doors, was apparently Gova's favorite place. The room might be just as her aunt left it a year ago, with her unfinished needlework lying in a basket by a well-worn chair. An old television sported a thick layer of dust. Heavily laden book shelves lined one wall, and dog-eared magazines were heaped here and there. A round floor pillow could have been a dog bed. The confusion gave the room a friendly, lived-in look, in spite of the high cavernous ceilings.

Another area of wall contained a collection of framed certificates and awards. Gova had graduated from the University of Mississippi with a degree in history and had won several awards for her work on the preservation of historical buildings. She taught tenth-grade American History and had won the "Mississippi Teacher of the Year" award in 1980. That her father was left out of the educational loop caused Dannah some concerns. He never went past high school and struggled all his life to earn a decent living

Why hadn't he taken advantage of the family money?

Both the den and parlor were darkened by drawn drapes. When Dannah parted the curtains, dust flew everywhere, causing a string of explosive sneezes. Dappled rays from the afternoon sun reflected on millions of swirling particles suspended in the air. In the new source of light, she saw two walls of floor-to-ceiling shelves, complete with a narrow ladder that slid on a rail. She examined her aunt Gova's books, hoping the titles might give additional insight into the woman. It was an eclectic collection books covering genealogy, local history, dream interpretations, psychic visions, ghosts, Native American lore along with several guidebooks to birds of Eastern North America. The title on psychic visions caught her attention and she pulled it from the shelf. "I'll take this one to bed with me tonight." An air-conditioning unit was blocking the bottom half of one window. Tentatively, she turned the switch to "cool." Surprisingly, the old compressor jolted to life and began to noisily spew out cold air.

The dining room was behind the entry hall and to the left of the den, its door beneath the second floor landing. And tucked beneath the staircase, there was a tiny powder room with a commode, pedestal washstand and a lovely antique mirror with a gilded frame. The room was tiny, but functional. Every inch of space was utilized and included a small coat closet wedged in behind the bathroom.

The colorful lead-glass chandelier was hanging above a trestle table in the dining room which was covered by a crocheted tablecloth and reinforced her perception of bygone days. There was even a large walk-in closet containing shelves stacked with delicately painted china dishes, elegant crystal stemware, a tarnished silver tea service, table linens, and a mahogany chest filled with equally tarnished silverware.

"Antiques. Probably valuable." She carried the tea service into the dining room and placed it on the table. "This is too pretty to hide. I'll add silver polish to my shopping list as well."

Dannah was struck by the notion that the floor plan of this house was strikingly similar to that of the Dunhill House. However, these rooms were much larger and on a grander scale. "Maybe all Victorian-style homes have the same general layout," she said, finding comfort in the sound of her own voice as it echoed in the silence.

The kitchen and breakfast room were last and the spacious area stretched across the entire rear of the house. The back door led into a screened-in area, then onto a flagstone patio. There was a tiny square mud room with three doors—one leading to the porch which wrapped around to the front of the house and one leading into the den. Behind still another door, was a steep, very narrow ascending staircase, wrapped in utter blackness. She imagined this was a servant's access to the second floor, but the darkness and musty smell, reminiscent of a funeral home, gave her second thoughts about exploring the area.

"I'll investigate it later," she muttered. "I'll need a flashlight."

An uneasy sensation engulfed her as she stepped in front of the kitchen sink. An unsettled knowledge flitted through her mind that something horrendous had happened on this spot. The apprehension was more like a nebulous nagging and wasn't at all like some of her other perceptions, which were more alive and carried a fresh immediacy with them. This impression was a little vague, more difficult to define, but, she could imagine light shining on a silver blade. Even the metallic odor of spilled blood seemed to be toying with her sense of smell. She stared down at the old linoleum floor whose colored design was nearly worn away. Mesmerized, she had trouble diverting her attention.

"The realtor said this place was 'sinister and foreboding.' Maybe. Maybe not." After forcing herself to shake off her edgy mood, she once again reached for Gunner, who was close on her heels. His presence was comforting.

The kitchen ceiling was inlaid tin pressed into a floral design. There were lots of cabinets and countertop space. A round oak table was nestled in the far left-hand corner next to a three-quarter circle of bay-style windows. An old rotary dial phone was on one of the counters. The line would be activated tomorrow. The avocado-green color dated the appliances to the nineteen-sixties or late fifties. A large, walk-in pantry was tucked beneath the stairwell and included a fairly new washer and dryer, no doubt a modern addition, while a second smaller pantry contained canned goods and such, along with a vintage vacuum cleaner, broom, dust mop and scrub mop as well. Dannah noticed that the floor of the pantry was made of wooden planks and contained a metal ring and hinges. She tapped her foot. It sounded hollow. After tugging on the handle for a few seconds, she noticed that the trap door was secured in place with about fifty or sixty very large nails. Her dad had called them "sinkers."

"Seems like overkill," she mused.

Although old, the refrigerator offered a reassuring hum. She peered inside. It was empty, but churned out plenty of cold air.

"A six-pack of diet cola would be nice." She closed the

appliance and scanned the room. "What do you think, Gunner?" she asked the dog, who was an attentive audience. "Can I manage to live alone in a house this big? Say, Gunner, do you have a girl friend or maybe a little sister?" Dannah laughed when he woofed softly in response and leaned down to give him a big hug. "I'm ready to be a responsible pet owner now that I have a home. Of course, I would need to fence the back yard."

Dannah returned to the main entry hall and started to climb the stairwell to the second floor, but decided that further investigation would have to wait until after a trip to the local superstore. The first item on her agenda was to fill the fridge and pantry and buy an assortment of light bulbs, paper products and cleaning supplies. And a cordless phone would be a necessity. Tomorrow, she would screw one-hundred-watt bulbs in every light fixture in the entire house and would offer up a quiet prayer that the ancient wiring wouldn't melt from the overload.

She left Gunner at the Dunhill House, then got in her car and headed for the nearest store. She shopped in frenzy, tossing a wide variety of items into the shopping cart, and running up a bill of over three hundred dollars.

Easy come, easy go, she thought as she pulled out her trusty credit card.

It was a chore stuffing all the sacks into her small vehicle. "I'll have to trade in my sports car for an SUV or a pickup truck now that I'm a homeowner. Oh, I love the sound of that."

Yes, she was definitely ready for the challenges which lay ahead, and in fact, welcomed an infusion of excitement into her dull daily existence. The safety net offered by her newly found wealth already was beginning to lighten the worry of finances that weighed so heavily on her shoulders.

***

The kitchen counters were piled high with plastic grocery sacks when the cell phone tucked in her handbag started ringing. It was Jason.

"Dannah, I got a late start. I'm just now getting through Atlanta. Traffic's a bitch, and I still have to get through

Birmingham. You okay?"

"Yes, thank you, I'm fine."

"Anything else happen last night?"

"No, but I had trouble getting back to sleep," Dannah admitted.

"So did I. You have no idea how upset I am that you were exposed to danger. Nothing like this has ever happened in our neighborhood."

"With Gunner to look after me, I honestly didn't feel like I was in any real danger. I'm sorry to say that my laptop computer was stolen as well. I left it on the coffee table in the living room last night. Maybe your homeowner's insurance will cover it."

"We'll call the cops when I get home, also my insurance agent. Never filed a claim before, but I think I'll need the police report to give them. Say, how'd it go at the bank this morning?"

"You're not going to believe this, but Aunt Gova wrote a will and left her house and money to me."

"What a surprise. You're going to be my neighbor? Permanently?"

"I don't know. If the house doesn't cost too much for maintenance, I might keep it."

"Hey, that's great, but last night was a damned poor welcome to the neighborhood. Listen, it will be after dark when I get home. Where are you going to sleep tonight? I don't want to scare you when I come creeping in after midnight."

"Your back door still has a big gaping hole in it, so I'd rather sleep here at the Wingate House. I haven't been upstairs yet, but I'm certain Aunt Gova must have a usable bed up there. If you don't mind, I'll keep Gunner with me."

"Be my guest."

"I'm falling madly in love with your dog and I think the emotion is mutual."

"He's a smart fellow. Appreciates a beautiful woman just like his master," Jason responded with a throaty chuckle. "See you tomorrow morning, Dannah, but not too early. I'm desperate for a few hours' sleep. Thanks for everything."

As Dannah hit the end button on her cell phone, she

glanced at her wrist watch. It was a little past five-thirty and she was hungry, not having taken the time to eat lunch. After putting away the groceries, she fixed a light dinner and sat down at the big oak table next to the bay window. Gunner was lying at her feet on a small throw rug when he suddenly sat up. He didn't growl, but his erect ears moved from front to side, as if trying to pinpoint the origin of a distant noise.

"What do you hear?"

The dog responded by standing up and striking a regal pose with his muscles tense. His eyes rolled upward to the ceiling.

Dannah strained to separate the normal sounds of outside activities from the silence within the house. "That's a bell—a very small one. Maybe Aunt Gova has a chiming clock upstairs."

***

Jason squinted into the setting sun as he set aside his cell phone and gripped the steering wheel with both hands. The corners of his turned-down mouth lifted in a rare smile. Dannah was going to be his new next-door neighbor—one who wasn't old and doddering. He pressed a little harder on the accelerator, forcing the needle on the speedometer to inch forward a couple of notches. There was a strange new feeling settling in the pit of his stomach that he was definitely unfamiliar with—an urgency to get home.

***

After washing the dishes, Dannah decided it was time to investigate the second story of this grand old house. "Come with me, Gunner. Let's check out the bedrooms. Maybe we can find a place to rest our weary bones tonight."

It was after six-thirty and the September sun was settling in for its nightly rest. A row of four light switches was on the wall at the base of the staircase. One controlled the front porch, one was for the two wall sconces where the hall narrowed, and the third lit the crystal chandelier hanging from the entry-hall ceiling. "This fourth switch...ah," she whispered half aloud. "This controls the upstairs hall." She peered up into the darkly shadowed area. Because of Gova's intense drive to be thrifty, there wasn't a light bulb in the entire house larger than forty watts.

She ascended the stairwell clutching the banister with one hand and a sack filled with one-hundred-watt bulbs in the other. The stairs curved gently to a landing level where stained-glass artwork covered a small round window overlooking the side-by-side driveways. The steps turned back toward the center of the house to the main hall on the second floor. Gunner was by her side making snuffling sounds as he thoroughly investigated the dust bunnies caught in the corner of each bull-nose riser. The stain on the old oak was nearly worn away by foot traffic. As she reached eye level with the second floor, Dannah noticed a pattern of footprints disturbing the thick layer of dust.

"Geez, bare footprints?" They were definitely feminine with a high arch and the pad of each slender toe plainly outlined. "Certainly not made by the maintenance man. I'm going to have to get the name and phone number of this guy and look at his feet."

The situation was screaming for a logical explanation, but only silently within her head. Her mental state was not ready to deal with the possible sources of the footprints. She grabbed Gunner's collar and went several steps higher. The footprints trailed from the rear of the hall to the top of the stairwell, then returned from whence they came. She stood quietly on the top step and looked around her. The stairs to the third floor were nowhere to be seen, but appeared to have been removed. The plaster on the walls and ceiling was poorly patched, and the lengths of hardwood planks on the floor didn't match either. "Very strange."

Carefully avoiding the footprints, Dannah and Gunner moved down the hall as near to the wall as possible. They inched past two bedrooms on the right, and one bedroom and one bathroom on the left, closest to Jason's house. She was gripping Gunner's collar so tightly that the chain links had made a painfully deep gouge into the flesh of her hand. The pain seemed to balance out her fears.

At the far end of the hall, a fourth bedroom had been converted into the storage area and next to it, a small, obviously rarely used bathroom. The white porcelain fixtures were heavily coated with dust and rust stains. The footprints disappeared beneath this door. There were no other marks displacing the layer of dust. The brass doorknob felt exceptionally cold to the touch as Dannah hesitantly wrapped her fingers around the tarnished metal. The door didn't want to open. Maybe moisture in the air had caused the wood to swell. She leaned in with her shoulder. Finally, after a mighty shove, the door flew open.

A musty odor accompanied by fear in its purest form came streaming out of the darkened room like morning fog sweeping across a field of newly planted cotton. It was a living entity, either seeking escape from its confinement, or food to feed on. Even Gunner was affected, rocking from side to side on his front paws, looking to her for guidance. Dannah refused to become fodder for its gruesome appetite.

She overcame her hesitation and peered inside, feeling proud that she was achieving some adeptness at managing what she perceived to be her totally unfounded fears. Footprints in the dust and a stuck door were hardly menacing. The two windows were boarded from within, allowing only a tiny bit of the waning light to seep in between the rough wooden planks. She found the light switch. The fixture was a bare bulb dangling at the end of a strand of frayed wire. The room was more like an oversized closet and was filled, from floor to ceiling, with a dozen or more old-fashioned trunks, tied or taped boxes, several lamps and pieces of out-dated furniture—end tables, headboards, even an old wooden rocking chair was lying on its side atop an antique cedar chest. The floor was covered with an old piece of carpet. Dannah groaned. It would take her months to sort through a hundred-plus years of castoffs and keepsakes.

As she started to retreat, Dannah noticed another door in the rear corner of the storage area. She studied the layout of the rooms and decided it was likely an entrance to that second flight of stairs she saw in the kitchen. She wound her way through the clutter and tried to open it, however, the door was secured with a hasp, loop and padlock. "I'll add bolt cutters to my next shopping list."

As she and the dog backed out of the storage room, a distant sound floated up from the main floor. The clock was chiming.

Three...four...five...six.

Another wave of emotion engulfed her entire body and caught her off-guard with its angry intensity. A shiver darted down her spine. "This is foolishness. That clock can't be chiming. The damned thing is broken. I'm letting my imagination run wild."

Her attention was drawn again to the footprints clearly outlined in the dust that paraded down the hall. She bent down on one knee and dragged her finger across the imprint. "No dust in the center. Like it could be new."

Pushing her fears aside, she continued with her investigation. In the largest of the bedrooms were a double bed, a night stand holding a hobnail lamp crusted with dust, a dresser cluttered with perfumes and lotions, a chest of drawers, and a small closet crammed so full of her aunt's belongings that the door wouldn't stay shut. There were clothes, purses, a weird assortment of hats and more shoeboxes than she cared to count. The ends of some of the boxes had been date marked with a felt-tip pen, others had names. Curiosity prodded her to open one. It contained old letters, pictures and newspaper clippings. She was sorely tempted to sit down and dig in, but forced herself to put a damper on her insatiable curiosity and wait until later. There were too many other chores that needed her immediate attention.

The main bathroom contained a cast-iron tub gracefully elevated on four clawed feet. "Geez, no shower." Dannah laughed out loud and the unaccustomed sound careened along the dusty, varnished wood floors. The linen closet in the bathroom contained a generous supply of neatly folded towels and bed sheets. Dannah twisted the faucets, stood back and watched as the pipes belched, quivered, and spewed rust-colored liquid for several minutes before the water finally cleared.

"At least the hot water tank is still working. Must be electric. Hmmm, if I knocked out the wall in the largest bedroom like Jason Dunhill did to his upstairs, I could build a walk-in closet and a huge master bath. Oh yes, and a garden tub surrounded by glass brick." Dannah laughed again, enjoying the friendly noise. "Maybe I shouldn't engage in any sort of emotional relationship with this house," she exclaimed. "Maybe I should simply live here a few months while I catch up on my reading and writing, and fix up the place so I can sell it."

It was getting late and Dannah decided to wait until tomorrow to finish her exploration. "Gunner, let's make one last trip outside. We'll lock up the house, then I'll take a bath and we'll go to bed early. I'm exhausted and I've got a lot of physical labor to do tomorrow."

She decided to sleep in what was probably Gova's bedroom. There was another window unit in this room and although noisy, it did a great job of cooling the area. After bathing and changing the sheets, she settled into bed to read for a while. As she grew sleepy, the book slipped down onto her stomach. "I think what I have is called 'touch telepathy,'" she mused aloud. "How convenient that it has a name. Of course, that doesn't account for the vivid dreams about the deaths of Daddy and Aunt Gova."

She rolled over and twisted the switch on the hobnail lamp, but it refused to extinguish. Groaning with exasperation, she rattled the base and it still didn't go out. Finally, she groped around the dusty floor and unplugged the lamp.

"With so many things needing repair," she muttered as she snuggled beneath the covers, "a well stocked tool box will be a necessity. Tomorrow, we go to the hardware store. Gunner, come sleep with me. How stupid of me to be afraid of you last night." He jumped on the bed, snuggled into the crook of her arm and lavished her with kisses. "Hmmm, much better than a cat."

***

Dannah awakened in the middle of the night, sat up in bed and glanced around her. The tenebrous corners seemed to harbor frightening shapes. Everything was unfamiliar. As she cleared the cobwebs of sleep from her mind, she thought she heard a noise. Gunner was reacting with perked ears and an inquisitive look, but no perceptible alarm as he had the previous night.

He has probably grown accustomed to the pop and groan of old houses, she thought. She was no longer afraid of the large dog, and in fact, was becoming fond of him and felt safe in his presence. The bathroom light had been left on for security and she could see the reassuring square of yellow slanting into the hall. The two dots of light brown above the dog's eyes created all sorts of interesting expressions. Prodded by her curiosity, she decided to investigate. She turned off the noisy air conditioner and strained her ears trying to separate the normal sounds of the night from anything out of the ordinary.

Could it be the chiming of the broken grandfather clock in the living room? Again? Or, could it possibly be the tinkling sound of a tiny bell she'd heard earlier? Her search of the second floor had revealed no other chiming clocks.

"Let's check it out." Dannah grasped Gunner's chain collar and they slowly descended the stairs. The squeak was louder than those in Jason's house. On the landing midway, she paused to stare out the window at the shared double driveway. It was two-thirty. The pale, octagonal-shaped beam of illumination from the hall lights shone through the landing window and onto Jason's white SUV parked in its usual spot. Gunner put his paws on the window ledge, looked out and wagged his tail.

"Jason's home," she told him. A sudden and unexpected feeling of safety drifted lazily throughout her body. Was it indeed safety, or some other warm and cozy sensation?

Before continuing with her descent, she peered over the banister into the hall below her. The front door was still closed, the wall sconces illuminated. The slip chain was dangling loose, swinging slightly as if set it in motion by an unseen hand or a gentle spring breeze. Had she forgotten to secure it in its slot? Had Jason tried to enter the house? Dust from the wood floor clung to the bottoms of her bare feet as she walked across the entry hall. A musty odor flirted with her senses, tickled the lining of her nostrils and made her sneeze

Achoo. Even her eyes watered and she wiped them with the tail of her pajama shirt. Her fingers trembled as she secured the chain, tested the dead bolt and strode into the living room. The silence was broken only by the click of Gunner's toenails on the wood flooring as he trailed behind her. She turned on a small table lamp and stared at the clock. One of the counter weights was still missing. The hands were still set on three-ten where she had previously set them.

Movement caught her eye. To the right of the clock, a rocking chair was gliding back and forth in the slow deliberate cadence a mother would use to soothe a cranky baby. Her entire body shuddered involuntarily as her mind raced frantically. She could not remember seeing the chair in that spot on her earlier forays through the main floor. She distinctly remembered seeing one identical to this upstairs stored in the fourth bedroom. Going back to see if it was missing was the reasonable option; however, reason and logic were escaping her right now.

"No, surely I must be imagining things," she muttered to the dog. "Let's go back to bed."

As Dannah climbed the stairs and reached eye level with the long expanse of wood that stretched the length of the upstairs hall, she noticed a second set of bare footprints on top of the previous ones, and on top of her own prints disturbing the deep overlay of dust. All the warmth in her blood was replaced by ice water. The chill of fear.

Fear, she noted, was cold, whereas terror caused the blood to rush and become overheated.

Chapter Eight
Thursday morning

Jason Dunhill sat up, rubbed at the grit in his eyes, then glanced at the bedside clock. Eight. He had slept like death itself. He had been so exhausted when he'd arrived home about midnight that he had gone straight to bed. He rolled out of the tangled covers, took a quick shower, shaved and dressed. His usual warm weather attire, when he wasn't teaching, was shorts, a tee shirt and sandals. He felt refreshed as he headed down stairs to check out his office and the extent of his losses. He groaned as he surveyed the papers that had been tossed around the room.

"It has to be Baxter. He's afraid I've uncovered something that puts him in a bad light," he muttered gruffly as he picked up the pages scattered across the floor. They were nothing more exciting than test scores from his latest group of grad students. None of the papers on his scientific article was among the debris. The large black zippered case holding all his system software was also gone, as well as his CD burner.

Anger exploded. Unspoken words pressed to be vented as he got in his car and drove straight to the campus.

Baxter's secretary delivered a hurried greeting as Jason strode purposefully into the familiar office. He slammed his knotted fist on the desk.

"You did it, didn't you?" Jason demanded.

"Did what?" Baxter stood up and adjusted his trousers over his belly.

His feeble attempt to fake innocence only intensified Jason's rage. "You broke into my house and trashed my computer."

"I don't know what you're talking about."

Jason stared into Baxter's watery eyes as the man fiddled with his tie. As if for the first time, he noticed Baxter's bushy white hair, pale grayish complexion and the weary slope of his shoulders. However, pity was not in his present range of emotions. "If you didn't do it, then you paid somebody else to do it."

Martha, Baxter's secretary, appeared in the door. "Is something wrong?"

"Damn right there's something wrong. Your boss is a freakin' thief," Jason snapped, storming out of the small office filled with unresolved fury.

***

Fifteen minutes later, Jason knocked on the kitchen door of the Wingate House.

"Come in," Dannah called out in friendly invitation. "I've got coffee ready and I can fix you some scrambled eggs and toast if you're hungry."

"Great, I'm starved." Gunner greeted him enthusiastically.

"Won't take a minute," she said with a smile as she dropped two pieces of bread in the toaster. "Where did you rush off to in such a hurry this morning?"

"I did something I probably shouldn't have done. I drove over to the campus and confronted Baxter. Of course, he denied everything, but he didn't look one bit surprised."

"Well, sometimes anger gets the best of us."

"I'll call the police as soon as I eat."

"Help yourself to some coffee."

As he stood beside Dannah, adding cream and sugar to his cup, he realized that she was much smaller than he remembered and a sense of protectiveness sprang to life. She gave him a shy glance as she whipped the raw eggs into an airy froth then poured them into the heated skillet.

Jason slouched in a chair by the huge oak kitchen table as he sipped his coffee and tried to calm down. It was difficult to maintain his anger with the morning sun shining in the big bay window to lend a cheery atmosphere to everything. He had been in this kitchen many times, over the years, to enjoy milk and home-baked cookies as a reward for doing small chores for Miss Gova. However, Dannah seemed to create a warmer, more welcoming atmosphere. Dangerous thoughts for a single man. "You're looking bright-eyed, cheery and, and very beautiful this morning."

"Thank you. I've been up since six. I scrubbed three

bathrooms and dusted all the wood floors. Footprints were everywhere. Did you check out the damage in your office?"

He nodded as he sipped at his coffee. "Yeah, it's pretty grim. The bastard put a virus into my computer." Both anger and hunger were temporarily forgotten as he watched Dannah float gracefully around the kitchen while fixing his breakfast. The self-assurance that radiated from her indicated she would be at home in a palace or a pig sty. Damn, the image he had hurriedly squirreled away in his head on Tuesday fell far short of the flesh-and-blood version of the woman. The knit tee shirt and jeans she was wearing hugged every curve with subtle seduction, and yet her manner of dress imparted a look of youthful innocence. Most of the career-type women he knew tried to hide their femininity beneath starkly tailored clothes, a severe hairdo, and unimaginative makeup. Dannah possessed a natural blush to her cheeks, pink-shaded lips, and thick, dark lashes circled her eyes. The charm and confidence with which she moved, at least in Jason's eyes, hinted of suppressed passion. He had been so consumed by his current research project that his social life had been nonexistent for nearly two years—thanks to one double-crossing gal named Liz Carpenter. Dannah presented a new, interesting and fascinating challenge. There was probably a helluva lot more hiding within than she was willing to reveal to a man she barely knew. He was captivated by this diminutive woman who could coolly handle what she did and not fall apart. Being a natural-born realist, he was seldom impressed by a woman. He had seen all kinds during his seven-year teaching career—from bored housewives, blatant husband-hunters, to wanna-be beauty queens looking for an easy course. This young lady was far different.

"I'm sorry you were subjected to the fright of a break-in. We've never had any crime problems in this neighborhood."

She turned to face him and delivered a devastatingly sweet smile that he felt all the way to his toes. "It certainly wasn't your fault. Besides, I survived. Thanks to Gunner, I never felt personally threatened. I was a little bit afraid of him at first—his size and impressive set of teeth—but I finally realized that he wanted to protect me and not attack me."

"I don't know many women who could go through such an ordeal and not come unglued. You are one cool lady."

"Thanks, but I might very well have come unglued if one of the burglars had tried to come upstairs. They were noisy and acted like they were fully aware that no one was home."

"Yeah, Baxter knew I was going out of town. I was arguing with him over the phone when you came to my door on Tuesday. He did the original work on the Chucalissa site, wrote a book and I guess he's worried about what I've uncovered. He and I have never been the best of friends; in fact, we've locked horns concerning curriculum on many occasions. But I never dreamed he'd go to such lengths to, to...." Jason's voice dribbled off, his train of thought derailed, when Dannah set a plate of eggs in front of him.

As he ate, Jason continued to tally even more of Dannah's visible assets. Her sparkling dark brown eyes had extraordinary depth, indicating the capacity to traverse a broad range of emotions, running the gambit from anger and defiance to friendly, to unknowingly sexy. That she wasn't aware of her satin sexuality made her even more intriguing. She sat down opposite him, her small hands wrapped around a mug of coffee, and a friendly smile parted her lips.

"I guess we should call the police and report the break-in," she said.

He nodded as he swallowed a mouthful of food. "I'm not looking forward to it, but it's a necessary evil."

"After they leave, we'll make a detailed list of all the stolen items. You'll have to give one to the insurance company. That, as well as the police report."

Jason finished breakfast, then made the call using his cell phone.

* * *

Several hours later, Jason, Dannah and Gunner sat on the front steps of the Dunhill House and watched as nosey neighbors walked or slowly drove by craning their necks to see what was going on. Police cars in this quiet neighborhood were a rarity. The repeated flash of a camera from within the house illuminated windows. Most of the morning had been spent waiting for the detective to finish his investigation. Finally, the head honcho appeared at the front door.

"Come into the living room. I've got some questions to ask. I'm Detective Jerry Bob Richards," he announced, ignoring the nicety of shaking hands. As he sank into one of the overstuffed chairs, he fiddled with a small tape recorder. "Let's begin with you, Missus Dunhill. Suppose you begin with Tuesday afternoon and retrace your steps."

"Wait a minute. I'm Dannah Wingate, not Missus Dunhill."

The detective arched a brow, shrugged and continued unflustered. "Whatever."

"I think we have to back up further than that," Dannah exclaimed as she settled on the sofa next to Jason. The detective looked like he might be a former Marine. His posture was ramrod straight, his body lean and his hair close-cropped in military style, with just a touch of gray at the temples.

"Okay, little lady. Since you told me earlier that you were on the premises alone when the robbery took place, why don't you tell me your side of the story first."

Dannah pulled in a deep breath and retold the story of coming to Oxford on Tuesday in search of her aunt, of learning about her death, setting up an appointment at the bank, and ultimately agreeing to house-sit and dog-sit for Jason, who needed to go out of town. She continued with a description of being awakened by the sound of broken glass, hearing what she thought were three voices, all the way to seeing the moonlight shining on a heavy-set man with light hair, and lastly, describing his car.

"Could you identify him in a police lineup?"

"I doubt it, I didn't see his face. Only the shape of his body and the way he moved—like he was limping. I know for a fact that I heard conversation from two distinct voices. The third voice was deep, raspy and coughed a great deal. I couldn't make out what he was saying. I was sitting on the top step of the stairwell with Gunner." The animal, who was seated by Dannah's feet, responded to the sound of his name and peered up at her.

"Why didn't you sic the dog on them? He looks mean enough."

"He wanted to go after them, but I was afraid they might have a gun, or some other weapon." Dannah smiled inwardly as she noticed the detective eyeing the large animal with a fearful glance. Obviously, owning a large and powerful dog such as a Doberman gave the owner a sense of superiority.

Jason interrupted. "Believe me, Detective Richards. All of my students and fellow teachers know I own this dog, and would not attempt to break into my house if my car was in the driveway. Although unwarranted, everyone is afraid of him. He goes on all my summer expeditions and is great protection for my tools and electronics."

Dannah continued. "After the break-in, I smelled cigarette smoke in Jason's den, and, later, Gunner found an empty cigarette pack outside in the yard. I laid it on the kitchen counter. Maybe you can get some fingerprints."

"Why didn't you call the police Tuesday night when the theft took place?"

"First I called Jason on his cell phone and asked him what I should do. He thought it would be best for him to make a list of what was stolen before we called. And...well, to be honest, I was afraid that you would ask questions I couldn't answer and think that I had no business being in the house."

"So, you and Jason aren't a couple?"

"Well, no." Dannah glanced nervously at Jason. "I just met him Tuesday afternoon."

Richards knitted his brows and turned his head to scowl at Jason. "Dunhill. Are you telling me you left a total stranger to dog-sit in a house filled with expensive computer equipment?"

Jason hurried to Dannah's defense. He put his arm around her shoulders and squeezed as he told what sounded like a convincing lie. "Dannah and I, well, we knew each other as kids. Yeah right, she's a Wingate. She would come down here from Memphis to visit her aunt during her summer vacations. But I hadn't seen her since she, she grew up."

"Yes, Detective Richards, just yesterday I learned that I've inherited the house next door from my deceased aunt." Dannah carefully skirted around the truth, trying not to tell any truly blatant fibs.

"So, Dunhill, what was stolen from your house on Tuesday night?" Richards asked.

Jason shook his head. "I haven't had time to take a complete written inventory. I was exhausted when I got in last night and went straight to bed. This morning, I did a quick survey then went—Well, I went over to Dannah's to make sure she was okay. I know my laptop is gone, three hunting rifles, a stack of photos, some important scientific papers, my CD burner and all my software CDs, including one program that cost two grand. I've got a really expensive piece of software that I use at dig sites to log the grid location of all the finds in virtual reality. Also, they trashed my big desktop computer by planting a virus. It corrupted everything. I'm really steamed over this. I could break Baxter's neck for committing such an underhanded trick." Jason smashed his fist into his open palm, barely able to contain his anger. "Doesn't the value of my property—stolen or damaged—put this into grand theft, or larceny, or something big?"

"I'll ask the questions. You give the answers." The detective snapped back at Jason.

Dannah added in, "Don't forget my laptop computer was also stolen."

Richards eyed her suspiciously then went into a flurry of note-taking. After a few moments, he directed his attention toward Dannah again. "Are you absolutely certain of all the facts you've stated?"

"Yes, I'm certain," she stated emphatically.

"I'll have your statement typed up and you'll have to come to police headquarters and sign it later this afternoon. Okay, Dunhill. Let's hear your side of the story. First, for the record, tell me what you do for a living?"

"I'm a professor of anthropology at the University."

"Do you know anyone who has a grudge against you— like a disgruntled student or a jealous coworker?"

"Like Dannah said, it all started Tuesday afternoon. First, I received a telephone call from Professor Bill Baxter, the department head, asking what I had uncovered during this season's dig. He's jealous and we argued. He probably thinks I want his job."

"Do you?"

"Definitely not. No desk job for me. I don't like the administrative details connected with teaching. Baxter manages forty classes—students and professors. Too much paperwork. Then Larry Henning, one of my students, came here to complain about a failing grade I gave, which prevented him from graduating. He took a make-up course during the summer, but failed again. Personally, I think he stays high on something—you know, like drugs."

"There are drugs on every campus in the country," Richards commented matter-of-factly. "From college down to middle schools and elementary."

"Well, he's also got a rich, overindulgent father. Larry likes to flash his big roll of money. Personally, I believe that struggling to get your education develops character. Some students take anthropology classes because they think it's easy. That it's only digging in the dirt and playing with bones. But that's not what this course is all about." After Dannah secretly nudged him, he took a deep breath and returned to the subject. "Anyway, I told him to go see Bill Baxter, the department head, about taking a make-up class under a different professor."

"So, this Professor Baxter and your former student are the two main suspects? Then there's a third unidentified male."

"I don't know who else has an ax to grind. Maybe it's one of Henning's drug-buddies. I'm supposed to make a formal announcement of my 'find' at a news conference on Monday afternoon. Baxter might have thought he could steal my artifacts and therefore stop my announcement, but they were in Athens being radiocarbon dated. That's where I was—Athens, Georgia."

"Did Henning know you were leaving town?"

"Baxter knew, but I didn't tell Henning. Although my suitcase was sitting in the middle of the front hall. He had to step around it to get in or out."

Richards glanced at the tape recorder, then continued taking notes, occasionally interrupting Jason. "Henning and Baxter—which one is heavy set?"

"Baxter. I left here around three o'clock on Tuesday afternoon. Like I said before, I got home around midnight on Wednesday. I was exhausted and went straight to bed. I drove sixteen hours in two days. And I made the same trip last Tuesday and Wednesday. Check my cell phone records. It will prove where I was when the calls were made."

"That's right," Dannah added. "I woke up about two-thirty to go to the bathroom and saw his car in the driveway."

"So, Miss Wingate, you spent Tuesday night here in Dunhill's house and Wednesday night next door."

Dannah nodded and announced with a touch of pride in her voice, "Yes, the house is mine now. Besides, the back door of Jason's house was broken—it can't be locked. So, I took Gunner with me and slept next door."

"I'll have both these statements typed up. I'll expect the two of you down at police headquarters sometime this afternoon. Bring your inventory of stolen goods." Detective Richards put away his tape recorder, pad, pencil and stood up. "Oh, and by the way, don't talk to either Baxter or Henning."

When Dannah glanced at Jason, the detective was quick to pick it up. "So, you already confronted one of them?"

"Yeah, Baxter. Of course, he denied everything."

"Not a smart move on your part. We don't usually do a full-blown investigation for a minor theft—"

"Minor?" Jason bellowed. "It'll cost at least six or seven grand to replace everything I lost. I don't know what the insurance will cover. You know, this isn't about me personally. It's about what I might have uncovered. I did this work in conjunction with a professor from the University of Arkansas. I've got to explain this to him as well."

"Is he a suspect?"

"Hell no. He lives in Arkansas. He handled the ground-penetrating radar."

"I'm a Mississippi graduate myself and I've kept in close contact with all the professors in the Criminal Justice department. I've even conducted some career seminars. Since you're a professor as well, maybe you'd like to have some of the grad students come in to collect all trace evidence. As you know, the city and county aren't large enough to have criminalists on the payroll. We have to use the State Agency from Jackson. If you'll agree to it, this is good practice for them. Especially since no murder is involved." The man shook his finger at nothing in particular. "You know, forensics is where the future lies. These days, crimes are solved under a microscope."

"Yeah, yeah, whatever." Jason was thoroughly exasperated.

"School isn't in session yet, so it'll be Monday before I can get them rounded up. Don't disturb anything. We'll be in touch with you."

"Say, are you going to question Baxter?"

"We'll need probable cause. First, let me see if we get any fingerprint matches."

"All teachers are fingerprinted these days," Jason added.

Everyone exchanged business cards. "Call me if you remember anything significant."

Jason and Dannah walked to the front door and waited for Detective Jerry Bob Richards to get in his car and leave.

"Let's have another look around my office," Jason suggested.

Dannah trailed after him and watched as he rummaged through all of his desk drawers. Finally, appearing defeated and bereft, he sagged into his chair and shook his head.

"Nope, they took everything. I'll have to rewrite the entire article and it won't make the November issue. My only lucky break is that the photo negatives are lying on my dresser in the upstairs bedroom. I'll get them developed next week. I had the pictures done by a professional photographer so the lighting would be just right for publication."

"What about the bones and artifacts?"

"They're safely locked in the glove compartment in my

truck."

"Give me paper and pencil and we can start on the written inventory right now."

"Good idea," Jason said.

Trying not to disturb any surfaces which might yield fingerprints, they made a list of everything stolen.

"Jason, I wasn't prepared for this turn of events. I need to go back to Memphis to pick up my desktop computer, electronic stuff and all my clothes. I'll probably put my furniture in storage. No sense paying rent on the place when I'll be living here. And, I need to do something about my dad's house."

"I'll be glad to help. Your new Corvette won't hold much and I have my SUV. It's dirty, but I can clean it up a little."

"I don't want to put you out."

"No problem. I owe you several favors, as well as the cost of a new laptop."

"I can wait until you get the insurance settlement. Right now, I'm not in the mood to work anyway. Besides, I have a big desktop model at home in Memphis. Hey, it's my turn to offer you and Gunner a place to stay for a few nights. You can't stay here until after the criminalists collect the trace evidence on Monday. You can sleep in my guest bedroom. We can drive to Memphis tomorrow. It'll probably take a couple of days."

"Oh wait." Jason slapped his knee. "I almost forgot about the cocktail party at the University Friday night. Attendance is required. It's an annual affair to welcome new members of the teaching staff. Will you go with me?"

"I hate to sound so typically feminine, but honestly, I don't have anything to wear. All my clothes are in Memphis."

"I can take you to the mall for a shopping trip. I'll even pick up the tab."

"You don't have to do that. What's the dress code?"

"It's not a satin-and-sequin affair. Whatever matches a dress shirt, tie and sport coat."

Dannah paused for a moment and after noting Jason's hopeful expression, she nodded. "Okay. We can go to Memphis on Saturday morning."

"Great." Jason and Dannah walked out of the office and into the entry hall of his house. "I feel like a first-class heel that you had such an ordeal with that obnoxious detective."

"No, I feel bad that the theft occurred with me in the house. I guess I should have done something to stop it."

"For crying out loud, you're only what—five-foot-three?" Jason put his arm protectively around her shoulders and squeezed a little. "You could have gotten yourself killed. Still, that cop had no right to grill you like that."

"I didn't mind. If the tables were turned and I was doing the interview for an article, I would have asked even more probing and personal questions, especially about the strange relationship between you and me. I would have jumped on that with sharpened claws. The detective is right. You shouldn't have left a stranger to look after your house and dog."

"If the house had been empty, then I wouldn't have had a witness to the robbery. Besides, Gunner likes you and he's a great judge of character."

A quirky little smile toyed around her lips, then she changed the subject. "Jason, is all your information lost?"

"I think so. I'll talk to Scott Miller, he's one of those computer-hacker-types at the University. He knows how to retrieve damaged data. I'll give him a call from your house. After all you've been through, I owe you dinner. I'll accept no excuse. We both need to eat. I'll even put on some decent clothes. Okay?"

"Okay, but let's don't go out. I'll fix us something."

"You don't mind?"

"No, I went to the grocery store yesterday and stocked my cupboards. They're bulging with good stuff to eat," she said, as they stepped into the warm, late afternoon sunlight. "I even bought a box of dog biscuits shaped like little t-bone steaks." Gunner was close on their heels, and began barking joyously.

"Watch out. He knows the words 'dog biscuit.' You know, it has been a tiring day and I'm not really in the mood to go out either."

"Great. Besides, I don't have any dressy clothes. But first, we've got errands to run." Dannah held up her car keys and rattled them. "Want to give it a whirl?"

His eyes lit up like a Christmas tree, and he responded with a very firm and loud "yes."

Before heading to the police headquarters downtown, Dannah told Jason that she wanted to go to one of those hardware superstores and put together a tool box.

"You gotta have a moderate-sized crowbar, a set of screwdrivers, pliers, socket wrenches—"

"Whoa. Why would I need socket wrenches? I don't plan on doing any auto repairs."

"They have dozens of other uses. Plus, you need a couple of hammers—claw head and ball peen."

"I need a good, strong flashlight. Oh, and how about bolt cutters? There's a padlock I need to cut through."

"Yeah, and this small ax."

"And a nice little red box to put them in. My very first tool kit," she exclaimed with a giggle. "This makes me an official homeowner."

"No, my little one. Not until you replace the ball cock in a leaky toilet."

Chapter Nine
Thursday evening

After leaving the hardware store, they drove downtown.
Police headquarters was a nondescript concrete building. Jason and
Dannah were escorted into a tiny office by Detective Richards.
Dannah was pleased to note that Richards had a picture on his desk
of his attractive wife and two bright-eyed children—it sort of
humanized him.

"Sit down," he ordered brusquely.

After reading her statement, Dannah asked, "Any idea
who these people might be?"

Richards rolled his eyes. "We'll do a thorough
investigation, then question all the known suspects."

"Probably a buddy of Henning," Jason interrupted.

After making a couple of corrections, they signed the
typewritten documents, filled out a stolen property form and drove
back to Azalea Lane. The ordeal had eaten up the entire day.

"Dannah, with all that's been happening, I think we should
lock your car in my garage. I'd feel terrible if it got trashed or
stolen."

"Will it fit?"

"My SUV won't, but your Corvette will. Let me run into
my house and grab some extra clothes."

Exhausted by the wild happenings of the last three days,
Dannah sat on the front porch with Gunner for a few minutes of
fresh air while waiting for Jason to come back.

"Why am I sitting out here instead of going inside?" she
wondered idly as she cast a glance over her shoulder at the dark
structure. "I'm not afraid to enter the house by myself. The rocking
chair has stayed put—I probably overlooked it on my first round of
exploration. It certainly can't go up and down the stairs by itself.
There are probably two of them," she continued with her
monologue. "I've dusted all the floors, so the footprints are gone.
Now all I've got to contend with is the old grandfather clock."

She absentmindedly stroked the dog's sleek, muscular

neck, happy to have his quiet companionship. The sun, low in the sky, was releasing its heated grip. Whereas the days of September were still hot, the nights were beginning to cool. The peaceful and lazy ambiance of this little country/college town was unnerving for her at first, being accustomed to the lights and noise of Memphis, but now she was developing a fondness for the quaint atmosphere. Neighbors were out walking their dogs, jogging with their headsets on, or taking the trash to the curb. A bucolic scene of small-town America of which she wanted to become a part. As she was enjoying the tranquility, one of those squeaky, pocket-sized dogs began barking at the front gate of her yard.

"Girlie? You Dannah Wingate?" asked the elderly owner of the noisy little dog as she hobbled down the narrow sidewalk closer to the porch.

"Yes ma'am, I'm Gova's niece."

"I'm Annie Fields. Me an' Gova was best friends. I live one street over on Daffodil Lane. This here's her dog, Pum'kin. Want her back?"

"No, thank you, I don't need another dog." She placed her arm affectionately around Gunner's neck and hugged him. He was grumbling softly over the tiny canine intruder.

"Just as well, I done got attached to her. She's a full-blooded Chihuahua, you know," the old lady stated with pride as she leaned on her cane. "You moved into the house yet?"

"Yesterday. It's going to take awhile to get settled in."

"You seen her yet?"

"Pardon? Seen who?"

"The ghost."

Taken aback by both the question and the answer, Dannah stuttered, "N-no, I haven't seen anything strange, but I've only spent one night in the house."

"You don't need to be afeared, 'cause Gova says she always took good care a her. She's a quiet one, no rattlin' chains or bangin' doors, an' always walks around the house barefooted an' wearin' her Indian garb."

"B-barefoot?" Dannah's heart began pounding furiously.

"Yep, wore a little bitty bell on one ankle. Gova told me

that on a quiet night, you can hear the bell a-tinklin.' She also said there's a second ghost that comes to the house occasionally, only he ain't that friendly. He smells bad an' he's all riled up 'bout something, but Gova never wanted to talk much about him."

"T-two ghosts?" Dannah hugged Gunner more tightly.

"That's what I said. Now don't you go a'lookin' for 'em. They'll find ways to get in touch with you. Did Gova tell you about the day she had the stroke?" Annie continued.

"No, she passed on before I had a chance to talk to her."

"Since I don't drive no more, couldn't go visit Gova in the old folks home, but we'uns talked might near ev'ry day on the phone. Been friends for might near forty years. I'm the oldest— thought I'd be the first to go." Annie rambled as she told her tale. "She tole me if'n it weren't fer the ghost, she'd a died right there in the den, long afore help could come, an' fetch her to the hospital. I wouldn't a found her till ten the next mornin' when we always had our coffee an' sweet rolls. Been doin' that fer years. Gova would grind the beans, brew the coffee—I like the amaretto flavor best— an' I'd bring my home-baked sweet rolls. Gova said it weren't one a them real bad strokes; 'course I reckon you couldn't a called it a good 'un neither. But she sorta slid outta her chair on to the floor in the den. She only had the one phone, an' it was in the kitchen. Don't know how she done it, but she done called 911."

"She? Gova?"

"No, silly girl, her mama, the good ghost."

"The ghost is her mother? Wait a minute, Miss what's-your-name?"

"Annie Louise. Fields is my maiden name. Was married once about forty years ago. Didn't last. He was only after my money."

"Miss Fields, are you trying to tell me that this female ghost dialed the telephone?"

"Ain't tryin' to tell you, I am tellin' you. It was her own mama. She didn't do no talkin,' jest dialed the number. Ain't that just the cat's pajamas? Wish my house was haunted." She cocked her head toward Jason's house. "I heard 'bout the break-in on the evenin' news. Don't believe nothin' bad 'bout the Dunhill boy.

He's from good stock. Honest as the day is long. The Dunhills is a fine family from way back afore the Civil War. They got nary a single ghost. Jason's a hard-working young man. You couldn't find no better husband."

"But-but, we've just met, we're only friends," Dannah protested.

"You see? If the Dunhills had a ghost, then the robbery wouldn't a happened. Ghosts would probably scare a burglar to death. You come to my house some mornin' 'bout ten an' I'll give you some a my sweet rolls. You like sticky buns with lots a pecans an' a dash of cinnamon?"

"Well, yes, I love them."

"I still make 'em, but it ain't no fun eatin' 'em alone. Come 'round to my house—707 Daffodil." She pointed to the direction with her cane.

"I'd love to. I'd like to learn more about my aunt."

"An' I'm just the one to tell you. Been nice talkin' to you, girlie. Come on, Pun'kin, let's go home."

As the old woman shuffled toward the sidewalk with her little dog, Dannah stood up and called out to her. "Miss Fields, wait a minute." The woman halted then faced her with an inquisitive arch to her brow. "I was just wondering if Aunt Gova ever talked about her brother, Coleman, he's my father, and I've always wondered…." The query died on Dannah's lips as the appearance of open friendliness slapped shut with hostile finality. Annie turned as quickly as her fragile bones would allow and hobbled away leaving Dannah with a queasiness in the pit of her stomach. "I can see that subject was distasteful. Wonder why Daddy was persona non grata with Aunt Gova?" Dannah returned to the front steps, sat down and placed her arms around Gunner 's neck, once again drawing comfort from him. "Tinkling bells? A barefooted ghost with the ability to dial 911? And a second ghost with a bad attitude? Well, I'm not ready to recognize that ghosts exist," she muttered. "Much less that they can call for an ambulance."

Dannah continued to ponder over the dramatic changes in her life, but she was ready for them. She was still recovering from the loss of her father. Theirs had been a close relationship, and yet emotionally very superficial. Coleman Wingate had not been a man to engage in frivolous conversations about the past. In fact, he was serious to the point of morose. Throughout her life, she never remembered her father ever laughing out loud or saying, "I love you." It was a mystery that she was determined to solve. And, she felt relatively certain that the answers lay somewhere within the walls of this house.

Chapter Ten
Same night

When Jason stepped onto the front porch with his battered suitcase in hand, he broke into Dannah's thoughts. "I see you've been talking to Miss Annie?"

"Yes, she's a fascinating woman with an equally fascinating tale."

"Neighborhood's full of 'em. According to her, there are ghosts in every house."

"Oh no. She told me that the Dunhill House has no ghosts."

"Ah, that's a relief."

"I'm afraid I might have nightmares tonight." Dannah joked as she unlocked the front door and they entered the darkened entry hall. She fumbled for the light switch. It hadn't taken her long to develop the habit of glancing into the living room to check on the rocking chair. It was still in the far corner looking oh-so-innocent. "What sort of food are you in the mood for?" she asked, anxious to change the subject. She was too mentally exhausted to engage in a war of words about good and bad ghosts.

"Anything. I'm not fussy when someone else is doing the cooking."

"How about salad, spaghetti, Italian bread and a glass of relaxing wine."

"That would be great. Does your phone work?"

Dannah nodded as they entered the kitchen. "Yes, they came this morning. They also hooked up the new cordless unit."

"Great. I'll use it to call Scott Miller. Hopefully, he can work one of his miracles." He dialed the number. "Scott? Jason Dunhill." Pause. "Damn, I made the evening news this quick?" Another pause. "Better watch your back, buddy. Apparently teachers can make some serious enemies." He laughed, then grew somber. "That's right, they left the tower, but installed a virus. If you can retrieve the data, I'd be eternally grateful." Jason made arrangements with his friend to pick up the computer late on

Monday after the grad-students collected all their trace evidence. After he hung up the phone, he turned to Dannah. "What else did they tell you at the bank yesterday morning?" he asked as he watched Dannah move around the large kitchen. Gunner lay on a small throw rug by the back door and followed every move she made with his large, adoring black eyes. "I know you said you inherited the house, but anything else noteworthy?"

"Truthfully, that was the shock of my life. As I explained earlier, my aunt named me beneficiary to her entire estate. I've not only inherited this house, but quite a bit of money as well. I also learned that she bankrolled my entire four years at UT-Knoxville. I can't believe my dad lied about something so important. He told me that he applied for scholarship money and it would cover the cost of my tuition. All we had to pay for was my books, room and board. This puts my whole relationship with him in a new, and not-too-happy light."

"She didn't live high on the hog. Never owned a decent car, wouldn't fix up the old house—except for the new roof. Since she was a school teacher for her entire career, I didn't think she had much money. Taught me tenth grade history."

"The banker called it 'old family money.' Whatever that means. Apparently, my father should have inherited half their parents' money when he turned twenty-one, but wouldn't touch it. Strange, huh? There are mutual funds, bonds and cash. It's not like winning the Super Lotto, but it's a nice windfall. At least, I won't have creditors banging down my door. I don't usually give in to impulses, but when I saw that red Corvette, I just had to have it."

"Nothing like a new set of wheels to brighten your spirits."

"That's very true, but it was before Daddy died. His funeral cost eight thousand dollars. Those two together were a near fatal jolt to my savings account. Now, his medical bills have just started coming in. Daddy didn't have much in the way of ready cash, or even supplemental insurance. I know I'm not legally responsible for all his bills, but I'd like to sell his house and pay off what I can."

"You thought your aunt was still alive when you came

down to Oxford?"

"That's right, I didn't know Aunt Gova had died. I called the phone number Daddy gave me, but the line had been disconnected, so I decided to search in person for my last living relative. Even though my father and his sister were not close, I did want to let her know he'd passed away. The fact that he studiously avoided her is just one of the mysteries I'd like to solve."

"You don't know the reason for their animosity?"

"No, do you?"

"Nope. I just ate her brownies and mowed the lawn."

Dannah paused to expel a sigh. "Gova told her banker that I'm the last living heir, so now I know for a fact that all the Wingates have passed on—except me. Since I don't have any brothers, the surname will daughter-out."

"No brothers, sisters or cousins?"

"None. Aunt Gova never married. My mother was from Kentucky and I never had any contact with her kin. However, I have traced her ancestry back for several generations."

"I think I'm going to like having you as a next door neighbor. We do have a common bond. I'm an only child as well. My parents died together in a pile-up on a foggy freeway and I inherited the family home. They were a rare couple. Married thirty-five years and still in love. I'm sort of glad they went together." Jason paused, then shook off his melancholy mood. "I've been told I have dozens of kinfolk—cousins, aunts, uncles on both sides of my family—but I don't know half of them. I've got an old uncle who can recite the entire history of the Dunhills and Lafayette County. He wrote a book on the family genealogy about twenty years ago, but, now, I think he's a bit senile, plus hard of hearing to boot."

"Aunt Gova has a copy of that book in her den." Dannah continued to talk as she set about gathering the ingredients for their meal.

"Yeah, I heard he sold about two dozen copies. I think he's coming down with Alzheimer's now. The last time I saw him, he didn't even recognize me."

"I was only eleven when my mother died, so I grew up

alone—just me and my dad. I guess that's why I wanted to have something on paper to show I do have blood kin, even if they're all dead. So, tracing my family tree became a hobby—Daddy always called it a 'foolish obsession.' In fact, he wouldn't even tell me the names of my grandparents. I searched the 1920 census records for Mississippi and found three Wingates—parents and one son. But I don't know if they were mine. I'm going to search 1930 census next. Genealogy is like putting together a giant jigsaw puzzle. Every little piece adds more light to the hidden picture, but the fun part is that it creates more questions than answers. It's sort of like following a trail of bread crumbs. You have no idea what you'll find over the next hilltop."

"Your single-minded determination is inspiring. However, as an anthropologist, I know you don't stop searching when you find one bone—no, you get greedy and want the entire skeleton, then you want to know how they lived, what they ate, so forth and so on."

She turned and looked at him, nodding enthusiastically. "Yes, it's the same when I'm writing an investigative report. I start digging for every scrap of information I can lay my hands on."

"So, you're alone and...unattached?" When she nodded, Jason smiled and stared into her expressive dark brown eyes.

"And you?" she responded.

"I'm single. I had a bad experience a couple of years ago when I went to Alaska. Not many women can handle the annual eight-week separation...that is, without straying. She got mad because I didn't call her every night."

"Daily phone calls from Alaska? That's ridiculous. Couples should make allowances for career decisions. I've had to go out of town several times in search of stories. It's what a person has to do to advance his or her career. If your girlfriend strayed, I'd say she never loved you to begin with." As the pasta was cooking, Dannah set the table and poured the wine. "You're going to get spaghetti sauce out of a jar tonight, Mister Dunhill."

"Does it come any other way?"

"I know how to make it from scratch, but tonight, I don't have the energy."

"You've been through a great deal in a short span of time."

"That is so true. You know something strange? I didn't even know until yesterday, when I saw the painting over the mantel, that my paternal grandmother was Native American. What a shock that was."

"Yeah, I remember hearing about her. You probably inherited your black hair and olive complexion from her."

"My dad also had dark hair and dark coloring."

"So did your aunt Gova. I'll bet she was beautiful when she was young. Can't understand why she never married."

"Maybe she never found 'Mister Right.' That is, if such a creature exists."

"Did you know that both of your grandparents were murdered?"

Dannah nearly choked on a swallow of wine. "Murdered?" she sputtered.

"Yep, in this house."

"You know, there's nothing I can put my finger on, but I had a creepy feeling about something bad occurring in this kitchen." She cast a tentative glance at the sink, then looked back at Jason. "When did it happen?"

"Before I was born. I think it was the early or mid-fifties. I don't know all the particulars, but I'll bet your aunt has some newspaper clippings stashed somewhere in this house. I recall hearing my parents discussing the incident. The police never found the murderer. They didn't have the technology to solve crimes back then—no Luminal, no DNA, no personality profiling."

"I did an article on the history of forensics a few years ago. Finger printing was the first forensic tool. The study of ballistics came as a result of the Saint Valentine's Day massacre. Witnesses said the police did it, but the bullets proved otherwise. Advances in the development of more powerful microscopes helped things along even faster. One by one new tests were developed. DNA typing was first used in England in 1986 to convict a rapist/murderer. Back around the turn of the century, police departments hired private investigators to solve murders and other crimes."

"You know a great deal about criminal history."

"I could bore you to sleep raving about police work. It's a fascination of mine. But, I never took any classes on the subject. I flopped around for a couple of years not having any specific major in mind. First I wanted to be a teacher, then a writer. I took mostly journalism classes, some history."

"You're young yet."

"I guess thirty isn't too old to go back to school," Dannah commented.

"I'm surprised. I thought you were younger than that. I'm thirty-two."

"Thanks for the compliment, but my thirty-first birthday will be in December." Dannah placed their salads on the table and sat down opposite Jason. "Geez, so much information coming so quickly has really caught me off guard. First the burglary, then the inheritance."

"After the way you handled the last couple of days, I can't imagine you ever being caught off guard in any situation," he said.

"After the shock of inheriting Gova's estate, not even Annie Fields' description of Gova's resident ghosts can phase me."

"Good old Annie Fields. She takes her nightly walk with that horrid little dog. Pumpkin must be close to fifteen years old by now. Annie is just as loony as your aunt when it comes to the subject of ghosts."

Dannah dropped her gaze to her plate and stabbed a piece of tomato with her salad fork.

"I'm sorry. That annoyed you, didn't it?"

"Well, yes, calling my aunt 'loony.' But...." She delivered her quirky little smile. "After all the talk about ghosts, it makes me wonder if Gova was senile, just plain crazy or if these strange beings really exist."

"Believe me, I've been digging up the bones of ancient Americans my entire career. When you're dead, you're dead. There is no 'in between.' 'Skeletons-in-the-closet' is just an old saying and has no basis in fact."

"You don't believe in the existence of ghosts?" she asked

with humor tugging at the corners of her lips.

"Absolutely not."

"The jury is still out for me. If I see one, then I'll believe it."

"Spoken like a true pragmatist."

"Gova wrote something just before she died. Her handwriting was really bad because the stroke left her with some residual paralysis. I glanced at it, but I can't make head or tails out of her hen-scratching."

"I'll take a look at it. I'm pretty good at deciphering ancient pictographs."

"Maybe it will give me a little insight into her personality." Dannah rose from her chair and retrieved a small spiral bound notebook from the kitchen counter. "See if you can figure it out."

"Your name is on the front—Dannah Nicole Wingate." Jason turned the page and studied the shaky writing for several quiet moments, then nodded his head. "Yeah, well, it looks like— 'read journal last page.'"

"That's it?"

"All you have to do is find the journal," he said, then bit into a crusty piece of Italian bread sending out a spray of crumbs. "Are you employed?" he asked after swallowing.

"Not in the strict sense of the word. I don't punch a time clock or go to an office, but I do work. I'm a freelance writer— maybe journalist would be a better title."

"What do you write about?"

"Everything. Mostly nonfiction. I used to be a reporter for the Memphis Commercial Appeal newspaper. Tuesday when I stopped by the paper to visit a friend, I was offered a new assignment to write an article on the education and psychological behavior of the profilers who work on serial-killer cases. Something with a new angle."

"There's an award-winning professor of criminal behavior at the University. Maybe you'd like to talk to him."

"I don't know, I've got too much on my mind now with the house and everything. Thanks for the offer, maybe later."

Dannah delivered a bright smile.

Jason laid his fork on his plate, picked up his glass of wine and held it aloft. "I'm truly pleased over the prospect of there being a later."

As they clicked their glasses, Dannah smiled over the realization that she was also pleased with the prospect of a future. "Here's to 'later'. So, tell me something about teaching anthropology."

"Nothing exciting to the normal person."

"You didn't get that tan in the classroom," Dannah responded with an alluring arch of one feathery brow. "You certainly don't look like any professor I studied under at UT-K. Most were either frail, pasty-complected young men with beards and braided hair or grizzled old men who mumbled through ill-fitting false teeth."

Jason laughed heartily. "Oh, how unflattering to the entire teaching profession, but yes, I've had my share of those. When I was in college I spent every summer on a dig, and now that I'm a teacher, I spend every summer with my grad students at a promising site somewhere in North America. Just got home a couple of weeks ago from Chucalissa."

"Somehow I can't imagine ancient cultures lying in the clay soil of Mississippi." Dannah returned his lazy smile with one of her own.

"They do, and in large numbers. North American anthropology has always been my passion. The new thing is to use ground-penetrating radar to find where the soil has been disturbed by habitation—fires, burials, temples. Human remains have been found along the banks of the Mississippi, the Cumberland River, and all the way up into the Ohio River Valley. In fact, I've just discovered evidence that can move the date from 1100 AD back to 900 AD. I just had radiocarbon dating done on two bone fragments, a pottery shard and a piece of charred wood I unearthed this season. When Dave Brookman called me from the University of Arkansas with his idea to use the radar at Chucalissa, I jumped at the chance. With that technology, you can visualize the artifact before you move one shovel of dirt. Baxter worked the site twenty years ago and declared there was nothing else to be uncovered. He's going to shit a brick. Excuse the profanity. Oh well, it's my turn to bore you to sleep talking about my research. We make a great pair, don't we?"

Dannah nodded. The same thought had crossed her mind as well. "As a matter-of-fact, we do."

"Never known anyone I could feel so comfortable with, and who has as much enthusiasm as I do about their work," he continued to ramble. "Most women I've met socially would rather put a bullet to their head than listen to me rant and rave about my profession. It definitely throws a wet blanket on any little fires of attraction that might be sputtering."

Dannah smiled, cocked her head slightly and looked at him in a new light—*little fires of attraction? Is that what's going on in the pit of my stomach?* she wondered silently. "No, no, it's fascinating. You're probably a very dedicated teacher."

"I try my level best to make my classes interesting. Webster's description of anthropology is 'the science of human beings.' I concentrate on the ancients. We have to know where we've come from to know where we're going."

"But, I thought only archaeologists dug for bones."

"Since the late sixties, the classification of courses has been in flux, what with interdepartmental wrangling, philosophical positions and quests for financing. Anthropology courses usually attract more students than either archaeology or paleontology. Nowadays, at least at my school, it's grouped with sociology. Archaeology is now broken down into several categories, even forensic archaeology. They're all wrapped up in proving that young King Tut was murdered. I have a friend who calls himself a bio-archaeologist. All he studies is how ancient peoples went to extreme measures to mold the heads of their newborns into bizarre shapes."

"You think of college as teaching only the old stuff, ancient history and the like. I had no idea the curriculum was on the cutting edge of what's going on in today's world. I thought everything was either black or white."

"It would be nice if it was. Next season I've been invited

to join the University of Virginia in their dig at the newly discovered fort at the old Jamestown site. Been lost for years because of the meandering of the river."

"Feather in your cap."

He nodded. "What I really wanted was to join the team searching for the Lewis and Clark winter sites and the burial place of Sacagawea. Everybody was clamoring for that appointment."

"She died really young, didn't she? After childbirth?"

Jason nodded. "Whoops, there I go again—expounding. I'm going to hush up and eat." He hungrily dug into the plate of spaghetti Dannah had set in front of him and was quiet for several minutes. He deftly twirled the slender noodles around his fork. "So, will you be staying in Oxford permanently?"

"The house needs to be remodeled from the inside out regardless of whether I keep it or sell it. That'll take at least a year or more."

"No sense in tying up your own money when you can get a special low-interest loan on a structure more than a hundred years old."

"I guess Wingate House qualifies. I'll check into it."

"That's what I did two years ago—rewired, re-plumbed, put in a new bathroom, new windows, new roof, central heat and air. The problem is that Azalea Lane has been designated an historical site. All renovations have to go through an Architectural Review Committee...a bunch of grumpy old men with nothing to do."

"Maybe you can recommend a reliable contractor."

"The same guy who did mine—Bennie Varossa. He's been the contractor for most of the old homes on Azalea Lane. He put the new metal roof on this house about four or five years ago."

"I like what you did to your master bedroom with the big closet and bath."

"Varossa designed and built it. He tried, but could never convince old Gova that the inside of Wingate House was in dire need of repair work. In fact, she wouldn't let anyone inside her house except Annie Fields. I've never been past the kitchen. Wait, I fixed her leaky toilet upstairs once. She was a strange lady and often exhibited bizarre behavior."

"And I'd like to know why. I've prowled through every room on the first and second floors and I haven't seen anything out of the ordinary. There is a storage room at the end of the upstairs hall that has me intrigued. There's another door at the back with a padlock on it."

They ate in silence for some time. sHaving bypassed lunch, they were both hungry.

"Tell me something," Jason asked when he finished his meal and leaned back in his chair. "I know you've only been in this house for one night, but how is your gut feeling toward this place?"

"I've got to admit that on occasion I do experience a little flutter of fear. I'm not used to such a big house or the creak and groan of old timbers. The real estate lady claimed the place felt sinister and foreboding to her. And yet, for some wild, inexplicable reason," Dannah's chin trembled slightly and her voice slipped into a whisper. "I feel like I've come home...that I'm...where I belong."

Jason looked at her and flashed a toothy smile. "Maybe you should listen to what this house is telling you."

Their eyes locked in mutual admiration. Something was different between them, viable, but not yet verbal. Sharply barbed words became softer, her demeanor mellowed, her laughter was swift and frequent, while shy glances were held boldly longer. Dannah surreptitiously studied Jason's warm eyes with blatant admiration. Wisps of plentiful chest hair peeked from the open collar of his casual shirt. He was handsome in a rugged sort of way, like the sun-bronzed cowboy actors in those old western movies on TV. There were tiny lines around his eyes—probably from squinting into the sun. In keeping with this tough-guy image, he wore no jewelry. In fact, she halfway expected him to swing into a saddle and ride off into the sunset. The handsome picture was completed with one unruly shock of wavy brown hair threatening to tumble over his forehead. The man literally oozed masculinity. In the beginning, she had found his intensity a little frightening. Now, she realized, he was deeply involved in his career.

Dannah retreated from his steady stare and lowered her eyes, studiously rearranging the food on her plate. "Thanks for the offer to take me to Memphis. I don't know why, but it's tough to admit that I need help. I guess it's the feminist movement. These days all women are supposed to be self-sufficient."

"Not when it comes to moving heavy furniture. Besides, classes don't start for another two weeks. I've already called the President of the University and asked him to postpone the press conference set for Monday afternoon because of 'unforeseen circumstances.' He's probably already heard about the break-in on the evening news."

"Do you think we need to ask Detective Richards for permission to go out of town? We'll have to stay overnight."

"Nah, to hell with him. He's got our cell phone numbers. Might as well go to Memphis as sit here twiddling our thumbs. The forensic people will be crawling all over my place taking pictures, getting fingerprints, vacuuming the carpet."

"I truly appreciate what you're doing. You're going way past being neighborly."

"I help out when I can. Minor carpentry and plumbing are just a few of my lesser talents. Most of our neighbors on Azalea Lane are in there eighties, but the old neighborhood is slowly giving in to the latest yuppie trend to buy and remodel old homes. Victorians and Craftsmen-style are very popular. Yuppies are the ones with the BMWs, Volvos and Land Rovers in the driveways."

"How long have you lived next door to my aunt?" she asked after a long silence while they concentrated on eating.

"Forever—I was born in that house. I went to college at the University of Georgia. You know how it is for teenage boys...I just had to leave home. Got my Masters' Degree at the University of Illinois. I thought I'd feel stifled coming back to Oxford, but when I was offered the job, I accepted without hesitation. For a while, I lived in an apartment closer to school, but after my parents died, I moved back to Azalea Lane. I've been the full circle and now I'm right back where I started from."

"At least you have roots. I don't have any."

"You have this house. Believe me, it's got a colorful

history."

"And I'm looking forward to uncovering it. Have you ever been married?" Dannah surprised herself by asking such a personal question.

"No, but came close." He shook his head and smiled at the same time. "Two years ago. She moved into my house. It was my idea for her to save rent money and have somebody look after Gunner. Couldn't take him to Alaska. Then, while I was gone, she moved her new boyfriend in with her."

"Into your house? Oh Jason, that's terrible."

"No, that goes beyond terrible. Dear Miss Gova was quick to give me all the juicy bits of gossip. I'm glad she did. I can hear her now—'Just dreadful. Their behavior was just dreadful.'" Jason stated in a comical falsetto voice. "What about you?"

She indicated no with a shake of her head. "Had a live-in for a while, but it didn't work out. Well, you know how that goes. Haven't even dated anyone in the last year. I'm not bitter toward men, I've just been busy. My dad suffered from congestive heart failure for a couple of years. I took care of him up until he passed away. To be honest, I'm not a nightlife person and detest the noisy bar scene. I never thought it was fun to sit on a barstool, drink too much and make inane small talk with total strangers."

"Me either."

"On Fridays the gang from the newspaper would meet after work at a local watering hole, but that was different. Everybody was friends. But even that gets old after a while. My former boss even tried to set me up with a blind date last week with a sportswriter guy, but, I don't know. It's so tough to get through that awkward 'getting-to-know-you' routine."

Jason winced with a surprising twinge of jealousy, suddenly unwilling to share her even with the past. "I think the unusual circumstances of our meeting have helped us circumvent that awkward stage. Don't you?"

Dannah nodded and smiled in agreement. "Lordy, I hate all those 'mind games' some couples like to play."

"Well, there comes a time in your life when you gotta leave all that kid-stuff behind, pick yourself up, shake off the dust and move on with living."

Their eyes joined for several moments and he felt a vague alliance with the young woman. Her head dipped and she nodded. "Odd you should use those particular words. Three weeks ago, while standing beside my father's grave, the same thought crossed my mind—'shake off the dust of sadness.' I'm all for getting on with life, but I've got to solve a couple of family mysteries before I can move forward." She lay her fork down and a charming smile lightened her face. "Speaking of mysteries, I can't help but wonder what Baxter could possibly want to steal from you? You're in academics, not corporate intrigue or high finance."

"That's what you think. A university professor's career lives and dies by making new discoveries, writing papers, and securing financial grants for research. That's how to attract the best students and keep enrollment high. The old saying is 'publish or perish.'"

"I guess I've shown my stupidity concerning the ins and outs of academia," Dannah responded with a smile.

"Not really. It's a world in and of itself. It all boils down to the fact that I made a discovery that will supersede Baxter's work from twenty years ago. I'm thirty-two and he's sixty-something."

"He probably hopes to find a way to discredit you."

"Sharp observation. However, everyone at the University knows he hasn't done any field work in the last ten or fifteen years. In fact, he's not far from retirement. I don't really know what his motivation is unless it's pure old green-eyed jealousy." Jason pushed away from the table. "Excellent meal. Thanks for going to so much trouble. Time to feed Gunner and take him outside."

"It may turn out that Gunner is the best detective of all," Dannah commented as Jason measured out his kibble. "He found the empty pack of cigarettes. I remembered you telling me that you had just mowed both lawns. The white package showed up in the moonlight."

"Gunner has a definite dislike for smokers. He sneezes and snorts whenever anyone lights up around him."

"I'm amazed at his intelligence. I've never been around

many animals."

Jason frowned. "What? No bird, hamster, dog or cat when you were growing up?"

Dannah shook her head. "Nope. Daddy would never allow it."

"I can't imagine growing up without a pet. There's an old saying: 'Until you've loved an animal, a part of your soul lies unawakened.'"

"Jason, that's a beautiful thought."

Chapter Eleven
Same night

After Gunner wolfed down his evening meal in typical doggy fashion, they went outside. The night was moonless and starless as Jason and Dannah stepped out onto the small porch and waited for the dog to complete his nightly ritual.

The only light came from the corner street lamp as it filtered through the wind-blown leaves of the huge magnolia tree, sending eerie shadows dancing about the area. A nippy breeze was blowing in little spits and spurts, tugging at Dannah's curls and molding the thin fabric of her tee shirt against her well defined breasts. In Jason's mind, she looked wild and unfettered, sensuous and ripe as she leaned against the porch railing. Her eyes sparkled with a vague promise, and the new and surprising ache to kiss her prodded him relentlessly. He made careful moves—nothing threatening—as he came up behind Dannah and crossed his arms over her breasts in a possessive manner, wrapping his hands around her bare upper arms against the hint of fall chill in the air. A slight shiver trailed across her shoulders. "Are you cold?" he asked and rubbed warmth into her cool and satiny flesh.

"No, not now," she said as she turned her head slightly toward his face.

She made no motion to resist, and in fact, relaxed against him, allowing the full length of her body to mold against his. The perfect fit of her fanny against his groin created an instant reaction. He nuzzled his face in her hair, inhaling the sweet, feminine fragrance of her.

She was keenly aware of all the sensitive places where their bodies touched, but had no inclination to pull away. As his response to her grew impossible to ignore, rare patches of embarrassment burned her cheeks and caused her to breathe in short, erotic little gasps. The safe haven she found within the circle of his arms was intoxicating—offering the sort of comfort she'd been deprived of for too long. It was insane to feel this strongly about a man she hardly knew, but there was no arguing with the reaction of her body. It had been a very long time since she'd felt such a powerful attraction to a man. Philip? Not even him.

Jason turned her around to face him. Only the rustle of the wind through the leaves filled the strained silence. For a few moments their eyes locked, each searching through a muddled mix of doubt and desire, with a liberal scattering of lust. Something connecting them sprang to life—tenuous, yet alive. Everything about them was abruptly altered. The carefully constructed barrier erected between them, as with all fledgling relationships, had crumbled and disappeared. With slow, almost imperceptible movements, Jason pulled Dannah even closer, then whispered seductively in her ear, "I'm gonna kiss you, girl."

His simple statement caused a complicated reaction in several remote areas of her body—finger tips and toes and those obscure places in between. When their lips joined, she experienced a jolting charge of electrical current passing between them. The kiss was casual at first, almost innocent and without demand, then slowly evolved and expanded with the unique thrill of their newness to each other. She parted her lips as an invitation for him to taste and explore. The kiss deepened and became as intimate as the sex act when the probing went past lips to her tongue. As her sleeping desires awakened, their connection became even heavier with the promise of more, and Jason's hands and arms completely encircled her, crushing her softness tightly against his firmness. His heat traveled both over and under her skin. The sharp pang of arousal startled her.

Melting from the fiery flames, Dannah responded by sliding her arms around his neck and molding her body tightly against his. Her fingers toyed with his hair at the nape of his neck, and for a few precious moments, she forgot the existence of all else but the sheer joy of their fresh and unfamiliar intimacy. She relished the luxury of allowing her mind to wander—wondering what would it feel like to lie next to him, with his hard masculine form next to her bare flesh.

After a rough ride through the raging winds of passion, she finally arrived at the calm, quiet eye of the storm, their lips still locked. She had spiraled through the many shades and hues of arousal and she didn't want to back off. She wasn't ready for romance, wasn't ready for a relationship, but she wasn't ready to push him away either. Unspoken words and unasked questions were racing through her mind. She hadn't been with a man in over a year and the temptation to allow herself this wild indulgence was overwhelming. Her desires were running rampant, battering her ability to resist. One more kiss like this might send her over the edge.

A little bit out of breath, their lips parted briefly. Jason murmured her name as he left a hot pathway of kisses down the curve of her neck. Shivering with the thrill, Dannah's head rolled back and she uttered a soft moan. His wide stretched fingers crawled up her spine and cradled her head as his lips claimed hers again. Gently holding her face between his hands, he kissed her again, this time with deliberately restrained passion, and yet, it left her breathless. She wanted to make the kiss last forever—free from the constraints of time and all the mundane troubles in her life as it inched forward in a mingled cadence of their beating hearts.

Reluctantly, Dannah brought her brain back to reality and broke away. Both were flustered over the intensity of their passion, and painfully conscious of their own quickening physical response. His was more obvious than hers. Jason swallowed hard, while Dannah flicked an imaginary crumb from her wrinkled tee shirt.

"Sorry, I probably shouldn't have done that. But...it just seemed...sort of...you know, right." He paused for a moment, at first serious, then broke into a broad smile. "Oh what the hell. Why not be truthful? I'm not a damn bit sorry." He lifted her chin with one hand, and with his thumb, smoothed out the furrows in her brow. "Don't frown," he admonished in a husky whisper. "I think something special and definitely out-of-the-ordinary just happened between us." He chuckled softly; his wine-scented breath tickled her cheek as his lips moved to caress her ear with another seductive murmur of words. "Now turn around or I'll do it again and stopping could become a problem."

Once again Dannah snuggled her back against his chest, mentally wallowing in her feelings of being safe and cared for. They stood there for quite awhile with Jason's arms across her breasts. They were both silent. Each lost in their own private thoughts, and yet warmed by a new and silent communication.

Something out-of-the-ordinary? Yes, indeed. If she were to rate the kiss, it would come out on the top of the heap.

As the earth released her daytime heat into the sky, jagged lines arced between the billowy clouds. The humidity was heavy. White lightning intensified the black of the nocturnal sky, while thunder rumbled in the distance.

Although loath to break the romantic spell, she felt a tight band beginning to constrict around her temples. "I feel a headache coming on. Must be the cheap wine, or maybe the tension."

"The wine was good so I cast my vote for tension."

"Probably."

"It's been one helluva busy week for you."

"You're right. Think I'll take a couple of aspirin and chase them with a glass of cold milk before turning in," she responded.

"A glass of milk and one of those tempting chocolate chip cookies I saw on the counter."

"I bought them for you," she said with a smile. "When I checked out your pantry, I noticed you have an affinity for cookies."

"For anything sweet." He clasped both of her hands and squeezed them with gentle pressure.

When she lifted her gaze to meet his, she battled with the fierce urge to sink into his arms and kiss him again. At six foot-plus, he towered above the top of her curly head and she felt surprisingly protected and secure with Jason, as though they had been best of friends for many years.

As soon as Dannah stepped into the kitchen, she heard the old clock in the living room slowly bong six chimes.

"That clock needs to be reset," Jason commented as he checked his wristwatch. "It's ten o'clock—not six."

"It's broken. It can't be running." Dannah could feel the blood drain from her features, leaving a chilled feeling. She had endured the frightening break-in, and yet, no matter how hard she tried, she couldn't argue herself through the foolishness of her panicky response to that stupid old clock. Immobilized by the nameless fear, her feet felt nailed to the floor, refusing to obey her command to move.

This is absolutely ridiculous, she argued silently.

"Sounds okay to me."

"Dammit, I'm telling you, it's broken." The hair rooted at the nape of her neck prickled like the primal response of an animal raising its hackles. Although it was a staggering thought that someone or something might be present but unseen, it was not necessarily terrifying. She was unsure if it was benevolent or malevolent. Fear and curiosity were joined by another even more insistent emotion—urgency. She was inundated by the pressing need to complete a task, yet unknown to her. "I feel as if we are not alone in this house."

"We're not. We've got Gunner and maybe a few mice."

"Come on. Let me prove to you that the clock is broken," she stated, then headed toward the front hallway with Jason and Gunner trailing behind her. The newly cleaned wall sconces cast their cheery illumination through the wide gracefully curved entrance. The beam of light fell across the worn carpeting in the living room, but was a long way from touching the clock standing against the far wall. Unfamiliar shapes lurked in the dark corners, and no amount of mental coaxing could force her to walk into that room.

Suddenly, a huge blast of thunder rattled the windows, followed by a deluge of rain splattering noisily against the windows and metal roof. The brass pendulum of the clock clanged against the two heavy weights dangling from their chains. Dannah threw herself into Jason's arms. Even Gunner was startled and barked at the sound.

Unperturbed, Jason untangled himself from her, sauntered into the dark parlor and switched on one of the small table lamps. He turned the tiny key and opened the glass door covering the clock. "You're right. It says three-ten, therefore it must be broken. One of the counter weights is missing. It needs three to run properly."

"So, how could it have bonged?"

"Well, we are sitting on the New Madrid earthquake

fault," he said with a whimsical smile. "Could have been a slight tremor."

"I'm aware of its history. The fault hasn't slipped in almost two hundred years."

"Well, maybe that blast of thunder shook the old house. Look, even the rocking chair is moving." He turned and frowned. "You're not afraid of this place, are you?"

"Of course, not. I won't let a few incidental sounds drive me away either," she stated with her chin jutted forward in defiance. "Retreating to the safety of a motel would be a disgraceful show of cowardice. Besides, if my aunt could live here for sixty-two years, surely I can survive."

"I would think so."

"Guess it's time to go to bed. We're both pretty tired."

"Do you want Gunner to sleep with you? I usually make him sleep on the floor."

"No, I let him snuggle in bed with me."

"You're spoiling him rotten."

"You're right. I give him one of those dog biscuits at bedtime." She reached into her pocket and pulled one out. "He loves them."

Jason, along with Gunner intent on his treat, followed Dannah up the staircase. She paused when she reached eye level with the expanse of hardwood flooring extending down the hallway to admire her handy work of earlier that morning. The floor was spotless in the glare of the bright lights she had installed—not a single footprint marred the shining surface. She continued on up, then turned to face Jason with a smile. "There are two guest bedrooms. Take your choice. Good night. Hope you sleep well."

"See you in the morning," he said with a husky voice, then catching her off guard, roughly pulled her into his arms and kissed her, long and with great authority. His left hand slid down her spine and pressed her body tightly against his own. Because she was so short and he was so tall, her feet left the floor. It was like floating in an erotic dream from which she did not want to emerge.

The luscious sensations he generated lingered long after

their kiss ended.

Chapter Twelve
Night and predawn

Too curious to sleep, Dannah picked out two of the shoe boxes from the closet, sat on the floor and began reading. The first one was marked "Michael" and contained mostly pictures and letters. "Oh my goodness. Aunt Gova had a boyfriend." There were photos of Gova, strikingly beautiful, along with a handsome young man in a military uniform. "Must have been during the Vietnam War," she mused. The letters from him were tied with a blue satin ribbon and Dannah decided not to read them, but to let the lovers have their privacy. Then she saw the yellowed newspaper clipping. "First local casualty, Sgt. Michael Daniel Duncan, dies in Vietnam War." Her fingers traced several small dots staining the paper. She knew with total certainty that they were Gova's teardrops speaking through the years.

The second box was dated in the early nineteen-fifties. According to the collection of newspaper articles, her grandmother, Rainy Skies, was planning to use her unusual psychic powers to help the police identify the man who had kidnapped several little girls from the area, raped and murdered them, then left their tiny naked bodies prominently displayed on various school playgrounds around the city. She and her husband, Jonathan Wingate, were murdered in their home the night before her appointment with the police. The police think the murders were the work of the suspect hoping to prevent her from revealing his name or description. The article went on to describe the bizarre brutality of the crime. Whereas the husband was stabbed only once in the chest, the woman had over sixty stab wounds in her body, indicating an intense level of rage. Oddly, the child killings stopped. The two children of the couple were in the home at the time the murders took place in the kitchen; however, according to their testimony, they were in bed on the third floor and did not hear or witness anything. The article went on to state that the two Wingate children didn't discover the bodies of their parents until the next morning. Neither the murderer nor the murder weapon was ever found.

"Hmmm, there are bedrooms on the third floor? Wonder why the door is padlocked? Maybe because the house is simply too large for one person. Gova lived alone for so many years."

When Dannah finally crawled between the sheets, her father's words kept circling in her head, "hopin' you wouldn't get burdened with 'em, but you're next in line."

Next in line.

Next in line.

"Mother. Daughter. Granddaughter. Geez, although I'm not Gova's daughter, I am the granddaughter of Rainy Skies. I guess that does make me next in line."

Rainy Skies was using her unusual psychic powers.

"Lord in Heaven. This is what's happening to me. It is real."

Gunner responded to her voice by coming to attention with his head cocked slightly to one side and his ears perked. She patted the bed beside her. "Come on, boy. You can sleep with me." The dog quickly obliged and snuggled happily in the crook of her arm. Dannah expected to lie in bed wide awake with gruesome thoughts about the murder of her grandparents in the kitchen below her occupying every inch of her brain, but fatigue finally pulled her into an uneasy sleep.

***

In the predawn hours, Dannah awoke in a clammy sweat. Her breath was ragged, coming in uneven gasps, as a cold fingers of fear pulled her to the edge of unexplained hysteria. She knew something was wrong. She glanced at Gunner who lay curled up beside her still sound asleep, blissfully unaware of any danger. Was it real or simply the workings of her overactive imagination? The clock glowed a green three forty-five. It was still dark outside. Blearily, she rolled out of bed and tiptoed into the hall. She didn't have robe or slippers. A small hint of noise was fading in and out, toying with her hearing like a cat with a luckless mouse. She peered down the stairwell into the entry hall, illuminated by the wall sconces. Nothing seemed out of place. The dog awoke and hurried to follow.

Slide, shuffle-shuffle.

The weird, inappropriate sound was similar to the hesitant gait of an old man. Could it be Baxter looking for Jason wanting to extract the ultimate revenge?

Slide, shuffle-shuffle.

Or...was something playing tricks with her mind? Was it nothing more threatening than the nightly hum of insects or the creak of old timbers? She returned to her bedroom and turned off the noisy window unit, went into the bathroom and splashed cold water on her face. She retraced her steps and stood at the top of the stairwell. The noise was indefinable—a swoosh of fabric, several footsteps, followed by the musty odor of times forgotten. She sneezed twice. Although she tried to ignore the prodding of her curiosity to investigate the source of the noise, the enticement to go downstairs was irresistible. She nearly stumbled from fright as she descended, one hesitant step at a time. On the landing midway, she peered over the banister into the hall below her. The front door was still closed; the hall was bathed in gentle light. However, the slip chain was dangling loose, once again swinging slightly as if set in motion by a diabolical hand. Had she forgotten to secure it in its slot? Had someone attempted to break into the house? She descended the remaining stairs, secured the chain and tested the dead bolt.

Nothing else looked out of place until she turned toward the dining room. She had left the small light on over the cook stove, but now saw only darkness. The door between the kitchen and dining room was one of those swinging contraptions that kept hitting the user in the face or fanny. She kept it propped open with a heavy stone brought in from the yard. Now the door was closed and the stone was shoved aside. It couldn't be an intruder. Both the front and rear doors were secured with dead bolts.

As though walking on egg shells, she cautiously approached the swinging door and pushed it open. Using her bare foot, she maneuvered the door stop back into position, peeked into the black hole that was her kitchen and slapped at the wall switch.

The light from the overhead fixture cast a brilliant, oblong pattern into the darkness, throwing her gently curving silhouette across the dining-room rug. She traversed the linoleum floor with a deliberate stride.

"Okay, so the bulb over the stove is burned out." Dannah left every light blazing in her wake as she retraced her path through the dining room, entry hall and to the archway to the living room. "That damned rocking chair again," she muttered. It was moving in that same rhythmic cadence. Back and forth. Back and forth with a slight squish of wood against wool carpet. She walked over to the chair and stopped its motion, then swung around and started to exit the room.

At first, it seemed insignificant, hardly worth her time to notice that the piece of Indian jewelry was lying innocently on the small round coffee table in front of the sofa. As if in slow motion, she picked it up and her thumb idly stroked the knobby texture of the beads while she hurriedly searched her memory.

Slowly, inexorably, a fog-shrouded image began to take shape in her mind. The jolting flash of light reflecting on a swiftly moving silver blade made her fingers spring apart, allowing the bracelet to drop silently to the carpeted floor. Her agile brain, prowling through her fears, searched for a tiny speck of logic. She stared at the artifact lying beside her bare feet as though it was an alien being that might suddenly burst to life and attack her. The remote sound of the tinkling bell and the swoosh of fabric continued to toy with her senses. A sudden chilling awareness of being watched by a pair of benevolent eyes flowed over her, but she was too terrified to turn around to face who or what might be behind her.

The bracelet had been moved from the corner cabinet. She and Jason had been in the living room just before going to bed and nothing was out of place.

"I might as well face it," she muttered aloud. The sound of her own voice had a calming effect, as if there was life amidst death. "There's a cognitive entity in this house. Something with the ability to reason and then act on deductions. So how can this spirit—something with no substance, no earthly body—have the ability to move tangible objects? Or to leave footprints? Where does the impetus, the solidity come from? Is it a poltergeist?" Her voice was little more than a rattled whisper as she bent to retrieve the bracelet.

According to what she had read, not all poltergeists are violent and destructive; however, those few written words did little to allay her worry. Dannah's cotton tee shirt felt like ice next to her hot skin as her imagination went wild and threatened her mental balance. And yet, through all these heart-thumping episodes, her steely determination to find the answers to all her questions remained steadfast.

Gingerly holding the item between two fingertips, she returned it to the cabinet and secured the small glass door.

The past. It's where tragedy lay hidden, waiting to be discovered, and Dannah Wingate was hellbent on finding it. As she turned to go back to bed, she ran into a hard, firm body and screamed.

"Jason! Lordy, you scared the hell out of me." Her heart felt like it was going to leap out of her chest. He was clad only in a pair of boxer shorts and she could feel the welcoming warmth radiating from his bare chest. She was wearing a thigh-length tee shirt and regardless of their provocative attire, she sank into his protection for a few seconds while she caught her breath. She locked her arms around his upper body, buried her face in the small patch of chest hair and held on tight. His coarse hair tickled her nose. She marveled over his shower-fresh aroma, a woodsy smell that always caught her attention.

"Sorry I frightened you, but Gunner came into my room and woke me. He was so agitated that I got up to check it out and saw your bed was empty." He grasped her shoulders and held her at arm's length. "That's when I got worried."

"I thought I heard a noise, so I came downstairs. I guess I forgot to secure the chain lock."

"No you didn't. I checked both doors before going to bed and everything was securely locked." He ruffled the curls on the top of her head. "Besides, Gunner would have alerted us if it was an intruder."

"Yeah, I guess you're right." If it were a flesh and blood

intruder, she thought. "I know there are dead bolts on both the front and back doors. But all that's been happening has me sort of spooked."

"You're not the only one who's rattled," Jason replied and kissed the top of her head. "I think it's safe to go back to bed now."

Dannah nodded her agreement, hit the switch that turned on the upstairs hall light—now sporting a one hundred watt bulb.

"I'll turn out the kitchen and living room lights and be right behind you," Jason said.

When Dannah was eye level with the upstairs hall, once again she could see footprints in the dust. Fingers of fear danced along her spine in an off-key cadence. "Dammit," she muttered. "I dusted all the floors this morning. They were spotless." And yet, she could plainly see the footprints left by her and Jason coming toward the staircase, but she also saw another set of small, dainty footprints parading in the same circle to and from the storage room at the rear of the hall. Gunner's paw prints went from left to right between the two bedrooms, then to the top of the stairs where he was patiently waiting, his short tail thumping against the floor and his eyes always on alert.

Jason came up behind and placed his hands on her shoulders. "What's wrong?"

"Dust," she replied, somewhat agitated. "I dusted all the wood floors this morning and now look."

"The house is old and smelly and needs a thorough cleaning from top to bottom—draperies, carpets and upholstery all create dust and odors. Even the heating ducts probably need cleaning."

"I may have to hire that platoon of energetic ladies who cleaned your house. They would probably want hazard pay for this place."

Chapter Thirteen
Friday morning
Oxford, Mississippi

He nervously fingered the two newspaper clippings and read them over and over.

July tenth. Miss Gova Marie Wingate died in her sleep at the Sunny Care Nursing Home. She was 62 years old and in poor health. A life long resident of Oxford, she leaves no kin. Miss Wingate will be interred at the Methodist Church cemetery next to her parents, Jonathan Wingate and his Native American wife, Rainy Skies. There will be no service. In lieu of flowers, please make a donation to the Lafayette County Historical Society.

"The first article says she leaves no kin," he muttered softly as he cut the most recent item from the morning paper. He had smiled when he initially read the first report, determined to buy the old house, but the second item in the Oxford Daily News ruined his mercurial good mood.

Andrew Mahoney, Trust Officer at the First Union Bank of Mississippi, told reporters today that he has located the heir of Miss Gova Wingate, who left her sizable estate to her niece, Dannah Wingate, of Memphis, Tennessee. Miss Wingate has decided to move from Memphis and take up residence in the last of the unrestored Victorian homes at 703 Azalea Lane. The Lafayette County Historical Society is thrilled that the venerable old house will finally have a young resident who will hopefully have an interest in its restoration. All the other Victorian-style houses on this block have already been restored.

He studied the picture of the old house in all its disheveled glory. Something caught his attention in the photo, causing him to pull out his magnifying glass. The face in the window. Even the film caught the phenomenon he had seen for himself on many occasions. Somehow the reflection of light on the glass combined with the imperfections in the wood boarding the third floor window from within created the illusion of a face of a man. Whose face? Salvatore Varossa, that's who.

Finally, he tucked the papers into a file folder and locked them in the bottom drawer of his desk, next to his 9mm handgun. He had been hoping that the blood line of the Wingates would finally die out, but he wouldn't be so lucky. Now there was another generation. The line of succession had to be stopped before she married, had children and perpetuated her evil abilities.

He still remembered his granny and the vacant stare in her eyes. Mary Ester Varossa might have been a beautiful woman in her youth when she, her husband and daughter immigrated to New Orleans from Palermo seeking a better life. Both she and his mother were traumatized when Salvatore Varossa disappeared without a trace. Benito Varossa never knew the man. The incident happened long before he was born. However, his picture had been prominently displayed by his grandmother. His mother, Catherine, had devoted her life to caring for the old woman—taking time out for a brief encounter that resulted in his own birth. He never knew the identity of his biological father. During his mother's last days, the same vacant stare took up residence in her eyes as well. Would he end up the same way?

There were times when he was nearly consumed by violent urges and strange but silent demands. He had never acted on them. However, as time passed, the urges had evolved into voices and their insistent challenges were getting harder to ignore.

He was cleaning out the old house to sell it after his mother's death when he found the box of newspaper clippings and his grandmother's diary. That's when the direction of his own life took a new and dramatic turn. He had a job to do. No one and nothing would get in his way.

The last words on his mother's lips were, "Find your grandfather's body. Lay him to rest in hallowed ground."

Spoken like a true Italian Catholic.

And, even after fifty years, he wanted to get to the bottom of this mystery once and for all. He left his big work truck parked in the company garage, got into his personal car and drove away...to watch and wait.

Chapter Fourteen
Friday morning

Jason was already in the kitchen filling the coffee pot when Dannah came down the stairs. They exchanged pleasantries over breakfast.

"Sorry I woke you last night. The robbery at your house still has me jittery. Even though there are dead bolts and chains on all the doors, anyone could break the glass to get to the lock." She tapped the side of her head. "I'm not going whacko, but, I thought it was happening again. Which is ridiculous because no one knows me in this town. In truth, someone has a grudge against you, Jason. I had no idea that life in the academic world was so fraught with danger."

"Neither did I. Of course, this is my first major discovery. There was a professor from Illinois who worked in the Gobi desert for five years before unearthing his new dinosaur. The guys from the University of Virginia have been searching for the Fort at the Jamestown site for more years than I can remember. I don't know how long Baxter dug at Chucalissa, but that was twenty years ago. I don't know the man's history and never cared to look it up. Although I did read his book. His research was good, but he should have dug deeper."

"Will he be at the cocktail party tonight?"

"You bet. It's a mandatory event."

Dannah sipped her coffee slowly and allowed her mind to wander. She was looking forward to the opportunity to shake Bill Baxter's hand to see what her new skill might produce. Maybe she could learn to live with it and become the master of her psychic abilities.

***

The trip to the mall resulted in a simply styled sheath dress made of a rich-looking fabric. The sleeveless black outfit came with a lightweight lacy jacket to use against the slight nighttime chill as fall weather began to make inroads into the Mississippi

Delta. She bought new shoes and matching handbag, and even purchased an inexpensive pearl necklace and earrings. She was pleased with the outcome, and judging by the look in Jason's eyes as she descended the stairwell, he was dazzled.

"You look gorgeous," he exclaimed.

"Thank you, Mister Dunhill. And your attire is a huge improvement over those tattered shorts you're so attached to." His brilliant smile and light blue eyes were in stark contrast to his deeply tanned skin.

The party was held in the campus art museum, which served as a huge lobby to the main library. Caterers had set up a cash bar and a table with an appealing display of finger food. All of the current teachers and assistants wore white name tags while the new additions to the staff wore tags of electric green. The pleasant mix of people ran the gamut of every ethnicity.

"Be nice to Bill Baxter," Dannah cautioned as they approached the bar. "I'll be forced to hide in the ladies' room if you create a scene."

"I promise to be on my best behavior. Well, I'll promise to try. I'll even introduce you as if nothing ever happened. However, I do plan on giving him a little food for thought." Jason paid for a couple of drinks and began to circulate with his free hand placed possessively around Dannah's waist as he guided her from one group to another, proudly introducing her to his coworkers as his "close friend and next-door neighbor."

After meeting and having a lengthy chat with the head of the Journalism Department, Dannah decided that going back to school for her Master's Degree would be a wonderful challenge. If she lived frugally, she wouldn't have to get a job.

When she and Jason finally approached Baxter, the older man appeared very much ill-at-ease.

"Baxter, I'd like you to meet a special friend of mine, Dannah Wingate. She's been my houseguest for the past week looking after Gunner while I was out of town. She just inherited the house next door to me."

"House guest? Wingate? Yes, yes, the old Wingate place." His eye lids fluttered nervously and he avoided eye contact. "I've never been inside; however, I'm familiar with it. I met Miss Gova when we both served on the Downtown Historical Restoration Committee. She was a delightful woman. Died a few months ago, didn't she?"

"Yes, and unfortunately, I never had the chance to meet her." As he shook hands with Dannah, she immediately noticed that his skin was very cold, dry and rough as his fingers closed around hers. In response to their connection, the images came quickly, ruthlessly invading her mind with his personal pain and plans for revenge all jumbled together without logical sequence.

—*Sweet revenge. Plot. Profound fear. A witness? New plan. Worry. Serious illness. Loneliness. Hopelessness. The color red. A large, hard piece of living tissue was slowly pulsating and expanding inside the chest, crowding discolored lungs and a sluggishly beating heart. Broken glass, a broken life and a broken heart—*

—and a broken train of thought when Baxter's voice interrupted the connection. "So, Miss Wingate, will you be moving to Oxford...uh, permanently?"

"Yes, I will. I'm finding both the house and the town are very hospitable." Dannah had witnessed enough and didn't want to experience any more of his thoughts and feelings. She withdrew her hand and grasped her purse, then nodded her head. "Nice to meet you." She looked up at Jason hoping he would take the hint to move on to another group of friends. He did.

***

"What happened when you shook hands with Baxter?" Jason asked as they exited the building two hours later.

"What do you mean?"

"I don't know. Your eyes sort of glassed over. Like you'd seen a ghost."

Dannah shrugged and smiled weakly over his reference to a ghost. It would be nice to unload her burden on this poor man, but their relationship had not reached the point for such an intimate revelation. "No, it's just that he reeks of cigarette smoke. Very unpleasant."

"The man went to hell after his wife died." Jason chuckled. "What was your overall impression of him?"

"He seems lonely and very worried." Dannah wanted to add that she experienced a twinge of sympathy for Baxter, but decided against airing her thoughts.

"Good," Jason snapped. "He better be worried. I'm going to nail him to the wall for what he did to my computer and all my hard work. By the way, you seem to be right at home among all the stuffy professors."

"With every day that passes, I'm beginning to feel more at home here in Oxford."

Jason brushed his lips across Dannah's forehead as he helped her into the car. "I'm glad."

Chapter Fifteen
Saturday morning

The next morning after breakfast, Dannah washed and dried their dishes. She felt well rested and was delighted to have slept through the entire night without waking up. "You might want to take a change of clothes to Memphis. It will take two days."

"No problem."

"I managed to find a mover on short notice and one who's willing to work on Sunday. And a realtor is going to meet us late this afternoon at my dad's house."

"I'm yours for the next two days."

"Thanks."

"I don't mind...honest. I usually play golf with my buddies on Saturday mornings, but I can bypass this week. My main objective in life is to whip Professor Krause just once before I die. Damn, he's a fantastic golfer. Not a great deal of power, but a ton of finesse."

"You must be one of those competitive sport-types. Always chasing after balls of various shapes and sizes."

"Yeah, and once a year, my buddies and I—driven by testosterone—tramp through the woods hell-bent on killing Bambi," he responded with a hearty laugh. "Then we sit by the fire at night drinking beer and talking about fast cars and loose women."

"I don't see any sport in that."

"You might be interested to know that Bambi has always managed to elude the cross-hairs of my rifle."

"Good for him."

"I'll get the last laugh," he stated with firm conviction. "You can't live in this town and not become an Ole Miss Rebel football fan. It's something in the air. After inhaling it for a while, you become addicted."

"Oh no, I'm a fan of my alma mater—UT. Go Big Orange."

Jason wondered if she would pursue lovemaking with the

same hot-blooded fervor she defended her own personal point of view. He lifted his collar away from his neck, feeling a rush of heat in spite of the air conditioning. During this lively exchange of exploratory small talk, he studied her with a critical eye and wondered about the extent of her wariness—a thin coating, or all the way to her core? It appeared to him that during their kiss the night before, he had managed to thaw a couple of inches. *Within her flower-like delicacy, this woman harbors some vicious thorns,* Jason quietly observed.

The essence of her abundant sexuality was magnified by her perfume, whose enticing aroma was whipping his pheromones into a frenzy. He would need to repress his emotions and get down to the business at hand.

***

Memphis, Tennessee

Dannah directed Jason to her father's little clapboard house on the east side of Memphis. "I hate asking you to do this. I feel like I'm dragging you into the muck and mire of my pitiful life."

"You don't have to say anything. I'm here because I want to be."

She mumbled a word of thanks and fell silent. He had no idea how reluctant she was to go back to the place where she grew up. There were no happy memories, no laughter, no gaiety, but when you're an only child, there was no one else to do the joyless task.

The contents of the mail box were spilling onto the sidewalk. Four or five desperate notes from the Post Office were tucked under the front door and sun-yellowed newspapers littered the porch. The grass was long, heavy with seed heads, and in the flower beds, weeds outnumbered the petunias and marigolds Coleman had so carefully planted in the early spring. As they entered the house, mice and roaches scrambled out of sight. Gunner made a mad dash after one of the vermin, but wasn't quite agile enough to make the kill.

"Geez, it smells awful in here." Dannah turned on the air

conditioning and threw open the windows, but the humid outside air offered no relief from the foul odor of decaying garbage. "I could kick myself for not coming sooner to clean up the mess. A quart of sour milk, egg shells, a tub of butter, a jar of jam, and an open loaf of bread. No wonder the mice were having a field day in here. Daddy was usually such a clean and orderly person."

"Not when you're in the middle of a heart attack," Jason commented.

A few moldy remnants of her father's scrambled eggs were still scattered on the kitchen floor. The handset of the phone was on the floor where he managed to call 911 before losing consciousness. Discarded bandages, packaging, vials and syringes were carelessly tossed around the room, unsettling evidence of the frantic effort of the EMS team to keep his damaged heart beating. Over a two-year period, Dannah watched helplessly as his health gradually deteriorated. The massive heart attack that landed him in CICU was the culminating event before he succumbed to death a few hours later. She still regretted the fact that the nurses sent her home and she had not been by his side to hold his hand when he passed to the other side.

Was he afraid to die? Or, had he made his peace with God?

Jason remained tactfully silent while she wrestled with her images from the past. He laid his large hand on her back with surprising gentleness and quietly asked, "Are you all right?"

With a weak smile, she pulled away from her miserable reverie and lifted her shoulders in a graceful shrug. "Yeah, I'm fine. It's just I have so many sad memories. My father was never a happy man. I can only hope that he's finally found peace from whatever demons or ghosts that were pursuing him."

He must have sensed that her declaration didn't need a response and changed the subject. "Hey, if the lawnmower works, I'll cut down the weeds while you work in the house."

Dannah was touched by Jason's thoughtfulness. His spontaneous offer to mow the grass almost brought tears to her eyes. She hadn't meant to make eye contact with him, but she lifted her head and met his gaze. What she saw in his sky-blue eyes was sincerity and solicitude, and she came very close to melting into his arms. The unspoken connection was still there—left over from the previous night's kisses. He was taking on hero status with his compassion, and for not asking too many probing and uncomfortable questions. He was far different from most of the men she had dated. Well educated, devoted to his career, yet down to earth, and obviously secure enough in his masculinity to exhibit his softer side. Although her emotions were too turbulent to deal with everything that had happened to her, she felt a growing affection for him overriding all other sentiments.

"Thank you," she finally whispered.

After he went outside, she filled a pail with soapy water and commenced cleaning, hoping the physical activity would keep the depressing thoughts at bay.

When she opened the door to her father's closet, she noted that he kept his clothes neatly placed on hangers. His Sunday suit was hanging on the door knob still in the plastic bag from the dry cleaners. She hadn't looked inside this closet in many, many years. Coleman Wingate had been a widower for so long, he had developed a penchant for neatness.

After she emptied the closet and packed his clothing in large plastic bags, she noticed a box on the top shelf marked "Important Papers" in awkward block letters. It was a shoe box for men's work boots. The cardboard container rattled as she lifted it. A strong image immediately slammed into her and, catching her off guard, shoved her over backwards and onto the bed. An image of—

—of a long, silver knife. Pure, raw terror. The knife was raised high in a two-fisted grip, then brought down and plunged into the back of a man bent over two inert bodies. What to do? What to do? Don't get caught. Blood flowing into an ever widening puddle—

Gunner whined and jumped on the bed with her. She gasped for air and blinked furiously, trying to remove every trace of the hideous vision. Reality seeped into her consciousness with the sound of the lawnmower outside the window. Her first impulse was to run out the front door and throw herself into Jason's arms where she could find temporary refuge from the reigning confusion. He probably wouldn't mind at all, but might ask for an explanation. Gunner continued to whimper and lick her face.

"Thanks for caring," she muttered and pulled herself together. It took every ounce of concentration and energy she could muster to hold at bay the upsetting images which niggled at her consciousness while she completed the cleanup job.

Finally, the place looked halfway presentable. Dannah signed a six-month contract with a realtor, then called a nearby church and donated the clothing and furniture. She also made arrangements to reroute the mail to her address in Mississippi and terminate the utilities and phone service.

"This is it," she stated, gingerly holding the old box with her fingertips. "This is all that remains of sixty-eight years of life."

"What's in it?"

Dannah rattled the securely taped box. "I don't know, and right now, I'm not ready to tackle another gut-wrenching stroll down memory lane."

***

It was dark when they entered Dannah's apartment; and Jason quickly surveyed the subdued quality of the furnishings. "Nice neighborhood. Nice place."

"When everyone hears the name Wingate, they think I'm related to someone rich and famous, but I come from humble beginnings. Not everyone named Vanderbilt is related to the Commodore. The Readers Digest picked up one of my nonfiction articles—they pay very well—so I invested in this condo."

"One of those fluffy little stories about PMS and the professional woman?"

Dannah clenched her jaw, wondering how he could make such an accurate off handed guess. "I was saving the money to buy a bigger house, then Daddy died."

"No rich boyfriends?"

Dannah flushed with indignation as she waved one tiny fist. "Why is it men think women are incapable of buying houses or making wise investments without their questionable masculine assistance?"

Jason threw up his hands. "Wait a minute before you launch into orbit. I'm not a chauvinist. I've always been sympathetic to the feminist movement. Women educators have enjoyed prominence long before anyone heard of the equal rights amendment."

"I'm sorry." She wilted. "Sometimes I get carried away. I had to put up with a bunch of overbearing baa...men at the newspaper. Every sentence contained a double entendre. They'd pat me on the fanny and say, 'Go get 'em, Tiger.'"

"Tiger? I like that nickname."

She gave him a chilling stare. "I don't."

"How about 'Pussycat?'"

"Don't like that one either."

"What did your father call you?"

Dannah softened and delivered a tentative smile. "'My girl.'"

"'My girl.' I like the sound of that even better."

The words carried a far different connotation coming from Jason's mouth than from her father's, and she liked it very much. Dannah felt a flood of comforting warmth invade her entire body pushing aside all her irritation. "I can send out for pizza, if you're hungry?"

"I can handle that."

"Sausage and mushrooms okay?" He nodded and she placed the call. "Takes about thirty minutes. Jason, I've enjoyed your companionship and value all the work you've done. You have the patience of a saint. Being single and independent means you have to be strong twenty-four/seven, never letting down your guard for even a second, and never, I mean never, show a smidgen of weakness."

"Whoever wrote that rule should be shot at sunrise."

"You're right. I've been handling everything alone for so long, it makes me doubly appreciative of you."

"Thanks, but you don't have to be alone any longer. Not unless you have some sort of burning desire to be secluded. After all, we're going to be next-door neighbors."

When Jason gathered her into his arms, Dannah willingly sagged into his chest and buried her face in the fabric of his shirt. The aroma of freshly cut grass overpowered the lingering summertime sweat—probably a trick of her mind over emotion. At this point in time, she'd like to stay snuggled in his arms forever—to hell with independence—and let Jason navigate all the ruts and potholes in the road of her life. But deep down inside, she knew that retreating and sulking weren't her style. She had always embraced life head on—good or bad, rough or smooth. She sighed deeply and pulled away. "I've been bitchy and I'm sorry. I've been riding an emotional roller coaster—ups and downs, life and death."

"I'm glad you used the 'b' word and not me. You need more fun and laughter in your life. And while we're at it, I could use a little of the same medicine. It's been a long, hot summer."

"Yes, it has," Dannah firmly agreed.

When the food arrived, they sat down at Dannah's kitchen table and clicked their cola cans together like wine glasses. "Here's lookin' at you, kid," he said in his best Bogart imitation.

She couldn't help but laugh and marvel over how much more relaxed she felt with Jason Dunhill sitting opposite her than when Philip Henderson occupied that very same chair. "I haven't done much laughing since, well, since Daddy died. August ninth to be exact. It feels good to laugh again."

He paused with his drink halfway between the table and his mouth. "I'm glad. Smiles look good on you."

"All of a sudden, I'm very hungry."

It was almost midnight when they finished eating, so they went upstairs to bed. "There's a small TV in the guest room and the bath is through that door. Everything gets cut off on Monday morning—water, utilities and cable. Do you mind if Gunner sleeps with me?"

"Okay, but you're spoiling him rotten. He won't like being relegated to the floor when things get back to normal."

Dannah halted in her tracks, turned and met Jason's intense gaze with deadly seriousness. "Normal? You know something, Jason? I don't think anything will ever be normal again."

Her words were delivered with a hint of desperation. Jason reached for her hands and held them, and when she tried to pull away his grip tightened. "Yes it will, and that's a promise. I've got a feeling that everything is going to be different when you move to Mississippi. Different, like better." He pulled her into his arms and kissed her.

They held the kiss until they were both out of breath. Dannah finally pulled away and tried to lighten the mood by tapping the end of his nose with her fingertip. "I like it and I'd like some more." She giggled softly. "That's my imitation of Lauren Bacall. You know that old song? 'They had it all, just like Bogey and Bacall.'"

"And so can we. I'd like to respond with something really clever and witty right now with some more snappy movie-star dialogue, but I can't find the right words. You leave me tongue-tied. So, I'll just say good night and pleasant dreams."

"If I had a choice, I'd vote for no dreams at all," Dannah responded. "Thanks. See you in the morning." She and Gunner retreated to her bedroom.

The layout of Dannah's apartment placed the two bedrooms upstairs at opposite ends, with the two bathrooms between them. Because her unit was at the end of the row, she had the added bonus of extra windows on the side. A small area tucked into a dormer at the top of the stairs served as her office with a desk, chair, file cabinet and her desktop computer.

Prodded by curiosity, Dannah opened the sealed box which she had retrieved from her dad's closet. The hand-beaded neck band she had seen in the painting of Rainy Skies was wrapped in a thin piece of tissue paper. It had been cut and the leather was stained—probably with Rainy Skies blood. As she handled the artifact, Dannah was aware of an odd, tingling sensation in her hands. Curiously, she didn't have any overt emotions concerning the viciousness of the murder which took her grandmother's life and the life of her husband. Possibly, fifty-something years was too long for there to be any residual psychic reaction for her to pick up. A second beaded band was also there.

This one had a tiny tarnished silver bell sewn into the design. An arctic blast of air chilled her to the bone as she recalled the conversation with Annie Fields. "...always walks around the house barefooted an' wearin' her Indian garb. She wore a little bitty bell on one ankle. Gova told me that on a quiet night, you could hear the bell a-tinklin.'" Dannah shivered uncontrollably until she dropped the band back into the box. The frosty breeze vanished, however, the brief experience was totally unnerving.

The numerous newspaper clippings were similar to the ones which Gova had, dated in the late nineteen-fifties and describing the murders. An old-fashioned pocket watch, engraved with the name of her grandfather Jonathan Wingate, lay in the bottom of the box. A ring with four slightly rusted keys was rattling around as well. There was also a copy of Coleman's birth certificate, his marriage license to Della Taylor, her own birth certificate and another confirming her mother's death. The box also contained documents verifying her father's stint in the Army when he fought in the Vietnam War. Not much to show for all his years of being on this earth.

Something else caught Dannah's attention. She thought it might be another newspaper article, but it was a heavy object wrapped in news print. A deep frown creased her features as she tentatively unwrapped the item.

"Why on earth would Daddy keep an old butcher knife? Ohmygod! There are two knives." Both were stained with blood. Whereas the blades had obviously been wiped clean, the time-darkened blood stains were deeply embedded in the wooden handle on the kitchen knife, and had also stained the leather handle of the hunting-style knife. The paper was dated April 13 1959. The same familiar cold chill washed over her.

Dannah caught a glimpse of herself in the mirror over the dressing table. It wasn't a pretty sight. Her eyes looked like cinders in a snowbank, sunken, hollow and darkly circled. It seemed as though fear and uncertainty had become her constant companion as of late, like living entities which skimmed over her skin then burrowed deeply into her flesh, finally coming to rest in and around her eyes. Could Jason see it? How could he possibly find her haunted, gaunt expression attractive?

As she stared at the two knives lying in her hand, cradled in a bed of yellowed newspaper, an amorphous vision fought to invade her mind—fuzzy, ill-defined. But she battled it back, refusing to allow its entry. Too vague, too wispy, too confusing and too long ago. Some little scrap of intuition told her that she would have to retreat into a deep trance to relive this event. She wasn't prepared to try it alone.

One corner of Dannah's lip curled into a half-assed satisfied smile. "Control. I do believe that I'm learning how to gain a little bit of control."

Carefully, she replaced all the contents of the box and secreted it in one of her suitcases, already packed with her clothing. She felt a powerful urge to scrub her hands, even though the newsprint had kept her from coming in direct contact with the two weapons. There was another urge striving for recognition. It was the desire to seek comfort by touching Jason, instead, she reached for Gunner and buried her face in his sleek neck. He twisted his head around and managed to plaster a wet kiss on her ear. His gesture of affection unleashed a torrent of cleansing tears.

***

Dannah liked to open the drapes after she turned off the lights. Her apartment was on the back row of the complex, and her second floor windows gave her an unobstructed view of the busy freeway as well as the nighttime sky. Stars twinkled like diamonds, their timeless permanence was a reassuring handle to grasp during all the demoralizing uncertainty which now dominated her life.

The nervousness she felt as she climbed into her familiar bed had nothing to do with Jason's presence in her home. It was apprehension concerning her dreams, that and a ton of fears and unanswered questions grinding through her mind. Finally, she drifted off into an uneasy sleep.

A loud pop cut into her restless slumber and she could plainly see a surprised victim staring down at the gaping hole in his chest as he fell against the oak kitchen cabinets and slowly slipped to the floor. Blood was pouring out onto a linoleum floor in an ever-widening puddle, and into a river of blood—

Her scream pierced the silence like a dagger. She awakened in a foggy haze, imagining that the damp perspiration covering her body was the brilliant red of fresh blood. The grisly image caused Dannah to sit up in bed and gasp for air. Gunner sat up as well and peered into her face with a concerned look in his huge black eyes. Her breath was ragged, coming in uneven gasps, as a cold cloak of fear lured her to the edge of uncontrolled hysteria. Awareness of time and place came slowly, tiptoeing along the fringes of delirium that had her trapped in between sleep and wakefulness. Once her eyes became focused, she looked at the time. It was three o'clock. She had not even recovered from the first avalanche of gruesome images when—

—another loud gunshot slammed into her mind as it tore into the head of a second victim. His body jerked backwards and fell onto a wood surface, his life's blood dripping between weathered boards—

The second shriek was so chilling, Jason nearly fell out of the narrow twin bed. In his sleepy-eyed haste to investigate the source of the sound, he lurched into the hall where a night light dimly illuminated the area to keep anyone from accidentally falling down the stairs.

"Dannah? Dannah?" He burst through her bedroom door. "Good God, what's wrong?" She was sitting upright, sobbing, almost hyperventilating in her struggle to breathe.

"A...a...a bad dream."

Jason sat on the bed and gathered Dannah in his arms. "Did you have a nightmare?"

"Y-yes, yes, t-two dreams." Her shoulders were trembling as she examined her outstretched hands, turning them over several times, searching for blood, wanting tangible evidence that it was a dream and not reality.

"Hey, are you okay?"

"No, I'm not."

As his arms encircled her in his sheltered haven, she buried her face in his neck, feeling like she had fallen from a great distance and landed in the safety net he offered.

"Everything's going to be okay," he whispered into her black curls. The fingers of his left hand touched the small of her back and crept upward to cradle her head in his wide-spread fingers. "My girl, my girl. Calm down, I'm here," he crooned in a singsong tone offering comfort.

Overcome by her frightening nightmare, Dannah locked her arms around Jason's neck and held on to him. Finally, the fear began to drain from her body and her tense muscles relaxed. She sank into his strong protection feeling remarkably secure considering how briefly she'd known him. A wave of ungovernable emotion tumbled down her spine and removed the last tattered vestige of restraint. She willingly allowed her physical needs to defeat her hesitation. The frightening residue of her dream prevented her from realizing their provocative situation. His bare flesh was warm and smelled pleasantly of soap and spicy male cologne. His coarse chest hair tickled her nose, offering evidence of being firmly planted in reality. "I'm sorry I woke you," she finally said.

"Don't worry about waking me. Just tell me you're going to be all right."

"I don't know," she responded in a muffled, little-girl voice.

He pulled away and gently tipped up her chin. "Do you want to talk about it?"

"No, not now. Maybe tomorrow."

She lifted her gaze to meet his. The brilliance of the full moon filtered through the thin curtains, allowing the delicate lights of the night to reflect in her eyes. She didn't often wear her vulnerability for all the world to view, but tonight, Jason could see the raw edges showing, and they were very much like his own.

"Don't leave me. I don't want to be alone."

"You don't have to be alone anymore."

"Oh, Jason. It's the dark, silent hours that are frightening and...and lonely. Hold me," she murmured in a quivering voice.

He became keenly aware of her warm flesh clad only in a gauzy bit of lace. He moaned as he gathered her to his bare chest and fought the desire to crush her in a tight embrace. The fragrance of her perfume wafted from her skin sending passion throughout his body, touching a place he kept well-guarded. Jason knew that he wanted to offer her more than a promise of temporary safety, he wanted to offer his love, comfort and his strength. He fell backwards and brought her with him, then moved his hands to lift her face and kissed her.

He was locked in a world of his own creation, certain in the knowledge that no one since the dawn of time had ever experienced this profoundly personal response. His past was forgotten, their future not yet contemplated; there was only the immediacy of his sexual desire blotting out the last shred of rational thought, and reality vanished in a haze of their hunger. Jason drew her into his whirlpool of feelings, and knew that their coming together would be the fulfillment of all the vague, restless dreams that had plagued him since he first laid eyes on her.

The slippery texture of her silken gown attacked every raw nerve ending and sent one clear message to his clouded brain. He was in physical pain from the urgency of his arousal and the act of pulling away would be heroic. "Dannah." There was deep fierceness in his husky voice. "Let me make love to you. I can help you forget whoever, or whatever is bothering you."

In the glow of the moon, she put her hand to his face and traced the outline of his mouth. His nibbling of each fingertip sent a fresh surge of fire streaking through her body. Her heart crashed against her ribs. She had been so long without physical love, every cell of her body was overwhelmed by the sudden demand to prove she was very much alive, still a vibrant young woman with strong desires. "Yes, yes."

He slipped the gown over her head and stepped out of his under shorts. He caressed her breasts, kissed every fragrant juncture of curve and plain, every peak and valley. Beneath his lips and his hands, heat consumed her body like a raging fever. When he moved on top of her, she greeted him eagerly, pressing against him, holding his swelling hardness in her hand. Dannah arched her back and thrust her hips forward. Her hands glided across his shoulders and down his back to cup his small rounded bottom and pulled him to her. She wanted him more than she had ever wanted any man in her entire life. His mouth traced a molten hot trail across her breasts, neck and to her waiting lips.

At the moment of their joining, vivid bolts of heat lightning arced across the dark sky sending sharp white daggers of light across the bed. The visual impact as he entered her was shocking and unexpected, ripping new emotions from the depths of his soul. No longer a blending of bodies, it became of melding of minds, of locked, love-ladened eyes. He lost himself in her softness, wanting only to bind himself to her for whatever time Fate allowed.

Dannah was more woman than he imagined could be contained in such a small body—earthy, hot and liquid, giving and so sweetly demanding. A fragile tigress, delicate yet rough and wild with her wanting. Soft little moans rumbled in her throat as they matched cadence, one with the other. He took his time, slow and easy. Tense from the pressure of holding back until she shuddered with pleasure, then he let go.

He held her tight while they briefly rested. They were carried away by one thrilling chill followed by another and another. Splintered splendor raced from tingling fingers and toes spiraling upward to burst into a million pieces of breathtaking joy. He knew it would be great with her, but he never imagined it would be this great.

There had to be a next time, and another, and another.

Chapter Sixteen
Sunday morning
Memphis, Tennessee

Even before she opened her eyes, Dannah knew that the heavy presence she felt beside her in bed was Jason Dunhill, not his dog, Gunner. She carefully turned her head to the left. The large animal was asleep curled up on her cast-off nightgown lying on the floor, his head pillowed on Jason's jeans.

Damn, she groaned silently as she turned again to stare at the ceiling. *What have I done?*

Of course, she knew the answer. She had made wild, passionate love to a virtual stranger. Wild, passionate, unprotected sex to be precise. Neither one of them had possessed enough common sense to think about something as intrusive as a condom. She certainly didn't keep a supply in her bedside table. She had stopped taking her birth-control pills over a year ago when she broke up with Phil. Since she wasn't dating anyone, she didn't see the need to put unnecessary chemicals in her body. She couldn't even blame alcohol for her aberrant behavior, having drunk nothing headier than a caffeine-laden diet cola.

She wondered if Jason was the sort of man who could make love with that much deep intensity, then laugh and walk away. At this exact moment in time it didn't matter, because every ounce of tension had flowed out of her body leaving her with that luxurious lethargy that comes from being a thoroughly satisfied woman. She couldn't begin to count the number of bone-wracking orgasms she had experienced during the three times they had coupled and made love, between short bouts of sleep. Whereas men were often accused of using women, the system could work both ways. She was fully prepared to accept the warm afterglow of passion without the usual flood of guilt.

Gunner sensed she was awake and put his paws on the side of the bed. The movement caused Jason to stir. He rolled over and cupped one hand beneath her bare breast. "Good mornin,'" he mumbled sleepily and started nibbling on her ear. "You are an amazing woman."

Dannah knew that if she didn't get out of the bed quickly, it would happen again. It's not that she didn't want him to make love to her again, but the fact that they might be bending the law of averages to the breaking point. She wasn't mentally prepared for an unexpected pregnancy. "We, we'd better get up," she stated and adroitly pulled away from him. "I'll take Gunner outside while you get dressed. The movers will be here shortly."

***

Downstairs over breakfast, Dannah decided to tell Jason the truth about her nightmares and visions. They had definitely arrived at a crossroad in their relationship. It was time to bare her soul. If he couldn't handle her psychic abilities, better to find out now before her heart got broken. In fact, it might already be too late. She fully expected him to label her insane and bolt for the nearest exit. "We need to talk," she stated as she pushed a steaming cup of coffee across the small kitchen table.

"Ooh Jesus, Dannah." He ran his fingers over the stubble on his chin. "This isn't going to be one of those bullshit, awkward-guilt-filled-morning-after conversations, is it? 'Cause I don't want to hear that it shouldn't have happened and it'll never happen again."

"No, no." As she shook her head, her uncombed black curls bobbed. "I have no regrets," she said, almost in a whisper.

"The way you shot out of bed like a rocket this morning and rushed to put your clothes on, I thought you were having major regrets."

Even though there was a lingering sense of sexual awareness dancing between them, her eyes nervously darted from side to side. "Uuh, for safety's sake. Jason, I-I'm not taking birth-control pills."

"Oh, Dannah, damn, I'm sorry about that. I'll make a trip to the drug store. I'm not one of those guys who always carry condoms in his wallet hoping to get lucky. If the unexpected happens, I won't walk away from you. I'm a man who takes responsibility for his actions."

"Look, we're both consenting adults. Plainly and simply, last night I was in need and you gave me exactly what I needed."

Jason reached across the narrow table and grasped her hands. "Last night was very special for me. Damn, you're every man's dream woman come to life. You have a marvelous and inquisitive mind, along with physical beauty and topped off by an abundance of passion."

"Thank you for the lovely compliment, but hold on a minute."

"I told you the other night that something special clicked between us."

"Oh Jason, they are beautiful words, but.... You're going to be the one having serious regrets when I tell you the truth...about me."

Jason stared at her with a quizzical expression for several seconds. The silence between them shimmered as real as a living being. "Okay, this must be one of those feminine guessing games. Because I'm still basking in the glow of your passion, I'll play along. You have a husband and four children in Texas."

"Noooo, I don't play games like that."

"You've spent time in jail?"

"Never."

"You've got some fatal disease and you're going to die in six months."

"Get serious."

"You're HIV positive."

"Not that serious."

"I'm trying. Okay? Let me have another guess. Insanity runs in your family?"

"Now, that's a possibility."

"Oh boy, I'm getting warm. Well then, you're probably an escapee from a mental hospital."

"No. Hush up and let me explain." Dannah tightened her lips to stifle a budding smile. *The man did have a wry sense of humor,* she thought. "I need to tell you the truth about me."

"Okay, I'm listening. What is this awful truth?"

"You see this calendar on the fridge?" She pointed. "I put

a big red X on July tenth. It was the day Aunt Gova died—although I didn't know it at the time—it was the day I started having visions, uh...nightmares."

"What sort of visions are you talking about? Aliens? Ghosts? Angels? The Virgin Mary making a plea for world peace?"

Dannah shook her head. "Please be serious. I have, uh...insights, uh...maybe you could call it a perception of what has happened or what might be happening. I call them 'pop-up visions' even though sometimes I'm asleep when I get them. It's something. An odd ability I think I've inherited from my Native American grandmother, through Gova. On the night Aunt Gova died, I dreamed that I died peacefully in my bed." Dannah fell silent for a moment, then decided not to tell him about seeing a hand reaching out to Gova from a bright light. "Then on the night Daddy died, I dreamed...more like a nightmare...that I was scrambling eggs in his kitchen when I had a heart attack. It was as if the events were happening to me, complete with the horrendous pain in my chest, falling to the floor, the ambulance ride. What I saw in my dream is exactly what I saw in his house—you saw it, too. After I woke up and went downstairs to the kitchen, the hospital called to say that Daddy had been admitted with a heart attack. He was weak and couldn't say much, but he did say, 'I was hoping it wouldn't come to you, but you're next in line.' He told me to go see Aunt Gova, she can tell me what I need to know."

Once again the silence became heavy and ominous. "Okay, so you woke up in the middle of the night on July tenth and discovered that you're psychic. Is that what you're saying?"

"I didn't know it at the time, but basically, that's exactly what happened. By the way, I prefer 'perceptive.' I've never been able to say that other word out loud."

"I thought psychics were born with their ability."

"That's what everyone seems to think. But mine appears to have been inherited through the maternal line."

His eyes rolled from side to side, then he got up from the tiny table and topped off his coffee cup. "This is a lot to dump on a guy."

"Yes, I know." Dannah closely watched the uncertainty in his eyes. "It's been a slow process for me to accept as well."

"Okay, I'll have to do a realignment of my thoughts."

"Yes, you will."

"Well," he drawled. "Daren managed to live with Samantha. Of course, she was a witch, not a psychic."

"You think I'm crazy, don't you? You called Aunt Gova loony, so you think I'm loony as well."

"Dannah, it'll take some getting used to. Maybe you do have some sort of ability that's slightly outside the norm. You're different than other women. Oh Lord, are you different. That's precisely what I love about you. Now, tell me more. Do you hear voices?"

"No. To date I haven't heard voices, but I do see actions and sense emotions."

"What do you see?"

"You sound so much like my old boss, Pete Jordan," Dannah muttered. "It's like a video tape—a very short scene that plays out in my head, sometimes repeatedly. I already told you that's what brought me to Oxford. I wanted to talk to Aunt Gova. I wanted to hear from her about what is being passed down in the family."

"Only she was dead."

"Apparently, Daddy wasn't aware of that."

"Dannah, get real. He was in denial. Obviously, since you are the only living Wingate relative, your aunt had to have died for this psychic power to come to you. And judging by your dad's warnings, he knew it, dammit, he knew it."

"I never thought of denial, but you're probably right. Daddy also said that it might already be too late." Dannah clenched one tiny fist and shook it in the air. "He was so damned bullheaded about revealing anything pertaining to Gova and his family."

"He probably didn't want to be around her because she could read his mind."

She reined in her anger and managed a half-smile. "You're very perceptive yourself."

"He also wanted to pass the buck and leave the explaining

to someone else. I'd also like to add that we're damn lucky Fate works in such strange ways to get two people together." He pitched his voice lower. "Especially when it's meant to be."

Dannah stared at him incredulously as her erratic emotions raced from gloom to glow. She was truly surprised by his response and couldn't believe he was being so receptive. "Are you taking me seriously?" When flustered, Dannah's artificially clipped speech reverted to her native southern drawl.

"Yes, I am. I'm dead serious." Jason paused to catch his breath.

The softness in his eyes made it difficult to maintain her annoyance. "Most of my dreams involve death, illness or strong emotion, such as rage. Some of the visions happen when touching something or someone."

"Can you...can you read my mind?" he asked hesitantly.

Now it was Dannah's turn to smile. "You don't sing in the shower."

His eyes widened in shock. "How did you know?"

"Gunner told me. No, I'm kidding. I can't read you or the dog."

"That's a relief."

"Thankfully, I can't read every person I meet. That would be very distracting. In fact, I think a psychic person would go totally insane if hundreds of visions were assaulting his or her senses all the time."

"Did you see something when you shook hands with Bill Baxter at the cocktail party Friday night?"

"Yes."

"What did you see?"

Dannah pulled in a troubled sigh. "Worry, fear. I feel certain that he was responsible for the break-in at your house. I also think he has lung cancer."

Obviously, Jason didn't have the time or inclination for sympathy. "Can you see faces?"

"Not the individual I'm inside of. So far, I have had no images of a face, only the emotion that lies beneath the face." Dannah studied Jason's odd expression and read it to be a suppression of laughter. "You can go ahead and laugh your head off—see if I care."

"I'm not laughing."

"Even before you told me, I knew that a murder or something else bad had taken place in the kitchen of Gova's house. I don't get that sensation anywhere else in the house except when I'm standing in front of the sink." Dannah rose from her chair and refilled her cup. "Thursday night, I read some old newspaper clippings about my grandmother, Rainy Skies. Back in the late 1950s, she was going to use her psychic powers to help the Oxford police identify a child-killer. Anyhow, the way I figure it is that the murderer must have read about her psychic abilities and decided to kill her before she met with police the following day and possibly revealed his identity. My dad and Aunt Gova were in the house at the time. I figure that Daddy was about fifteen or sixteen and Aunt Gova was about eleven or twelve. All these years have passed and the case has gone unsolved. However, the child killings did stop. I swear I'm going to get to the bottom of this if it's the last thing I do."

"How are you going to solve this fifty-year-old murder mystery?"

"I don't know yet. But I need to know for certain if I've truly inherited this ability from Rainy Skies. And the push to do something is nearly overwhelming me."

"Once again, I'll say that because of the fire in your eyes and the determined set of your chin, I have no doubt that you will succeed at anything you attempt. I also understand your father's observation of foolish obsession."

Dannah waved her hand as if brushing something aside. "I'm also going to have to do some deep thinking about my relationship with my father." She took a deep breath and leaned against the back of the wooden kitchen chair. "Yeah, I know all of this must sound strange and absurd to you. It sounds that way to me as well."

Jason shrugged. "Not necessarily. Parapsychology is a respected discipline taught in many universities. As I mentioned before, I can arrange for you to see Professor Albert Krause—he's my golfing buddy. He can tell you all you want to know about psychics and psychic abilities. He's the professor of Abnormal Psychology, but I know for a fact that he dabbles in the paranormal. We play eighteen holes at the country club almost every Saturday and he's told me some strange stories. Maybe now you'd like to meet him and talk to him."

"'Maybe' is the understatement of the year. Yes, now I'm ready. Oh, Jason, thank you. I would appreciate that opportunity. But, there's more. I haven't told you everything that's been going on in that house."

"Like what?"

Dannah locked gazes with Jason for several seconds, weighing her options. There was only so far a person could push believability...even her own. She waved a dismissive hand. "Never mind. That's enough for now."

"You can't stop now. You have to tell me everything."

Dannah hesitantly recounted her experiences with the clock, the footprints in the dust, the piece of jewelry and the rocking chair. "It all seems to tie in with my weird conversation with Annie Fields."

"Good ole Miss Annie. Has she related all her stories about how the house is haunted by restless souls?"

"She said there are two ghosts in the Wingate House, but I'm trying to convince myself it can't be possible."

"I think you're trying to create something threatening where nothing exists."

"Even the realtor said the house seemed sinister and foreboding."

"Don't pay any attention to what other people say. It's probably nothing more than your galloping imagination. Look what you've been through in the last month. I harbor no doubts about your level of intelligence. Moving into one of these ancient mausoleums masquerading as a house would be enough to scatter anyone's senses."

"You think I'm making this up? Is that what you're implying?" she asked.

"No, not about your psychic abilities, but there's got to be a plausible explanation for all the other stuff going on. Maybe it's nothing more than the fluctuations of your hormones." Jason patted her hand with a friendly gesture, but Dannah jerked away.

"Why do all men want to attribute everything to hormones? You should have to ride this monthly roller-coaster to hell. Please, don't get patronizing with me. Can't you understand? The educated and rational side of my brain doesn't want to believe in such foolishness as ghosts and psychic visions."

"Well, maybe it's only a temporary condition and eventually they'll go away."

"This isn't fatigue or hormones. Apparently, I've inherited a little bit more than a house. Yes, some of my visions are like dreams, but sometimes I'm wide-awake. Of course, I appreciate logic, but there may be occurrences which defy our current knowledge. Anything is possible. Who knows, maybe there are lost souls trying to reach out to the living."

"The ghosts were invented companions for a lonely old lady."

"No, there's more to it." Dannah set her cup on the table and once again prompted Jason to look into her eyes. "Annie Fields said that one of Gova's ghosts was her mother."

"One of the ghosts?"

"The second one has a bad attitude. According to the story, the day when Gova had the stroke. She was alone in her den and yet someone used the phone in the kitchen to call 911."

Jason battled laughter. "Her mother called 911?"

"You have no right to be judgmental. I know this sounds totally unbelievable to you, but I felt something the moment I walked into that house."

"Good or bad?"

"Neither. More like a need to do something unfinished." Dannah's expression grew serious. "Jason, on the night your house was broken into?"

"Yeah?"

"When I sat in the chair behind your desk?" Even though skepticism was painted all over his face, she was determined to plow on. "I had another vision. Bill Baxter sat in that chair, and I can tell you something else about him."

All the humor disappeared from Jason's eyes. "What?"

"Hopelessness, loneliness—lordy, so much loneliness—and with some rage mixed in. The most prominent thought that popped into my head when I sat in the chair was...was revenge and...and murder."

Jason was aghast. "Revenge against me? He wants to murder me over a few bones and chards of pottery?"

"I can only tell you what I read in his thoughts." Dannah looked down into her coffee cup, then lifted her head to stare into Jason's wide, unblinking gaze. "The nightmares I was having last night when you came into my room were about two men being murdered."

"Murdered? Who?"

"Unfortunately, I don't know who, it was too dark. And I'm fairly certain that there are two separate individuals."

"Do you know when?"

She nodded. "Probably last night when the dream occurred. I think it was about three o'clock when I woke up screaming."

"I didn't look at the time. Do you have any clues as to where this incident took place?"

"In a kitchen—either yours or mine. One body is leaning against a kitchen counter, the other on the back porch—half in and half out of the back door. It was sort of fuzzy. I could see the victims, but not the murderer, because I was in his head at the time."

"Do you recognize any faces?"

"No, it was too dark and there was too much blood. I read in a book somewhere that I might be able to see his face if he looked in a mirror."

"Do you think that would work for you?"

"To be honest, I don't know."

"What exactly did you see?"

"I can't remember every little detail. A gunshot to the chest, another to the head. A lot of blood. Look, I'm new at this psychic thing. I haven't learned how to handle it." She raised her hands in a helpless gesture. "If I could just grab hold of the image for a few more seconds and study it...but, I can't. It comes and goes too fast."

"So, you honestly believe that what you dreamed has truly taken place?"

"Yes, I do."

"Let's call Detective Richards and tell him."

"No. Definitely not. I'm afraid he'll just laugh at me. Besides, I don't have enough confidence in my abilities just yet."

"I think not calling the police is a big mistake."

Dannah's chin trembled. "I'm afraid of ridicule if I'm wrong and I'm equally afraid of being correct."

Jason sighed heavily, then tipped up his cup and finished the coffee. "Tell you what...let's move away from this subject right now. Temporarily. Okay? We'll learn if this is fact or fiction when we get home this evening."

"You're right. Talking, guessing, arguing and wondering will get us nowhere."

"We also have some important relationship concerns to discuss later. Come on, let's start to work, get you packed and moved to Oxford."

They spent the rest of the morning stuffing Jason's vehicle with as many of Dannah's clothes and possessions as possible, but the cloud of skepticism between them remained alive and viable.

Chapter Seventeen
Late Sunday night
Oxford, Mississippi

Because they had to wait until late afternoon for the movers to finish packing and loading Dannah's furniture, it was nearly midnight when Jason guided his Ford Explorer into the double driveway between the Wingate and Dunhill houses. Dannah had fallen into a light sleep and Jason placed a gentle kiss on her lips to awaken her. "We're home," he whispered.

Dannah stretched and yawned. "I like the sound of that word. Home." Gunner stood up in the back seat and stretched as well.

Jason gently touched her chin and pulled her around to face him. Her features were partially hidden in the mottled shadows coming through the windshield. The pale moon cast a weak sprinkling of light on her small dainty hands folded in her lap. "Before you say a word or move a muscle, I want you to know that last night was very special for me. Definitely not a one-night-stand. You were wonderful, exciting, more woman than I ever imagined could be contained in such a small package. We were as visually and physically intimate as a man and woman can possibly be. But intimacy is verbal as well as physical and you never uttered a single word—well, maybe a couple of sighs. I appreciate you being honest with me this morning. And yes, I want honesty from you, but Dannah, I want more than candor. I want to know everything you're feeling and what you're thinking. Maybe I'm being selfish, but I want it all from you—with nothing held back. I want to get to the woman beneath all that bravado."

Dannah's heart was pumping so hard, the rushing blood made her ears ring. His honest statement shoved her threatening tears onto her cheeks. She hated herself for such a stereotypical display of feminine weakness. "I know...sometimes I have trouble expressing myself, putting my feelings into words. I grew up in a very sterile household—just me and my Dad—and he was short on dialogue or any display of affection. I tried to show you, to let my actions speak when words failed."

"For such a mouthy broad, it's hard to believe you can ever be at a loss for words. Look at me," he gently ordered. "Say the words and I won't ever try to touch you again. I won't like it, and I'll argue like hell, but I will honor your wishes. Dannah, answer me."

In the dim moonlight, their gazes joined. She felt his hand touch her hair and it created a shivery tingle. She responded by stroking the strong line of his jaw. "I can't say that. You made me feel like a thirty-year-old virgin, like I was making love for the very first time. I was so knocked over by new feelings and new thoughts, like I'd never been so close to perfection. Like I could touch the stars and tackle the world. As though nothing as mundane as words were needed. Like saying, 'Oh baby, you're the greatest,' would have cheapened the experience." Her voice dipped into a husky whisper. "You fill all the places where I'm empty. I felt totally joined with you. There was a oneness I never dreamed could be possible between two separate beings. Especially, since...well, since we've only known each other less than a week."

Jason was stunned speechless by her response. He gathered her in his arms and kissed her soundly. "I want us to be a permanent thing."

"And I want to be certain these feelings are real and not just salve for my loneliness. I want to know this is not just a rush of over-heated hormones, or the alarm ringing on my biological clock. I've fought all my own battles for so long. I've earned my own living, made my own friends, made some mistakes and a few enemies along the way. I want to believe we can have a future together, but I need my own identity, my independence."

"Dammit, Dannah. I don't want to own you. I'm not asking you to take up golf, deer hunting or anthropology. I want you as a lifetime partner, as equals, sharing our dreams and passions for living. I want the freedom for both of us to pursue our careers and still come home at night to each other. Home, family, the whole nine yards."

"I guess we'll both have a heap of adjusting to do. I don't know, maybe we can teach each other how to trust again, how to build a life and a relationship that respects both of our careers."

Jason got out of the car and walked around to open the doors for Dannah and Gunner. He pulled her into his arms, leaned down and nuzzled her ear. "Let's have a repeat of last night."

His whispered words set the surface of her skin aflame and launched a railroad of chills racing along the pathway of every nerve. They kissed again, his mouth open slightly, and it left her wet, rattled and breathless. Without even realizing it, she tipped her hips forward, her wanting of him was so fierce and compelling. She locked her arms around his neck, stood on her tiptoes and whispered in his ear. "Yes, I'd love to have an instant replay."

"Do you want to check out my house first to see if anyone was murdered while we were gone?"

She shoved both fists against his chest. "You are impossible! You're making fun of me again."

"No, I'm not. I'm serious."

As she took a step toward the Wingate House, she stopped. "Jason, wait a minute. I left the front porch light on when we left yesterday."

"Maybe the bulb is burned out."

"No, I screwed in a new one. I also left the front hall lights on."

"I've got a big flashlight in the back. Let me get it."

As they unlocked and opened the front door, the cloying, metallic odor of blood, body fluids and death greeted them. The stench was heavy in the hot interior as they stepped into the entry hall. Gunner began making whimpering sounds, sensing something was terribly wrong.

Dannah flicked the switch and the six new bulbs in the hall chandelier lit up. She extended one arm to force Jason and the dog behind her and stood statue still, allowing her keen senses to come into play. Even though her ownership of the house was brief, the location of each item of furniture, each lamp and each area rug had been firmly imprinted on her mind.

Her gaze slowly swept the area...the turret to the left, the curved stairwell, the hall table and lamp. The living room was to the right...the sofa, the two side chairs, the coffee table, the stately grandfather clock, the curio cabinet.

Wait. Something was missing. The rocking chair. The wooden rocker she had seen in the far corner on Friday night was gone.

Fear was a silent invader. Dannah reached back a second time and grasped Jason's hand. "Hold on to me," she whispered.

Jason held tightly to both Dannah's hand and Gunner's collar as the trio hesitantly walked through the dining room. The soft buzz of flies floated in from the kitchen.

Jason stopped and looked at Dannah with disbelief "Sonofabitch! Your dream was correct. I think there is something or someone dead in there," he whispered. "Maybe we shouldn't look. Maybe we should call Detective Richards first."

"Not yet, I want to see if my vision was correct."

"You're a glutton for punishment. Okay, let's go inside...carefully."

"I keep that swinging door propped open with a rock. Now it's closed."

All Gunner's obedience training was temporarily forgotten as he started barking furiously, struggling to wrench free and blatantly ignoring Jason's repeated commands. It took both hands to hold him back. "Something bad is behind that door. Just be careful what you touch."

Dannah pushed against the swinging door with her butt and patted the wall until she found the switch. The overhead lights flooded the kitchen. She blinked against the brilliant glare of fluorescent bulbs until her eyes adjusted. The back storm door was hanging open, the flimsy screen door was ripped from its hinges and was lying outside on the porch. She could see a pair of lifeless legs lying over the doorsill. The body of a young man lay on the linoleum floor in a huge pool of blood. His head was propped against the oak cabinet beneath the kitchen sink, a flashlight lay a few inches from his left hand, the fingers of his right hand were still clutching the handle of a small handgun. His body was just beginning to bloat. Flies buzzed around his eyes, nose and mouth.

Jason turned away, but Dannah couldn't drag her eyes from the macabre sight. His face was mottled with bluish red blotches of color, his lips were purple, his clouded eyes were open, staring into nothing. There was a noticeable hole in the victim's chest. The sickening details would be forever etched in her brain. The victim had been standing up when shot. Blood splatter and bits of flesh from the exit wound were all over the counter top, sink and wall.

"Do you know him?" she asked.

"Yeah, it's Larry Henning," Jason muttered. "Jesus, I've never seen so much blood."

"The bullet probably severed his aorta and he bled out. There's another victim on the back porch." Dannah carefully tiptoed around the debris of broken glass to look. "It's Baxter—I recognize his white, bushy hair. He's also dead—shot in the head." Her voice sounded strange even to her own ears, as though it belonged to another person.

"What were they doing in your house?" As she moved to approach Henning, Jason reached out and grasped her arm. "Wait," he said while still trying to subdue his agitated dog.

"I've got to touch both of them."

"No, no, stay away. You might screw up some trace evidence. There's a shoe imprint."

In the viscous and slimy liquid that had congealed on the linoleum floor, there was one very distinct marking left by the sole of the killer's sneaker. Two other imprints leading to the back door were smudged.

She turned to look into Jason's eyes, which were filled with both fear and concern. The compassion in his voice and his calm demeanor allowed her to relax, unwind and concentrate. "This is something I have to do. Go ahead and call Detective Richards."

Reluctantly, Jason pulled his cell phone from his pocket and walked back into the dining room, leaving her alone with the bloated bodies of Lawrence Henning and William Baxter.

She searched deeply trying to grasp a tiny bit of calm, then approached Henning from the left side. Dannah was careful to avoid stepping in the blood. She reached out and, from a safe distance, placed her hand on the young man's shoulder. Even through the fabric of his shirt, she was mindful that his flesh was cold and firm. Steely self-control settled over her as the images flowed into her mind. Once again, she was hit hard by the same vision that had visited her the previous night. But this time, she experienced the fear, shock and surprise the victim felt. Awareness came in explicit flashes as she battled to recapture the images of—

—mission accomplished at the Dunhill place. Looking for something to steal. Go next door. No lights, no cars. They're in Memphis. Silver—lots of it in the dining room. Kitchen. Look for plastic bag to carry it. Sound. Surprise. The flashlight. The face. Who-the-hell? The first shot he fired missed the mark, then the gun jammed. The next gunshot was both felt and heard simultaneously. His hands and body went limp. Please call for help, he had asked his uncaring assailant, but there was no response—only an empty stare from his attacker. Death approached with full awareness of its coming—

Shaken, Dannah stepped back, however, the victim's burning pain lingered inside her own chest, distant, but nonetheless real.

"The police are on their way," Jason said after he finished making the phone call.

"I don't think Larry Henning knew the identity of his attacker," she whispered.

"Are you certain?"

She nodded. "He fired the first shot, then his gun jammed."

"Those little 25mm automatics are not reliable. Were you inside Henning's mind...even though he's dead?"

She nodded again. "Yes, and the visions were crystal clear."

"What else did you see?"

"The attacker. He was illuminated in Henning's flashlight. The man had black hair, with a touch of salt-and-pepper at the temples. Tall, mostly slender except for a small round tummy. Like a 'beer-belly.' Dark complexion—maybe something ethnic, like Mexican, Greek or Italian. He was wearing jeans, a short-sleeve, plaid shirt and brown leather work boots—high tops, just above his ankles."

"I don't know who that might be."

"Let me touch Baxter."

Jason shook his head. "No, let's get out of the kitchen."
He still held the dog's collar in one hand and put the other around
Dannah's shoulders and led her into the living room. "Gunner is
freaking out. I've got to run next door and put him in his crate. I'll
only be a minute. Will you be all right here? Alone?"

"Yes, I'll be okay, honest." As soon as Jason disappeared
out the front door, Dannah walked back into the kitchen and
carefully bent over Baxter. He had been shot at close range. The
bullet had entered just above his right eye and exited at the back of
his head. The blood splatter indicated that Baxter had also been
standing when shot. Dannah's hand was trembling slightly as she
gingerly touched the dead man's shoulder. The rush of images
slammed into her—

*—single gunshot from a distance. Then another. Hurry to
see what's wrong. Damn fool kid went next door to find more loot.
Grass was slippery and damp with dew. Back door. Young Larry
was dead. No doubt. Fear running wild. Stranger. Gunshot.
Welcome to the darkness. No more pain and loneliness. Peace at
last—*

Dannah walked into the living room, completely shaken
by her experiences. She chose one of the Queen Anne side chairs
and sat on the edge of the seat with her hands folded primly in her
lap, her head bent in silent prayer as she challenged her Maker to
take away this unwanted power. Either that or grant her the ability
to handle it with greater finesse. Although Dannah had been raised
a Catholic, right now she wanted to keep her mind in neutral and
not think about religion or the pain and mental anguish of the two
victims. Her nervous glance circled around the room. The
grandfather clock was silent, the hands still pointing to three-ten;
the piece of Indian jewelry was still inside the corner cabinet, its
glass door securely locked and the rocker was still missing. She
didn't take the time to ponder over errant furniture.

Several minutes later, Dannah was still sitting on the chair
trying to collect her thoughts when Jason came crashing back

through the front door, breaking the disquieting silence.

"Sonofabitch! Someone broke into my house again. This time they went upstairs and stole my negatives. Then the bastard took a baseball bat or crowbar and smashed my CPU and monitor into a pile of useless rubble. Nothing can be salvaged now. Nothing." He pounded his head with the palm of his hand. "Damn, what a dunce. Why didn't I lock everything away?"

Dannah tried to shake off her ties to the murder scene and return to the present. "Because the brilliant Detective Jerry Bob told you not to move anything. That's why." She frowned as she fought to concentrate. "But, Jason, how did Baxter know where the negatives were? How did he know we weren't home?"

"Well, my car was gone and yours was hidden in the garage, but that's still a very good question."

Dannah shook her head from side to side then slapped her hand across her mouth. "Oh damn, I just remembered one snatch of conversation I heard during the initial robbery."

"What?"

"Jason, somebody put a bug in your den. I'm sorry that I forgot to tell you. The high, whiney voice said, 'You gotta hide the wire.' We talked about the negatives being in your bedroom and about us spending the night in Memphis while we were doing the inventory of stolen property."

Jason rubbed at his temples. "I can't believe all this is happening. Why on earth were Henning and Baxter here in your house?"

Through the niggling onset of what would no doubt evolve into another violent headache, Dannah recalled her vision. "Henning was looking for something to steal. He knew we were in Memphis. That's what he was thinking about before he died. He probably found Aunt Gova's silver tea service in the dining room and went into the kitchen to find a plastic bag to put it in. That's when he crossed paths with the intruder already in the house. When Baxter heard the shots, he came to investigate and he was shot as well."

As sirens in the distance became louder, Jason rolled his eyes. "Yeah right, wake up the entire neighborhood."

***

It was nearly dawn and the police still hadn't finished. Once again, Detective Jerry Bob Richards sat down with them, this time in Dannah's living room. It was *déjà vu.*

"We have to wait on the coroner. He's in another part of the county," the detective explained. "He might not be able to give us an accurate time of death because of the heat, and we won't have the results of the autopsies until Monday morning, maybe later. Because the fly eggs have had time to develop into maggots, I think the victims have been dead for at least eighteen hours, possibly longer. However, we'll have to get the State Crime lab to supply an entomologist to look at the bugs."

"I turned off the air conditioning because I was going out of town," Dannah interrupted. "The wiring in this house is very old, and I'm afraid of fire."

Richards droned on as if he never heard her. "Method of entry was the same as the break-in at Dunhill's house last week. The screen door was torn from the hinges, then a pane of glass was removed from the storm door to give access to the lock. Of course, that's a fairly standard method for home invasions."

"I think they broke into my house before they came here," Jason added. "This time they stole my photo negatives and looks like they took a baseball bat to my computer."

Richards nodded. "Yeah, I saw a baseball bat lying on the back porch. We'll check it for prints. I'll send a crew over to your place to look for evidence."

"I can't figure this out," Dannah interrupted. "The Wingate House has been empty for a year, then all of a sudden there are two break-ins in one night."

"Easy to explain," the detective responded and pulled a newspaper article from his black leather organizer. "The bank manager gave a statement to the newspaper about Miss Gova Wingate leaving her 'sizable estate' to her niece who will be moving here from Memphis. It was in this morning's paper."

Dannah quickly scanned the article, then rolled her eyes. "Oh geez, what a stupid thing to do. Complete with a picture of the house and the address. Might as well advertise this place as ripe for rip-off."

The detective was interrupted by one of his female coworkers who whispered something in his ear. Richards looked at Dannah's small feet, then at Jason's larger ones. "Okay, Dunhill, we need to collect your shoes." The woman placed his sneakers in a paper sack, then left the room. "They dug a 9mm slug out of the wall. Must have gone straight through the guy. Do you own a weapon?" He directed his question to Jason.

"Well, yeah, I do have a 9mm pistol in my bedroom closet. But it hasn't been fired in months."

"It's next to the bed in the guest room. I got it out after the Tuesday night robbery."

"We'll test it. There was also a 25mm slug in the opposite wall. We'll test both of you for gun powder residue."

"So, where does that leave us?" Jason asked the detective.

The stern-faced man arched an eyebrow. "With a great many unanswered questions."

"The murder had to have happened late Saturday night while we were out of town," Jason explained. "We spent Friday night at the campus cocktail party where we saw Baxter. We were in Memphis all day Saturday and Sunday packing Dannah's belongings for the move here. They're in the back of my Explorer right now."

"I know. I saw the bicycle strapped to the roof of your car," the detective added. "Can you prove your alibi?"

Jason gasped with shock. "Alibi? Am I a suspect?"

"You did have a strong motive. You were pretty angry over the break-in and loss of your computer data. Maybe you caught him in the act with the baseball bat and shot him. I'll send a crew next door to search your house for any evidence of a crime scene. However, the blood splatter pretty much proves the murders were committed here. Another theory could be self-defense. The kid did have a gun in his right hand."

Dannah shook her head and ventured a comment. "No, no. I'm his alibi. He was with me the entire time. We drove to Memphis on Saturday morning, cleaned out my dad's old house and talked to a realtor about putting it up for sale, then the pizza delivery man came to my apartment around 11:30 Saturday night. The movers came this morning about nine to put my furniture in storage. We didn't get back here until nearly midnight. The murder happened around three in the morning—that's about twenty-four hours ago."

"How do you know that?"

"I, uh, well, I can figure these things out as well as the police."

The detective shook his head and rolled his eyes. "Look, I'll need the names and phone numbers of all individuals you claim to have seen. However, Dunhill, you still had time to drive from Memphis Saturday night, murder Henning and Baxter, then drive back before sunrise. It's not that far." Richards stood up and slipped his trusty little tape recorder and note pad in his pocket.

As Jason sputtered, searching for an answer, Dannah rose from the sofa and stepped into Richard's personal space. Even though her diminutive stature was far from threatening, her expression and voice were firm and filled with authority. "Jason and I slept together on Saturday night—all night. I'm his alibi."

The tall, lanky detective peered over Dannah's curly head and gave Jason a knowing glance and a sly wink. "Man, you work fast, Dunhill. You two just met on Tuesday afternoon and you screwed her on Saturday night?"

From the corner of her left eye, Dannah was only barely aware of Jason erupting from the sofa. She saw his knotted fists as he covered the short distance in two giant steps. He punched the detective square in the jaw before she could gather her senses and react. Richards staggered backwards several steps and fell hard into one of the antique Queen Anne chairs. The legs of the old chair gave way and the man ended up sprawled on the floor amid of heap of torn upholstery and jagged wood.

"Dunhill, that little deed could get you into a heap of trouble," he said, rubbing his sore jaw. "Assaulting a police officer is serious business."

"So is your filthy mouth," Jason muttered between clenched teeth.

Suddenly, the tinny sounds of the old grandfather clock reverberated in the temporary silence as it bonged six times.

Richards scrambled up, straightened his clothes and glanced as his wristwatch. "It's only three o'clock. You need to get that clunker fixed." He rubbed his elbows which took the brunt of his fall.

"Oh, if you only knew," Dannah muttered softly.

"Don't leave town again—either of you. That's not a threat. That's an order."

Just as Richards was leaving, the coroner arrived. He set about his gruesome task of taking photos, examining the body, recording the ambient temperature and the temperature of the victim's liver. Dannah surreptitiously watched with an occasional peek around the door frame from the dining room. When Henning was rolled over, she saw the Kodak envelope sticking out of his back pocket. The coroner took some pictures, then wrapped the corpse in a body bag and left without saying a word to Dannah or Jason.

"I think your negatives are in Henning's pocket. Were they in a Kodak envelope?"

Jason nodded. "They'll probably give them back to me eventually. Now it'll be after the first of the year before I can get my article published," Jason said as they followed the officials out the front door. "Looks like we'll have to spend the night at my place."

"The police have sealed your house as well."

"I'll go inside to get Gunner and another pair of shoes."

"Now I feel like I have no home at all. Home is a place that's comforting and familiar. Wingate hasn't earned that title as yet."

"Let's go get a cup of coffee and some breakfast." When she nodded, Jason put his arm around her shoulders and guided her back to his vehicle. "You shouldn't have told him we slept together."

"Maybe, but you shouldn't have hit him."

"Couldn't help myself. I guess I had a rush of testosterone to protect 'my woman.' I'm truly glad that Gunner was at home in his crate. He would have taken a sizable chunk out of the man." Jason helped Dannah into the front seat, then went into his house to get Gunner and another pair of shoes. When he slipped into the driver's seat he said, "I'll have to call the University President and postpone my announcement indefinitely. Can't very well gloat over a discovery when there's the cloud of a murder hanging over my head."

"You'll be cleared," she stated emphatically. "Besides, they're going to find my fingerprints on your pistol. Remember? You told me to get it out of your closet in case the burglars returned. I took the gun out of the bag and handled it. Believe me, once they have the autopsy reports and talk to our witnesses, they'll know that Henning and Baxter were murdered on Saturday night when we were in Memphis."

Jason stared into the darkness and slowly nodded his head. "Yes, I did have time. I could have driven to Oxford, committed the murders between midnight and three in the morning."

"Jason, we made nonstop love. Well, I did fall asleep once."

"Yes, and once during the night I got up. Gunner was acting restless, so I put on my jeans and took him out for a short walk."

"Three hours isn't enough time."

"How can you be so sure I didn't commit the murders?"

She lowered her head and looked at him through her long lashes. "Just because. I told you what I visualized last night. I had the dream about three in the morning. That's when the murders happened and that's when you were in my bedroom. Also when I touched Henning and Baxter, I'm convinced I saw the face of the murderer. I just have to figure out who he is."

"Hopefully, the investigation will exonerate me."

"It will."

"Can you read the future?"

"No, I can't. When the realization dawned on me that I might truly be psychic, I looked up the word in the dictionary. It's a sensitivity to supernatural forces outside of physical science and has nothing to do with foretelling the future."

"I don't care about any of that. I only care about us." Jason pulled her into his arms and kissed her. The inside of the vehicle was silent except for the rustle of fabric and the intake of air. Gunner stood up in the back seat and poked his long muzzle between them, whimpering softly. "I do believe he's jealous." Silence settled between them as he looked at her quietly for several minutes, not really wanting to break the magic spell. The old saying that it is darkest before dawn was proving to be true. Only the pale green dash lights illuminated their faces. "Dannah? Do you believe in love at first sight?"

"Well, maybe not first sight, but...but... maybe second or third."

"I think I'm falling in love with you," he whispered.

"Oh, Jason."

"It was that morning after the first break-in, when I got back from Athens. You looked so damned cute in the kitchen, so comfortable with the domestic scene—like one of those TV sitcoms with a husband, wife and a couple of kids. You're so talented in a dozen different ways. Most women of our generation don't even know what a skillet is, much less how to cook an egg in it. Today's career women are so damned selfish about their own goals—stock broker, accountant, teacher, office manager, whatever—they have tunnel vision. They don't know how to exist in a real world with real-world emergencies." He fell silent for several tense moments. "You must have magic powers—you've turned me from a man into a marshmallow."

"From my point of view, you're very much a man. A kind, good man."

"I love you because you're you, not because you can cook an egg. Damn, I'm all tied up in knots and nothing's coming out right. Oh, forget it."

"I don't want to forget it. I've waited all my life for this sense of belonging to someone special—like you. I'm sort of in a mental muddle right now. Until I get all this craziness sorted out, I can't commit to anything...even though I want to very much."

"I'm not the kind of guy who says, 'I love you' at night, then 'goodbye' in the morning."

Jason stared straight ahead, but Dannah could see the muscles tensing in his jaw. She put her hand on his arm. "It's very sobering to learn that you could love me...especially knowing what you now know with this psychic stuff, this house and everything that's happened. I'm truly screwed up, and I've screwed up your life as well. None of this would have happened if I hadn't barged into your life."

"That's not true. This started because of my discovery at Chucalissa and Baxter's jealousy. You had nothing to do with that. You've been a wonderful coincidence."

"It's the Wingate House. It's holding a secret."

"To hell with the house." Jason twisted in the seat and gathered Dannah into his arms and pulled her tightly against his chest. One hand dug into her curls and tipped her face up. "You're not sleeping alone...not tonight or any other night." He kissed her, pouring his heart into the act.

Dannah pulled away a few inches, wanting to catch her breath. "You know something? I'm not the least hungry...for breakfast."

"How about a motel with room service?"

"One that allows dogs," Dannah stated emphatically. "We're a threesome now."

"A permanent threesome," Jason added.

Chapter Eighteen
Monday afternoon
University Campus

"Glad to meet you, Miss Wingate." Professor Albert Krause rose from his chair and extended his hand in greeting. "Jason tells me you're a writer from Memphis."

"Yes, freelance. I appreciate your taking the time to see me," she responded with a smile, noting he was neither old nor young, but lost somewhere in his forties. Although he was tall and mostly slender, the faint beginnings of a tummy were straining the bottom two buttons of his white oxford-cloth shirt. His collar was unbuttoned and the knot in his tie was pulled loose and askew, creating a rumpled look. The professor's office was a shamble of overstuffed files, books, and scattered scraps of newspaper clippings, while stacks of video cassette tapes were piled on every available table and shelf. She couldn't resist the temptation to stare at the clutter with discernible distaste.

"You're a Capricorn."

"Well, yes," Dannah stuttered. "How did you know?"

"Just a lucky guess. Most Capricorns are offended by clutter. Jason also told me that you've just inherited Wingate House."

"Yes, and I've had some unsettling experiences there."

"Some local people claim Oxford's antebellum homes are a virtual hotbed of ghosts," he explained. "The truth is, they're everywhere. Even pictography of ancient civilizations described ghosts. There's something in the human psyche that makes us all cling tenaciously to the idea there's life after death. Ancient Egyptians, for example, took their beliefs in an afterlife to extremes, going so far as to sacrifice servants so the deceased royalty would have someone familiar to care for them."

Professor Krause was a squirrelly sort of guy with quick jerky movements, Dannah observed. He wore thick, dark-rimmed glasses which he constantly pushed up his bony nose with the middle finger of his right hand. Except for his deep tan, he didn't look athletic and she was having difficulty with the image of him as a whiz at golf.

"I'm embarrassed to be discussing the subject of parapsychology on a serious level. I'm not an escapee from the local cracker factory."

"I understand your trepidation."

"Professor Krause, what started you in this line of work?"

He reared back in his chair and propped his feet on his desk. "Are you sure you want to hear the story?"

"Yes, it might help me get over my fear of telling my own tale of woe."

"My great-grandmother possessed psychic abilities. The story handed down in my Jewish family is that she had a vision a few days before the Germans started gathering up the Jews for extermination camps. She loaded the family into an old 1934 Polski-Fiat and drove to France where she and her children escaped to the United States. When I learned the family history, I became engrossed in the psychic phenomenon. I teach criminal psychology—the paranormal is sort of my side interest."

"You're not psychic?"

"No, wish I was."

Determined not to cave in, Dannah breathed a sigh a relief. "Professor. I, uh, I think I have some level of psychic abilities."

"Jason didn't tell me that."

"I told him everything, but I guess he's not comfortable with it...yet. The dreams and visions are bothersome, and truthfully, I've been driven to exhaustion from lack of sleep. These experiences, whatever you want to call them, began on July tenth, which was the very night my Aunt Gova Wingate died at the nursing home here in town. Then later, in mid-August of this year, on the night my father died, I dreamed his heart attack was happening to me." She hesitated, wanting the inflections in her voice to recreate the fear as she felt it. "It was awful. I was in horrendous pain. I remember dropping a skillet full of scrambled eggs, calling 911, the ambulance ride. Then after I woke up, I got a phone call from the hospital about my father being admitted because of a heart attack." Even retelling the dream caused little beads of sweat to develop across her forehead and in the deep cleavage between her breasts. She paused to gather her composure. "When I got to the hospital, my dad was insistent that I go see Aunt Gova—who lived here in Oxford. She was his sister; however, they were estranged. He said she would explain things to me. He also said, 'I was hoping you wouldn't get burdened with them, but you're next in line'."

The professor leaned forward, his fingers steepled at chest level. "This is fascinating. Most individuals with psychic abilities are born with the knowledge, and learn to develop it as they mature. I've never heard of the talent being passed from one generation to the other—especially later in life. How old are you?"

"Thirty."

"What is the line of descent?"

"My grandmother, to her daughter—who is my aunt who never married—then to me. When I got to town, I found out that my aunt had passed away on July tenth—the day my dreams began—and that I had inherited her house. Apparently, I'm her only blood kin. Well, when I walked through the house, I got this unsettled feeling when I stood in front of the kitchen sink."

"Involving violence?"

"Yes, the flash of light on the silver blade of a long knife, blood. However, the vision seems faded somehow, indistinct. As though it may have happened in the distant past."

"What do you feel when you walk through other rooms in the house?" he asked.

"Good feelings. As if I've come home."

"Are these night dreams or day dreams?"

"I get both. My father's death, as well as Gova's, came to me at night. Sometimes, especially when I shake hands with someone, I get flashes. I even get visions concerning serious illness."

"Are you psychic with everyone you meet?"

"No, only if the illness is severe or their rage is intense. I guess you've read the news report about the murders that took place on Saturday night inside my house."

"Yes indeed. I heard about it on the evening news. What a

tragedy. I saw Baxter, you and Jason as well at the welcoming party on Friday night. That house certainly has a violent history. Did you notice the picture in the newspaper?" The professor shuffled through the clutter on his desk, found the article and handed it to Dannah. "Look at the third floor window. It's boarded from within."

She studied the image for several seconds. "Oh, my goodness. Definitely looks like a face to me."

"That's what I thought. Does it look familiar?"

Dannah shook her head, then told him about her conversation with Annie Fields that there may be two ghosts inside the house. "One is a man with a bad attitude, the other is Aunt Gova's mother—Rainy Skies."

"Typical story of good against evil."

She backtracked to explain how she met Jason, his archeological discovery, the break-in, the destruction of his computer and scientific article.

"The article in this morning's newspaper seemed to indicate that Jason might be a murder suspect. They claim he had a strong motive."

"I'm certain he'll be cleared. Jason and I went to Memphis on Saturday and Sunday to empty my apartment. While there, I had a vivid dream as the murders were taking place. Jason was sleeping with me at the time, so he couldn't have committed the murders."

Krause maintained a noncommittal appearance and settled back in his chair. "It appears that the majority of your psychic experiences or phenomena concern things or people associated with Oxford or in your house."

Dannah's jaw gaped open. "Ohmygod, you're right. You're absolutely correct. I never noticed the connection. Then there are the footprints in the dust, a tinkling bell, the chiming of a broken clock and a rocking chair." She explained them in greater detail.

"These phenomena can fall into several different categories. Some call it touch telepathy. Some visions and dreams relive a forgotten incident from the past, while others often foretell the future. As Shakespeare said, 'Tonight's dream is tomorrow's reality.' Someone or something is trying desperately to get your attention."

"Yes, I do have a sensation of a job that needs to be done."

"I need to warn you, Miss Wingate, that getting too deeply immersed in a psychic episode can be very dangerous for you."

"For me? How?"

"You need an anchor, a lifeline, someone who can pull you out if you get in too deeply."

"Pull me out?" she parroted. "You mean there's a possibility that I can't emerge on my own?"

"Correct. You need someone with a strong personality— like Jason. He's very dynamic. One of the most popular teachers on the University staff. Tell me some more of your background."

"You see, genealogy has been a passion for me, but my father steadfastly refused to give me the names of his parents. Only when I inherited the house, did I learn that my grandmother was Native American."

"Maybe your grandmother was a tribal shaman."

"I don't know if she was one herself, but a newspaper article stated that she was descended from a line of Chickasaw tribal shaman."

"That would explain a great many things. My gut reaction is that when your aunt died, the ability passed on to you—the only female, blood-related descendant. Please understand, there's no scientific evidence to back up this theory. Miss Wingate, have you seen any apparitions in the house?"

"See? You mean I might actually see a...creature, or a thing?" A fluttering sense of alarm floated upward from her stomach.

The professor laughed. "It's entirely possible, and sometimes accompanied by a strange odor."

"Occasionally, I feel like I'm being watched."

"Do you feel threatened?"

"No, I don't...well...a little bit. There are other emotions lurking beneath my occasional bouts of fear. The realtor made an interesting comment. She said, 'It isn't the friendliest house I've ever been in.'"

"My studies seems to indicate that ghosts generally haunt the place where they died. The study of paranormal activity is an imprecise subject. However, my research seems to indicate that these apparitions aren't random, but occasioned by a definite purpose, something compelling, possibly some unfinished business. Other scientific data indicate that some ghosts were victims of violence, murder perhaps, and want to come back to identify their killers. Others are trapped in this 'undead state' because they failed to complete their life's work. It may sound humorous to you, but some spirits don't know they're dead. They're caught in the cracks, so to speak, and instead of walking toward the light on the other side, they try to return to the living world. Some ghosts are driven by love that refuses to die—a love so powerful they can't bear the separation."

"The problem is that I don't know who the cast of characters are in this family melodrama. Tell me, professor, are there good and bad among ghosts?"

"Yes, indeed. I've read there's a spirit on the Carolina coast who warns the living of an approaching hurricane. It's said there's one old house located on the beach which has survived many vicious storms without so much as a shingle out of place. As you can see, ghosts and poltergeists don't abide by our worldly rules."

"P-Poltergeist?" Visions of Hollywood horror films careened through her mind.

"Don't be afraid of the label. Poltergeist is based on a German word meaning noisy ghost."

"Aren't they dangerous?"

"Yes, some can be so intent on revenge against the living they go to violent extremes—but not like they are depicted in the movies. I wish I could give you some good hard answers, but I can't."

"Amazing. Before my own experiences, I was first in line to laugh off ghost stories, but after these last few days, I'm about to change my mind. There's also the problem of the broken clock. Every so often, it chimes six times, even though it's an impossibility."

"Maybe a ghost is making the clock chime to get your attention."

Dannah drew in a deep breath. "He or she has certainly accomplished that. Thank you, professor, it felt good to unload to a sympathetic ear."

"You're very welcome. When all this murder-business is done, I'd like to do a walk-through," Krause added.

"And I'll be delighted to have you. In spite of its history, Wingate is a wonderful old house. I don't know how to explain it, but it has this crazy magnetic attraction for me. It's a strangely comforting feeling that 'I'm-where-I-need-to-be.'"

"Tell me, have you studied the entire history associated with this house?"

"I only learned that I inherited the house last Wednesday." Dannah fumbled in her purse. "Please, I'd like you to read this 1959 newspaper article."

The professor nodded as he read, then stared at Dannah with a smile. "I'm very familiar with this case. It's a 'cold-case-file' that's going to be the subject of a class this semester in the Criminal Justice Department. They've been dying to get their hands on this one, but out of courtesy to your elderly aunt, they decided to wait until she passed away. All the evidence is going to be re-examined, chewed up and spit out. DNA profiling will be done on all the saved blood samples. They're going to do the works. Believe it or not, I had planned on getting in touch with you to discuss this matter when I read that you had inherited the old house. It would be wonderful to have your permission for the students to study the actual crime scene after all these years."

Dannah fell silent for several long, drawn-out seconds as she thought about the two knives she had found. Should she tell him? And if she didn't, would she be guilty of withholding evidence?

"Miss Wingate?"

"Oh, sorry, my mind was wandering."

"I think my mind would be going astray as well under your circumstances."

"Professor," Dannah hesitated, then decided that truth was the best policy. "Professor, when cleaning out my dad's house on Saturday...I found two large knives hidden in a box—a butcher knife and a hunting-style knife. I think they might be murder weapons because there are blood stains on them."

Krause's entire demeanor became brighter and he rubbed his hands together like a happy kid. "This is wonderful news! Miss Wingate, you've got to become a part of this investigation and speak to the class."

"Yes, of course, I'd be thrilled to."

"Then we can tour your house. Hopefully, the investigation will reveal some new clues. This is going to be an exciting semester."

"Would you happen to have any photos of the 1959 crime scene?"

"As a matter-of-fact, I do. Just last week I collected all of the evidence from the police archives. They're extremely graphic. Think you can handle the blood and gore?"

Dannah nodded. "I've seen those kinds of photos when I worked at the newspaper."

The professor rose from his desk and dug into a large box. "Just bring them back to me by next Monday when classes start. You know, my dear, I keep thinking that maybe your ghost is the murderer who himself was murdered."

***

Dannah was physically and emotionally drained by the time she left the professor's office. "Ooh damn," she muttered as she sank into the soft leather seat of her 'Vette with Jason behind the wheel. "My brain is suffering from overload."

"Let's go home."

"Lordy, I really love the sound of that word. By the way, where is your office?"

"Right next to Bill Baxter's—second building down. I'll bet his secretary is upset. They've worked together for twenty years."

"Maybe you'll be promoted to department head."

"I hope not. I'm not ready to give up teaching to be a desk jockey." Jason patted the cell phone in his shirt pocket. "I got a call from Detective Richards. My house has been released. Your house is still sealed as a murder scene. According to Richards, it will be another day or two before we can get inside and clean up the mess."

Gunner raced through the house after he was released from his crate, obviously happy to have the opportunity to stretch his legs.

"Make yourself comfortable, Dannah, while I take Gunner outside, then I'll fix us a couple of sandwiches."

Sinking deep into the plush sofa, Dannah kicked off her shoes and curled around a pillow. Jason returned shortly and placed a tray loaded with sandwiches and glasses of milk on the coffee table. He collapsed beside her.

"Has it been a tough day for you?" he asked.

"Exhilarating but exhausting," Dannah said with her lazy-lidded eyes half-closed. "The professor was incredible and gave me a wealth of information. It'll take me days to digest it all. I can't thank you enough for arranging the interview. We must have spent three hours together. He also gave me a stack of books to read."

"There are numerous advantages to living in a college town. When I moved back to Oxford from grad school in Illinois, I thought I'd feel stifled in such a small city, but there's so much here to feed a hungry mind."

"The professor told me that the Criminal Justice department is going to re-open the Wingate murders as a cold-case file. All the old evidence has been saved. It's been in storage for fifty years. He's invited me to become a part of the class."

"Whoa, that's going to be interesting."

"Jason, I told the professor something I haven't yet told you."

"Uh-oh, more confessions?"

She nodded a little guiltily. "Something I don't think I'll reveal to Detective Richards—at least right now."

"A fifty-year-old murder might not fall under his

jurisdiction."

"You're wrong," she stated emphatically. "There's no statute of limitations on murder."

"So what is this new information?"

"Evidence. I found two knives hidden in a box in Daddy's closet. They both have blood stains."

"What about your psychic visions? Do they reveal anything about the weapons?"

Dannah shook her head. "They might if I really concentrated, but the images are very dim. I guess because it happened a long time ago. I don't know what to do. The professor said that if I get too deeply immersed in a vision, I might not be able to get out unless I have help, a strong life-line."

"This is your party, so I'll dance to your music."

Dannah flashed a broad smile and sank back into the comfort of the sofa. "I'm a little too tired to tackle anything like that right now."

"What's in that?" Jason pointed to the big brown envelope lying on the coffee table.

"Pictures. Take a look."

Jason withdrew the stack of photos and grimaced. "Oh geez, this is awful. Ruins my appetite."

"It's my grandparents' murder scene. Thought maybe if I handled and studied them I might get some sort of image. But not now, I'm way too tired." She took a bite of sandwich and washed it down with a big gulp of milk. "I can't believe I sat there in Albert Krause's office and had a serious discussion about ghosts—and with a straight face no less. Geez, I hope nobody at the newspaper ever hears about this. I'd never live it down."

"Speaking of the Memphis newspaper, your old boss, Mister Jordan, called on your cell phone while you were in with Krause."

"Pete? What did he want?"

"Apparently the story about the murders at the Wingate House was picked up by the wire service. He was worried."

"I sent him an email the other night and told him I had an appointment with the bankers."

"I brought him up to speed about your inheritance. Apparently you already told him about your psychic visions."

Dannah nodded. "After Daddy died, he's all I had left. He's been like a father to me."

"You can call him back tomorrow."

"Thanks for talking to him. I didn't want the cell phone ringing right in the middle of my interview."

"How old a guy is he?"

"Old enough to be my father. Don't tell me you're jealous."

"No, no of course not." Jason bluffed innocence.

"The Professor thinks it's entirely possible that my grandmother, Rainy Skies, could have been the shaman of her tribe, and that possibly she passed her psychic ability to her daughter, Gova, and when Gova died without any children, then it passed to me as the only blood relative."

Jason picked up another sandwich. "I don't know about inheriting this Indian witch doctor thing. It sounds a little farfetched."

Anger flared, lifting her into a defensive posture. "You only know about bones—not souls. Why don't you believe in Krause's explanation? You told me he's an expert in his field."

"He is, but that doesn't mean I agree with some of his offbeat theories. I have my own beliefs concerning this subject."

"Are your beliefs more meaningful than his or mine? Do you have to be right all the time?" Again indignation flashed through Dannah's eyes, but it quickly dissolved, beaten down by weariness. "You promised not to laugh," she muttered as she sank deeper into the cushions with a defeated sigh and a whipped-little-puppy-dog look that evoked in Jason a strong urge to nurture.

"Hey, I'm sorry. I guess if this was happening to me, I'd be calling Los Angeles for the 'Ghostbusters'."

"You're doing it again—making fun of me." There was an endearing but impish look on Jason's face that made it difficult for her to sustain a high degree of annoyance.

"You've got to admit, this does have comedic undertones. Like an old John Belushi movie."

"The professor said something that wasn't one bit funny—'Maybe your ghost is the murderer who himself was murdered'."

"Now I'll accept that as 'almost' logical food for thought."

"But not very pleasant. If Rainy Skies and Jonathan Wingate were murdered, then their killer was murdered... Jason, my dad and Gova were the only ones in the house. Daddy was only fifteen or sixteen."

"Not a pretty picture. Maybe he killed the guy who killed his parents. Stranger things have happened."

Maybe your ghost is the murderer who himself was murdered. That gruesome thought planted by Professor Krause kept rattling around in her brain. "I don't even want to think about the possibility of my father being a murderer."

"It would be self-defense."

"Would it be considered self-defense if he was stabbed in the back?"

"I think so. After all, you told me that Rainy Skies had sixty stab wounds. Maybe your dad caught this guy in the act and the murderer was so busy with his raging anger that he didn't hear Coleman Wingate sneaking up behind him."

"Why didn't Daddy tell the police?"

"He was just a kid, he was afraid. Back in the forties and fifties, cops were painted as tough cookies in the movies. They always interrogated the suspect in a dark room with only one light bulb shining in his face. And the bad guys always got sent to the 'big house' to 'fry in the electric chair.'"

"You watch too many old movies."

"It's a 'guy-thing.'"

Dannah pressed her fingertips against her temples, trying to fight the awful probability that her father may have killed someone. "I feel another headache coming on. Lordy, I'm so exhausted." She reached up and tweaked his nose, trying to lighten the mood. "Although we've spent a great deal of time in bed, we haven't done much sleeping for the last three nights."

"And I'm ready for more."

"Sleep?"

"No, not sleep," he commented jokingly.

They both hunkered down deeper into the sofa cushions and Jason watched as she relaxed in his arms, the tense lines on her face smoothed into honey-beige satin. Dark, lush lashes brushed her cheeks, and her slightly parted lips looked luscious and pink. Rumpled curls teased her ears and caressed her neck with hair so black it swallowed the light, then threw it back in the deep rich color of a midnight sky. Perfectly rounded breasts rose and fell as her breathing slowed and she unwound. Her blouse was untucked. Jason visually stroked every contour from her nose to her toes. Dannah was a petite package containing the total essence of her gender—strong, yet sweetly vulnerable. Even disheveled, she looked so beautiful and so undeniably desirable. He could feel the tingling beginnings of arousal and fought the temptation, engaging in a fierce battle to restrain himself from acting on the potent impulse to make love to her—right here, right now. As if two days of incredible lovemaking had never happened, he was still hungry for the physical connection with her.

"Whatcha thinkin' about?" she whispered.

"Us. Our future."

"Me too," she responded. "I know we have a future together, Jason."

"I'm glad you've come over to my way of thinking. I used to think I was too busy to have a relationship, too wrapped up in my work, but you've made me realize that I've been living a hollow existence. Work, eat and sleep. You said it the other night—it's the dark silent hours that are so lonely."

Reflected colors from the muted television danced about the room, revealing the tumultuous emotions emanating from her wide, brown eyes. He held her face between his hands and kissed her—a hard, crushing embrace that took his breath away and sent his pulse soaring into warp speed.

The ringing phone jolted the lovers out of their reverie. Jason groaned as he unfolded his long legs, got up and walked into his den. He returned a few minutes later with a stricken look on his face and raw exhaustion weighing down his shoulders.

"What's wrong?" She stood up and rearranged her clothing.

"That was the University President. I've been relieved of my teaching duties until the matter of these murders is resolved."

"Oh Jason. You're innocent. We've got to do something." She rushed to him and he opened his arms to enfold her. "Whatever happens, we'll face it together," she muttered into the cotton fabric of his shirt.

"I don't know what they'll do with the students in the Anthropology Department. I have a full schedule of classes. Who'll fill in for me? You know something?" Jason released her and glanced at his wrist watch. "It's only four o'clock. He's still in his office. I need to talk to the University President face to face. I don't know what they've been saying about me on the TV and radio, but I want to set the record straight with him."

"That's a good idea." Dannah glanced at the cluttered coffee table where Jason had tossed his keys. "Why not drive my car?" she suggested as she dug into her purse. "Your car is still packed with all my worldly possessions."

"Want to go with me?"

"No, I'll stay home with Gunner."

"Don't do anything foolish while I'm gone."

"What do you mean?" she asked, her eyes wide with innocence.

"Just sit tight. We've got a great deal to discuss when I get back. I'm not usually wordless, but this entire situation has gone too far." The difference in their height was proving to be a liability as Jason bent into a graceless angle to kiss her. He was engaged in a private war to dampen his passions. He gave in to the distracting urgency of his need. He swooped her into his arms, carried her back into the living room and collapsed into the sucking comfort of the sofa cushions. "I think I can handle anything with you as my partner." Jason kissed her, pouring all of his emotion into their connection, then grasped her shoulders and held her away from him. "I'll be back in a couple of hours. Stay out of trouble."

A loud, firm knock on the door interrupted their actions and thoughts. Gunner started barking and headed for the source of the sound.

"Sonofabitch, who could that be? I hope it's not that

damned detective again." Jason strode across the living room to the entry hall and opened the front door.

"Jason, remember me? I'm Bennie Varossa, owner of Varossa Construction Company."

Once his eyes had adjusted to the gloom on the front porch, he recognized the man. "Oh yeah, yeah. Gunner, quiet!"

"I was looking for the new owner of the Wingate House." He pointed to Dannah's house. "I wanted to talk to her about remodeling."

"Come in, come in. She's here with me."

"I wanted to be first in line for the job," Bennie explained as he entered the house. "You know how much I love these old Victorians."

Jason glanced at Dannah as she came into the entry hall and wondered why she looked so strange. "This is Bennie Varossa. Varossa Construction. He did a super job on the renovations of my house."

Bennie extended his hand in greeting.

Dannah hesitated with her hand about six inches from Varossa's, but didn't know how she could graciously avoid the inevitable handshake. Her mind moved in slow motion as the stranger's large fingers wrapped around her much smaller hand. His flesh was cold, hard and rough with callouses. The vision sliced into her consciousness with surgical precision and played out before her opened, but glazed eyes—

—*his curiosity about the house. Searching for his grandfather's body. Surprise. Gut reaction to reach for his gun. Surprise again to see someone else. Squeeze the trigger another time. Fleeing into the darkness. Remorse? Not a single shred of remorse hiding in the nooks and crannies of his convoluted mind. The corridors were dark and frightening, lined with many closed doors—*

It was several long and awkward seconds before Dannah could snatch her hand from his grasp. And it took even longer to break eye contact, as she was mesmerized by his unwitting revelations. She finally lowered her gaze to the floor and spotted his brown leather work boots. He was a man hiding many secrets, but with an equal number of questions begging for answers. "I-I don't feel like talking about this today," she stammered, then fled the room.

Puzzled, Jason shrugged. "You know how women are. She's real upset over the fact that a couple of people were murdered in her house. We'll be in touch with you later."

After Varossa left, Jason followed Dannah into the kitchen. "What in the world is wrong with you?"

"It's him. I saw him fire his gun twice. He murdered both Larry Henning and William Baxter."

"That's absolutely ludicrous. No, no, no. That's impossible," Jason shook his head vehemently.

Dannah was adamant and her small hands were knotted into fists as she gestured. "Think about it. Why would a business man seek out a new client just two or three days after an unsolved double murder was committed in the house he wants to renovate? It makes no sense at all."

"Bennie Varossa is not a murderer. He's a respected man in the community and runs an established construction company. Dammit, Dannah, he hires about thirty men. He's a go-getter when it comes to business and wants to be first in line for the job. Your aunt Gova never let anyone inside the house—except me and Annie Fields. I distinctly remember seeing them conduct all their business on the front porch. He was probably wondering what she was hiding inside. And now, so do I."

"Jason, I saw his face when I touched Larry Henning. Varossa did it. I saw him fire the weapon. And what's so awful is... that... " She sucked in a gulp of air in an attempt to calm herself. "He knows that I know."

"When you shook hands?"

"Yes, I could read his thoughts. I know for certain that the murders were spur-of-the-moment and definitely not premeditated. He broke into my house to look it over out of pure curiosity. He must have stumbled across Larry trying to find something valuable to steal. He shot him. He didn't mean to, but Larry was high on drugs and brandishing a gun. Larry shot first, then Varossa fired. After hearing two shots fired, Baxter probably came to investigate the sound, then he was shot. Although it was not planned, he doesn't feel one smidgen of remorse over taking human lives."

"Could he read your thoughts?"

"He knows about the psychic powers that Gova had. He suspects that I might have inherited them."

"Well, if his shoe print matches, then he's the guilty party."

"I saw something else disturbing—a long dark corridor with many doors and I have a feeling that each one is hiding a secret. Mentally, he's a very sick man."

"How could you possibly know something like that?"

Dannah halted. She couldn't tell Jason the final bit of information. That Varossa was determined to kill her, to stop the line of descent. A deep frown was entrenched across her brow, as she marched back into the living room with Jason trailing behind her. She sank into the sofa and folded her arms around a pillow. Gunner climbed up beside her. "Jason, he's looking for his grandfather's body. He thinks it's hidden somewhere inside the Wingate House."

"But that would mean...Oh Jesus."

"I know. It means that Daddy did kill the man who killed Rainy Skies and Jonathan Wingate and that his body is hidden somewhere inside that house. The problem is... I can't go to the police and tell them about my vision. They'd laugh, or worse, try to have me committed."

"They might consider it." Jason's forced laugh was humorless as he looked down at her. "I've got to run my errand. I'm going over to the campus to see the University President. This is important to me. Why don't you ride along?"

"No, I'm exhausted. I'm going to take a bath and change into clean clothes."

"Promise, promise, promise you'll behave yourself. Please. Stay here and lock the doors. Don't go anywhere and don't let anyone inside this house."

Dannah rolled her eyes up at him and nodded. "Okay, I'll try."

"Do more than try, Dannah. You may think you're

independent and invincible, but you're not. You're in an extremely vulnerable position right now."

She wouldn't meet Jason's stern gaze. Instead, she wrapped her arms around Gunner's neck. "I promise. Gunner will take care of me."

"Somehow, I don't think that's the answer I'm looking for. If my career weren't at stake, I wouldn't leave. Won't you change your mind and go with me?"

"No, you go on. I'll be okay."

She watched out the window until Jason backed her car out of the driveway and left. She snatched up the car keys to the Explorer. "I've got a little errand of my own to run," she stated aloud. "Come on, Gunner. The weather's cooled off, so you can ride with me."

Chapter Nineteen
Monday evening

Bennie Varossa was shaking as he hurriedly fled Dunhill's house. His knees were rubbery, barely able to uphold his considerable weight as he staggered to his truck. His hands trembled as he struggled to separate the ignition key from the others on the ring. The engine sprang to life and he slipped the gear shift to drive. Too rattled to concentrate, he couldn't even make it to the next corner, but was forced to pull over and stop. His knee nearly gave way as he applied the brake. Unable to calm his wracking tremors, he bent his head over the steering wheel and squeezed his eyes closed. He tried to clear his mind, but unfettered images were taking control.

It was the same scenario as the one five years earlier when he first contacted Gova Wingate about putting the new metal roof on her house. When they shook hands, the old woman had held his too long, too tightly, and then there was that same shocked but knowing look in her eyes. It was as if she had peered into his soul and read his thoughts and feelings. His grandfather had met the first generation psychic, now he had met the next two generations. Their eyes told the story. Most of the time they were a rich mahogany brown, but when a connection was made, when they were employing their power, the color evolved into pure black, a seemingly endless pool of evil. The wickedness must be stopped.

Movement in the rear view mirror caught his attention. The vehicle was easy to spot with the bicycle still strapped to the roof. The driver was preoccupied and had not even glanced at his huge white pickup truck with his company name emblazoned on the door.

***

Dannah spotted her convertible parked in front of the main Administration Building, then drove on past it and to the buff-colored brick building Jason had pointed out earlier. She grabbed her empty briefcase, fluffed out her hair, and pulled her expired press card out of her wallet. She left all four windows part-way down for Gunner, then marched into Baxter's office with all the brass she could muster.

"Good afternoon," she smiled at the secretary and swiftly flashed her press card, then put it away. "I'm assistant to Pete Jordan, editor of the Memphis Commercial Appeal newspaper. I'd like to interview Professor Baxter about his work at the Chucalissa Indian site."

"What's your name?"

"Nicole Win... Winters."

"You drove down from Memphis today?"

"Yes."

"Then you haven't heard that Professor Baxter was murdered on Saturday night."

Dannah feigned shock. "Oh, no, Miss—"

"Martha Anderson."

"Oh, Miss Anderson, I'm so terribly sorry to hear that. You must be devastated."

"Yes, we were very close for a very long time. His wife has been dead for several years. No one on campus knew it, but he had just been diagnosed with lung cancer. He was due to have surgery and start chemotherapy next week." She gestured to the boxes scattered around the room. "I've been packing some of his personal belongings. I don't think I can bear to stay on."

"I guess this has been a wasted trip. I'm sorry to have disturbed you."

"No, no. Tell me exactly what you want to know."

"All about the professor's work at Chucalissa. Right now, the site is a tourist attraction and we'd like to have a little history of the place. The city is gearing up for a big advertising campaign next spring to tout all there is to do in the area for vacationers."

Martha's mood brightened and she happily launched into a long dissertation concerning her employer's talents, his accomplishments, how much he was underrated and a long list of Baxter's health problems. Dannah managed to keep the conversation going a good thirty minutes with several artfully crafted questions.

"Would you like to have a copy of his book on Chucalissa?"

"Yes I would."

"There are a few extras in the storage room. I'll be right back."

While she was gone, Dannah sat down in Baxter's chair behind his desk and soaked up several minutes of his private thoughts. She was feeling extremely satisfied with herself as she emerged from Baxter's office with new insight into the man and possible reasons for his smoldering jealousy against Jason. She didn't even feel guilty and surprised herself that she could tell such a string of lies so glibly.

The long hallway was dark as she hurried for the exit with book in hand. A pale pink haze was all that remained on the western horizon of the setting sun as she skipped down the steps toward Jason's Explorer, still packed to the hilt with her possessions. She was intent on digging the car keys from the bottom of her handbag, when Gunner began growling. Just as the dog broke into a frenzy of barking, she attempted to turn. It was too dark for a reflection in the window glass of the man behind her, but even with her eyes closed she could see a clear image of his face and knew his cruel intentions. A huge hand clamped around her mouth. She tried to scream, dropped her ring of keys, book and briefcase and began to claw at the strong bare arms encircling her.

Bennie Varossa.

—End of the line. No more psychics. No more Wingates. Find my grandfather's body. Stop the voices. Subdue the rage—

Gunner managed to angle his head and neck through the narrow window opening and clamped his powerful jaws on Varossa's wrist. The man yowled with pain, but didn't release his grip. Holding Dannah fast with one arm, he delivered a brutal slap to the side of the dog's head with the other. Pressed tightly against his body, she could feel the 9mm pistol stuffed into the waist band. In a flash, she knew with absolute clarity that it was the weapon that killed Henning and Baxter.

Keep a cool head! Don't panic! She kept those thoughts foremost in her mind as Varossa quickly wrapped silver duct tape around her mouth and wrists and threw her onto the floor of his pickup truck. Her purse still hung over her shoulder. If she could get to her cell phone, she could call for help.

Chapter Twenty
Monday evening

With a grim expression deeply burrowed into his features, Jason paced the floor of his living room. Anger and worry were at war inside his head and the battle escalated as the clock continued to tick. However, his annoyance and anxiety could not stand up to the powerful realization of how deeply his love for Dannah had grown in such a short length of time. There was no way to doubt the sincerity of his feelings for her.

"Where the hell did she go? Why didn't she leave me a note?" he muttered as he walked back and forth across the length of his living room. "And where the hell is Gunner? She doesn't know a damn soul in this town. Well, there's the banker, the realtor, Professor Krause. And she did meet Bennie Varossa. Oh Jesus, no. Surely she didn't go to his office to confront him. No, no, she wouldn't do anything so dangerous."

He looked as his watch for the twentieth time—almost seven o'clock—then rummaged through his wallet and other belongings looking for the business card with Dannah's cell phone number. He couldn't find it anywhere. The phone was probably still sitting on the console of his vehicle. "What sort of devilment could she be into?"

Finally, Jason got into Dannah's 'Vette and drove by the office of the Varossa Construction Company, then back to the University campus, where he saw his Explorer was parked in front of the Anthropology building. When he spotted his keys and Dannah's briefcase lying on the ground under the driver's side door, he broke into a cold sweat. Gunner was standing on the front seat barking, panting and obviously agitated.

When he released Gunner from the vehicle, the dog began sniffing the ground and continued barking. "Damn, she's got to be here somewhere. Gunner, find Dannah." The only trail for the dog to follow was into the office building. Jason was right behind his dog taking the stairs two at a time as Martha was exiting the main entrance. "Where is she?" Jason demanded.

"Where is who?" Martha countered with a distracted frown.

"Dannah Wingate."

"The only person I've seen is Nicole Winters from Memphis. She left almost an hour ago."

Jason pointed to the items beneath his car. "This is as far as she got." His hands were trembling as he fumbled with his cell phone and Detective Richards' business card. "Meet me on campus in front of the Anthropology building," he instructed. "And hurry. Dannah's been kidnapped." As Jason punched the end button, he saw blood droplets on the window and down the side of the driver's door. Even in the gray haze of evening, the red blood stood out plainly against the white of his vehicle. Terror raced through him.

***

"Okay, what's the big emergency?" the detective asked as he rolled out of his car.

"I told you, dammit! Dannah's been kidnapped. The only person with a grudge against her is Bennie Varossa."

"Varossa? The local contractor? Why?"

Jason took a deep breath and hurriedly explained the entire situation, including a quick description of Dannah's psychic abilities.

"Sonofabitch," Detective Richards drawled. "She thinks he murdered Henning and Baxter?"

Jason nodded. "Not just 'thinks.' She saw him do it...saw it in her mind."

"But how?"

"I'll let Dannah explain that. Look, I think she still has her purse with her and her cell phone is inside. Would it be safe to call her?"

"No. Varossa might turn it off, or worse, he could throw it away. As long as it's turned on and with her, we can get a general idea of where she is from the satellites. Wonder where in the world he would take her?"

"Back to the Wingate House," Jason stated with firm

authority.

***

From her crunched position on the floor of his pickup truck, Dannah could plainly see Varossa's face. The muscles in his jaw were alternately relaxing and tensing. She could watch the blood pumping through his carotid artery, prominent on his corded neck. The 9mm pistol was still tucked behind his belt; the extra flesh on his belly partially enveloped the weapon. As the sun began to set and his grim visage became deeply shadowed, the moments ticked into eternity. Blood actively dripped from the deep bite wound Gunner had inflicted on his right arm. She didn't need to touch him or use her psychic abilities to know what he wanted and what her ultimate Fate would be.

A narrow alley behind the double row of stately Victorian houses on Azalea and Daffodil Lanes was a leftover from the days when the trash was collected from the rear of the elegant homes. Bennie Varossa's hefty pickup truck barely fit between the lush weeds that had grown into good-sized bushes. She could hear the branches scratching the doors as he eased down the alley. He never uttered a word during the entire trip.

Varossa's hand was rough as he wrapped his strong fingers around her upper arm, dragged her across the bench seat and onto the ground. She struggled to maintain her balance. Varossa smashed his way through the broken fence and pulled her toward the rear of the Wingate House. Her purse, its strap trapped by her bound hands, had fallen from her shoulder and was spilling its contents—her wallet, sunglasses and cell phone—onto the ground.

With the onset of evening, the ancient trees in the old neighborhood and the lush green grass had blended into a deep shade of gray. Although birds had ceased singing, a dog barked somewhere in the distance.

Dannah used her moist tongue in an attempt to loosen the tape around her lips. Varossa was a bear of a man with a massive amount of strength. He kicked in the back entrance, which was nothing more than a sheet of plywood nailed in place by the cops.

Once inside the house, Varossa looked for the kitchen light and turned it on. He then ripped the silver tape away from her face, yanking several locks of hair with it. She yelped with pain.

"Shut up, bitch. You're supposed to be the new psychic in the Wingate family. Now you can tell me where my grandfather's body is. I gotta sneaking suspicion it's somewhere inside this house. That's why the old woman wouldn't let nobody in here to remodel. Where's the body? Where's the body?" he asked a second time.

"What body?" Dannah responded with all the feigned ignorance she could muster.

"You know damned well what body. My grandfather— Salvatore Varossa. I know he was murdered in this house in, in, can't remember the year. At least fifty."

Dannah's mind raced. The grandfather clock began chiming. No matter how farfetched Jason might think the explanation, she knew with full certainty that it was the angry ghost of Salvatore who caused the clock the chime. The chiming went past six, and then past twelve before finally stopping. Bennie Varossa appeared too centered on her response to notice the noisy clock.

"Answer me," he demanded.

Fearing he was going to get even more violent, she finally nodded toward the pantry. "In there. His body was buried in the root cellar. Below the pantry. But, but—" Before she could finish the sentence, he disappeared into the tiny room and found the light switch. A forty-watt bulb dangled from the high ceiling on a long wire. The boxes and cleaning supplies in the pantry began to fly through the air. "Wait a minute," she yelled. "The trap door is nailed down. You'll need some tools. I... I don't have any. You'll also need a flashlight as well. I don't think there's any light down there."

"I got a tool box in the truck." He waved his balled fist in her face. "Don't move a muscle while I'm gone."

She cowered, hoping to look helpless. Dannah's wrists were still behind her back securely taped, but her legs were free. She got to her feet and, side-stepping the huge puddle of Henning's dried blood still on the floor, awkwardly picked up the new cordless phone and, with it behind her back, managed to feel the keys well enough to punch in 911. She laid the phone on the counter and whispered into the tiny mouth piece, "Send police to 703 Azalea Lane. Back door." Then she pulled the handset into the silverware drawer and pushed it closed with her butt. She quickly returned to the floor where Varossa had put her, up against the refrigerator. A plan of action was quietly and methodically taking shape.

It took about three or four minutes for Varossa to return with his heavy tool box. She tried to calculate how long it would take the emergency operators to forward her call to a patrolman and how long it would take for a unit to get to the house and figure out that something was wrong.

Where was Jason? Was he still at the college talking to the President? Did he see Gunner and his car parked in front of Baxter's office? Has he seen her briefcase and the keys? Would he put two and two together?

Keep a cool head! Don't panic! Those were the thoughts she was mentally clinging to right now.

As Varossa rummaged through his tool box for a pry bar, Dannah hoped to slow him down with some conversation.

"Mister Varossa, how do you know that your grandfather died in this house?"

"My grandmother--his wife--found out that he was a serial killer. He talked about the psychic Indian woman who was going to help the police identify him. After he read the newspaper article, he took his hunting knife and left the house. She never saw him again. The dying wishes of both my mother and grandmother were to find his body and bury him in hallowed ground—a Catholic cemetery. I'm going to keep their wishes."

"You can't just show up at the mortuary with a fifty-year-old corpse. They would have to call the police."

"I'll bury him myself at night."

"You can't bury a murderer in hallowed ground. God wouldn't approve of that."

"If you follow the rules, God is forgiving. My grandfather

was sick...in the head."

"What about me?"

He stopped what he was doing and stared at her with a half-smile and a predatory gleam in his dark eyes. His hand moved down to his crotch. "Yeah? What about you?"

Dannah knew he planned to rape and kill her. "I haven't done anything to you."

"The power you have is evil."

Without another word, he set to work. The rusty nails didn't give up their hold on the wood without a noisy complaint. To fight panic, she counted each squeak—forty-nine, fifty, fifty-one.

"There," he grunted contentedly, and laid aside his pry bar.

The trap door was glued in place with fifty years' worth of dust, dirt, debris and floor wax. Varossa fought and finally lifted the hefty pantry floor amid the angry squeal of rusted hinges. The musty smell of mildew floated upward. Dannah pushed against the refrigerator and levered her body upright and on to her feet. As he got down on all fours and intently peered into the blackness of the root cellar, Dannah kicked him as hard as she could. Caught off balance, he tumbled head first into the gaping hole, and the trap door slammed closed on top of him. With her hands still taped behind her and her empty handbag flying in the wind, Dannah ran as fast as she could out the back door into the darkness and down the driveway toward the street. She slammed into Jason's body so hard they both fell to the ground. Almost hysterical with relief, she started babbling, "I pushed him into the root cellar. Be careful, he's got a gun."

Dannah was teetering on the brink of tears as Jason removed the tape and swooped her into his arms. He sat down on the back steps of his house with Dannah in his lap while the police rushed into the kitchen and apprehended Varossa. "I told you not to leave the house. Why did you pull such a stupid trick?"

She looked into his clear blue eyes. "Because I love you."

***

"So, here we go again," Detective Richards stated as he plopped down on the hard sofa in the living room of the Wingate House and began fumbling with his tape recorder.

"You've been here so often, I'm going to start charging you rent," Dannah replied with a caustic tone. "What can you pin on Varossa to keep him in jail?"

"Kidnapping, assault with a deadly weapon, carrying a concealed weapon, violating a crime scene. Just to name a few."

"Don't forget to take an impression of his shoes and do a ballistics test on his 9mm."

"I don't need you to tell me how to do my job, Miss Wingate."

"I'm not, but I do have access to some knowledge of the crime."

"Mister Dunhill explained that to me, but I'm not quite ready to accept it."

"You know something strange, Detective Richards? I don't know that I'm ready to accept it either. So, what did you find in the old root cellar?"

"Nothing particularly noteworthy."

"Nothing?"

"Well, some trace evidence," he responded, acting a little fidgety.

"Like what?"

"The forensic people say it looks like what might have been a considerable amount of dried blood mixed with the sandy soil, but no body. I don't know what's going on here, but Varossa keeps babbling about the body of his grandfather who disappeared fifty years ago."

"Yes, a double murder was committed in this house back in the late fifties. Professor Albert Krause collected all the old evidence. It's going to be the subject of a class this semester."

"We're going to do another interrogation after he's booked and gets his arm stitched. We'll try to get this matter cleared up."

"Don't let him cop an insanity plea. He killed both Henning and Baxter in cold blood."

The detective stood up and slipped his tape recorder into

his coat pocket. "I'll be in touch with you later. You can't stay here. The crime-scene investigators still have some work to do. Don't leave town and please leave the detective work to us."

Jason had been quiet during the entire exchange. He stood at the front door with his arm around Dannah as they watched the man leave. Dannah's shoulders sagged. "You have no idea how exhausted I am."

"Let's go get a bite of breakfast, then we'll go home to my place. I have to look after Gunner."

"Was he hurt? Varossa slapped him in the head pretty hard."

"He's okay. Gunner's tough and so are you. I don't know how you managed to keep such a cool head."

"To be truthful, I don't either. By the way, what did the University President tell you?"

"He admitted that he acted too hastily. I'm reinstated. I have my own question—what were you doing in Baxter's office?"

"I wanted to sit in the chair behind his desk and see what I could pick up. So I devised a little story to tell his secretary and she obliged me."

"What did you learn?"

"He was in a great deal of pain. Some of it emotional over a wasted life and a great deal of physical pain over his declining health. Jason, he wanted to do more research, he wanted to be out in the field with you, but his joints were wracked by arthritis. I think he was more jealous over your youth, fitness and energy than anything else."

Chapter Twenty-one
Tuesday night

She was drifting in a dreamy state—not quite asleep, but not quite awake either. A warm breath of air tickled her ear, sending little ripples of desire skittering across her skin.

"Hello, sleepy head," a deep male voice whispered.

Dannah yawned and stretched. "Hmmm, Jason. What time is it?"

"Seven," he responded.

"Seven?" She squinted her eyes toward the window. "What happened to the sunshine?"

"It's seven in the evening."

Dannah shoved him aside, sat up in bed and looked around her. "How long have you been up?"

"A couple of hours. I've already had my shower and dressed."

She was surprised to discover that she was totally nude in Jason's huge king-sized bed and hurriedly wrapped the sheet around her bare breasts. "Where are my clothes?"

"Downstairs in the living room. You sort of passed out on my sofa from lack of sleep. Couldn't wake you for hell or high water, so I undressed you and put you to bed. Although I did sleep in the same bed with you, there was no funny stuff. Honest. Well, not because I didn't try, but you wouldn't wake up. Don't you remember anything?"

"I remember that Detective Richards kept us up half the night with questions, questions and more questions."

"After he left, we went out and ate a late dinner, or maybe you could call it an early breakfast."

"Yes, I remember that. Things get fuzzy after we got home."

"You slept damn near round the clock. Richards called about noon. When they tried to interrogate Varossa a second time, he clammed up and called his attorney."

"They couldn't get a confession?"

"Nope. In fact, the lawyer posted his bond and Varossa was released."

Dannah swung her feet over the side of the bed forgetting all about her nudity. "What? He's out?"

"Sweetheart, they have to gather their evidence and present it to the District Attorney before they can swear out a warrant for murder. They have to match fingerprints, do ballistic tests. You know the routine. And it has to be done by the state crime lab. So far, there isn't a shred of evidence to connect him to the crime scene or the victims."

"What about all those other charges? Kidnapping? The concealed gun?"

"The hearing on those charges was this morning. Bail was set high, but apparently he had the money to get free. Dannah, basically Oxford is still a small town with small-town attitudes and values. Varossa is a highly respected business man. The evidence isn't in yet. This isn't the big city capable of a six-network media blitz."

"He did it. He killed Henning and Baxter."

Jason shrugged. "Unfortunately, I don't think the ravings of a fledgling psychic will count in a court of law."

"But-but, he did it," she stammered. "And I didn't feel a shred of remorse coming from that man."

"Richards said Varossa kept saying that he was looking for the body of his deceased grandfather in the root cellar. He told them about the old unsolved murder. At first, Richards didn't know about the old case."

"To be honest... I thought the body might be there. Or, what's left of it."

"No, but they did find evidence that a body might have been buried there a long time ago."

"I think the old man is somewhere inside that house."

Jason paused, then asked, "Can you think of food and murder at the same time?"

"Yes, I'm starved."

"While you take a shower, I'll fix something to eat. We can talk over coffee."

"That's a deal, but I need some clean clothes."

"I brought up a couple of your suitcases."

Her cheeks were rosy and her hair still damp when Dannah came down to the kitchen in the Dunhill House. It wasn't nearly as large as hers; however, it had been beautifully modernized. She was greeted enthusiastically by Gunner. "Is this your idea of a healthy meal? Fresh coffee with stale donuts?"

"The cops brought them last night. I can fix you a bowl of corn flakes or some scrambled eggs."

"No, I'm hungry enough to eat a cow."

"We'll go out for a steak dinner. Let me grab my car keys."

The night was cool and dark. Jason's Explorer was still full of Dannah's belongings, so they drove theCorvette. Gunner leaped between the bucket seats and into the tiny rear area.

"I'm so proud of you, Dannah. Damn, you missed your calling. You should be a homicide detective, or maybe one of those FBI profilers."

"No, I don't think I could take a steady diet of serial killers and dead bodies. I'm proud of Gunner." Dannah rubbed his sleek neck with both hands and accepted a face full of kisses. "He did his best to protect me. If I had lowered the window a little more, he would have jumped out and attacked Varossa. That man must have a serious wound on his wrist."

Jason nodded.

"When can I get back into my house?"

"It's been released. While you were sleeping, Richards sent over a crew specializing in hazardous materials. Hazmat. Henning was an IV drug user and his blood could have been carrying the HIV virus, hepatitis, whatever. The Wingate House is all clean and awaiting her new owner."

"The answer to this mystery lies somewhere inside, but, first, we've got to find Gova's diary. The last thing she wrote before she died was 'read the last page.'"

"After we eat, then...we'll search the house."

"Jason, I know you can't comprehend my motives," she said with a small catch in her voice.

"Believe me, I'm trying."

"I have to know if my dad really did kill Salvatore Varossa."

***

Against the moonless sky, the old Wingate House took on a sinister air. Not a single light was burning. The tall structure looked like something from a medieval castle, or maybe a Stephen King novel. The three-story peaked roof of the turret disappeared into the dreary night sky. The dark red bricks with their gray painted trim melted into the night. There was a hint of fall in the air. The crisp, cool feel of night air infiltrated the thin cotton fabric of Dannah's tee shirt. She was happy to have Jason by her side and was ready to face the fact that she had truly fallen in love with him.

Jason retrieved the set of keys from Dannah's purse. Because the police had replaced the sheet of plywood across the opening of the back door, they went around to the front. He entered first as Dannah hung back on the threshold, holding on to Gunner's collar until the reassuring wash of light spilled into the entry hall. Dannah tried not to look to her right, but her line of vision was irresistibly drawn to the old wooden rocking chair in the far corner of the living room.

Dammit! I don't need this hassle right now. I'm going to nail the rockers to the floor, she thought grimly.

They made their way back into the kitchen turning on lights along the way. Of course, both bodies were gone. The place smelled of bleach and ammonia. The trap door to the pantry was closed. Everything looked so deceivingly normal. She released the dog.

"Where do you think we might find her diary?" Jason asked as he placed his left hand on the back of Dannah's neck, weaving his fingers in her thick black curls.

"Judging from my own experience with diaries when I was a kid, I say it's either in her den or her bedroom. She wouldn't have to hide it because she lived alone. I kept mine under the mattress so my dad wouldn't find it."

A thirty-minute search of the bookshelves and end tables

revealed nothing. "We can't give up yet." Dannah finally sagged into the big, over-stuffed chair in front of the TV. Her hand idly reached for Gova's fancy work placed casually in a large basket to the left of the chair. She lifted the fabric and rubbed the delicate embroidered stitches with her fingertips. Suddenly, the knowledge came to her in a brilliant flash. The small diary with a picture tucked inside lay at the bottom of the basket. "Ooooh, I found something. It's the diary." A picture of Dannah—about age ten— and her mother and father looking much too formal, was tucked between the pages. Della Taylor Wingate had been a beautiful young woman, and Dannah idly wondered what had attracted her to Coleman. Yes, he was handsome when young, but even then, there was no hint of a smile on his face. She hurriedly flipped through the pages of entries to get to the last sheet. She read aloud.

Dannah, my dearest niece. If you're reading this, it means that both me and my brother are dead and gone. It also means that The Power has come to you.

Use is wisely, use it sparingly, and never begrudge it.

Although Coalie wouldn't agree with me, I think you should know the truth about what happened in this house that April so long ago. Go to the third floor. The front stairwell has been removed, but you can break the lock at the back of the storage room on the second floor. All the answers lie up there. Sweet girl, there is so much I wanted to explain about The Power, but Coalie refused to let me see you.

Love, your Aunt Gova.

When the tears fell, Dannah quickly wiped them away. "Let's go to the third floor."

"How do we get there?"

"We'll need the bolt cutters, a flashlight, and maybe an ax. Come on and I'll show you." Jason followed Dannah up the front stairwell to the midway landing. "If you look at the layout, you can see where the staircase once existed. It was removed and the ceiling boarded up. You can also see where the paint and the newer hardwood flooring don't match. The servants' stairs up to the third floor are behind the storage room at the far end of the hall and the door is securely padlocked." When Dannah reached the mysterious room, she placed her hand on the knob. The door opened a little more freely this time.

Once again, she felt the cold and the danger, and glanced at Jason to see if he sensed it as well. His expression was benign. She entered the dark and forbidding area and found the dangling light bulb. The room was as she remembered—the old lamps and furniture. "There's the door," she said, pointing toward the back of the room.

"I think your bolt cutters will do the trick. The lock looks old and rusty."

Gunner scratched at the door and whined as Jason struggled to break the lock. Finally, he forced the door open. The narrow staircase was draped in cobwebs. Dannah tried the light switch, but nothing happened. Squeezing past them, Gunner darted up the dark passage and within a couple of seconds began barking furiously.

"Let me go first with the flashlight, Dannah. You stay behind me. Come back here, boy. Settle down. Damn, he knows there's something up there."

"Yes, I can feel it too" she muttered.

Dannah lifted her gaze to study the narrow stairwell. The dark walls seemed to swallow the light. Each riser groaned as it reluctantly accepted their weight. There were two bedrooms, one bath, and a sitting area in the turret on this third floor. It was obvious from the decor that the first room belonged to Gova, who must have been a preteen with dolls and cheerleader pompoms. The bathroom fixtures were in bad shape after fifty years of neglect. She tried several other light switches as they searched, but none worked. Gunner was clawing at the opening to the second bedroom, which was blocked by a dozen or more hefty one-by-eights.

"Whoever put up these boards, didn't want them taken down." Jason groaned and grunted as he spent another thirty minutes prying each of the boards free.

When there was an opening large enough to accommodate his body, Gunner wiggled through the space, raced over to a bed and continued yapping. In the murky darkness, Dannah could tell by the decor that the room had belonged to Coleman—who had played on the high-school baseball team. A smell, a subtle musky hint of decay harassed her nostrils.

The narrow beam of Jason's flashlight swept across the room. Dannah screamed. Jason ordered Gunner to come and sit beside him.

Lying neatly on a narrow bed was a fully articulated skeleton, the bony fingers of one hand splayed out on top of an old, leather-bound journal, while the other hand loosely clutched the brass weight from the old grandfather clock.

"Jesus H. Christ. Another body."

Chapter Twenty-two
Oxford, Mississippi

"I guess we better call the cops... again."

"No, not yet. Let me read this diary first. They'll probably take it away as evidence." Dannah gingerly lifted the bony hand, removed the small journal and began to thumb through the pages. "Gova must have written this when she was much younger. The handwriting is very good."

They sat down on the floor beside the bed and Jason angled the flashlight so Dannah could read. Gunner curled up beside them, but kept his eyes glued to the skeleton, as if he thought it might rise up. As she read Gova's journal aloud, the scene unfolded in stark reality.

It was mid-April and I was in my bedroom on the third floor doing my school work when there was a tap on my bedroom door.

"Gova? Did you hear a noise?"

"No, I didn't hear anything."

Coleman scowled at me, but I always ignored him. "Well, it sounded sort of like a scream or somethin' like that. I'm goin' downstairs to see."

"Coalie, Mama told us we couldn't leave our rooms until we finished studying for our final exams next week." By the way, he hated his nickname. I called him that just to make him mad.

"Don't care."

He was a stubborn kid. "You're not leaving me behind. I'm coming, too."

"We'll go down the back stairs to the kitchen. Be quiet," he ordered.

I was right behind Coalie as we crept down the steps. I never heard such sounds before. Guttural groans that seemed to be rising up from Hell. He cracked the door and peeked in. The brutal, bloody sight was playing out in front of my eyes. That split second was forever burned into my mind. Coalie was an inexperienced sixteen, and I was only twelve. A large man was bent over our parents. Mama was face up, her arms splayed out, lying on top of Dad who was face down on the floor. Blood was everywhere. Mama was still making some funny sounds, but didn't have the strength to fight the man who just kept stabbing her and stabbing her. It was like something out of a horror movie.

We both saw a large butcher knife sitting on the edge of the stove. Without a moment of hesitation, Coalie tiptoed into the room and picked it up. Grasping the handle with both hands, he plunged it with all the strength he could muster into the back of our parents' murderer. The man uttered a slight gasp of surprise. First, he tried to turn around, but slumped on top of Mama and Dad, then rolled over to one side onto his back.

I was too shocked to cry or make a sound. All I could do was watch. Coalie stood there still holding the bloody knife. The room was deathly quiet, only some raspy sounds coming from the stranger as he breathed his last. Coalie leaned over to look into his face. His eyes were open. All of a sudden, his hand snaked out and grabbed Coalie's wrist, then he gurgled and died.

I screamed, then the old clock started chiming. It was six o'clock.

We looked in his wallet. His name was Salvatore Varossa. Mama had only told me a little about The Power as I was growing up. I knew it was supposed to come to me when Mama passed on, but I thought I'd be grown up—not twelve years old. When I touched the dead man, I knew he'd killed all those little children. Mama was going down to the police station the very next morning to try to use her psychic powers to identify him.

Neither me nor Coalie knew what to do. I wanted to call the police, but Coalie said no. Finally, we dragged the body to the root cellar. We buried him, then nailed the trap door closed. While I cleaned up everything in the kitchen, Coalie just sat there on the floor rocking back and forth and staring into space. I tried and tried to convince him to call the police, say it was self-defense, but he wouldn't let me. He was afraid the police would think he killed all three of them. Of course, that was stupid. He made me wait until morning before making the phone call. He made me lie and tell them we didn't hear anything because we were way upstairs on the third floor. I was just a little girl. I didn't know I should have disobeyed him.

Because Coalie and I were still minors, the executors of Mama and Dad's estate hired a nanny-housekeeper to live with us. Coalie called her "our jailer." She was supposed to stay until Coalie turned twenty-one, but we went back to court to have the nanny removed when he was eighteen, saying that Coalie was plenty old enough to look after us. Besides, I was able to take care of the house and cooking. The bank took care of all our expenses and gave us a weekly allowance.

Eventually—I think it was three years later—after we got rid of the nanny, we hauled the body upstairs to the third floor, boarded up all the windows, removed the third floor stairs and padlocked the doors in the servants' stairwell. Coalie kept the keys.

He got mad at me because of my visions. Couldn't tell him anything or he'd fly into a rage. He wouldn't touch Dad's money— thought it was cursed. Wouldn't go to college. When our father, Jonathan Wingate married Rainy Skies, our grandfather disinherited him. Said he didn't want Indian blood mingling with the royal blood of England. But the yellow fever took both Holcomb Wingate and his wife Bethaloma. We were so young. I don't even remember our grandparents. Since our dad was an only child, the money came to him anyway.

I think Coalie was always ashamed of our Indian heritage, mostly because Mama had The Power. She liked to wear her traditional leather clothing around the house, and—unless she went out—was always barefooted. Sometimes, when she would chant a song, Coalie would get so mad he would stick his fingers in his ears so he wouldn't have to listen. She used to sit in the rocking chair in the living room and tell us stories about when she was a little girl. Mama also took me to the reservation once a month to visit her father up until he died. Coalie wouldn't go.

Coalie didn't carry his guilt very well, even though I kept telling him it was self-defense.

When Coalie turned twenty-one, he left and moved to Memphis. I rarely heard anything out of him after that. Only a

*letter now and then when he occasionally needed extra money,
then again when you, Dannah Nicole, were ready to go to college.
I was happy to pay your tuition. You are the only family left.*

*Coalie never did understand or seemed to care what I had
to give up to protect him. He told me I couldn't let anyone inside
this house. Things would have been different if Michael Duncan
had lived. My life would have been much better. We were engaged
to be married when he got home from Vietnam, but he was killed in
the war. I planned on telling Michael what Coalie had done, then
going to the police. Yes, I would have done it for Michael. I don't
think your father would have gone to jail, but it was something I
worried about.*

*Dannah, The Power is a magical thing once you learn
how to control it and not let it control you. You won't be able to
read the future such as predict the winner of the World Series.
Modern day psychics call it "Touch Telepathy," but it extends
farther than that. Yes, you'll be able to feel strong emotion when
you touch something or someone, but it's the dreams I always
found most bothersome.*

*There were times when I thought I might want to help the
police solve some crimes and missing persons cases, but the
memory of what happened to my parents was just too strong to
overcome.*

Be very careful how you use The Power.

*There have been two ghosts in the house. One of them is
Salvatore Varossa. He's Old-World Catholic and angry because
he didn't have a proper funeral and burial. I'm sure once this is
taken care of, that his soul can be put to rest. Mama is the other
ghost. I think it's because she never had the chance to fully explain
things to me, and now, sadly, I've never had the chance to explain
things to you. Be happy.*

Dannah closed the diary and let it slip into her lap. "Well,
that's a great deal to be digested all at once."

"Yes, but it answers most of your questions. And, we
found the missing weight for the old clock. It'll run properly now."
Jason stood up and extended his hand to Dannah to lift her from
the floor. "Let's go downstairs and call the police."

Gunner had come to attention, striking that now familiar and regal pose when he was straining to separate ordinary sounds from the unusual. He began to growl, the rumble growing louder.

"So, here you are." The voice and jerky path of a second flashlight announced the shocking presence of another person.

Jason swung his body around to face the door, his flashlight following the swing of his body. The circle of yellow glinted on a pistol and the contorted face of Bennie Varossa. The scene played out within the confines of Dannah's startled scream. The sleek body of the valiant Doberman Pincher arched through the swath of light with his mouth agape, aimed at the gun. The shot rang through the silence of the darkened rooms on the third floor.

Chapter Twenty-three
Wednesday morning

The sky had barely turned pink with dawn as Detective Richards pulled onto the crumbling concrete driveway. His weariness was obvious as he rolled out of his vehicle clutching a styrofoam coffee cup and a bag of donuts. "Don't you people ever sleep?" he asked, obviously grumpy from lack of rest. "What now?"

"Well," Jason began, not bothering to get up from his chair. "The EMS crew just left with Bennie Varossa. He was bitten a few times, then fell down a flight of stairs. He might have a broken arm as well. And...we also have another dead body."

"Not exactly a body," Dannah added from her spot on the floor.

"If it's not a body, then what am I doing here for a simple assault?"

"Come on upstairs and I'll show you." Dannah led the way with Detective Richards trailing behind her.

Richards twitched his nose against the musty smell. "Whoa. Guess we'll have to call in a forensic anthropologist for this victim. I don't know how we're going to identify him."

"We know who he is. He's Salvatore Varossa, Bennie's grandfather. His wallet is in his pocket. Oh, and there's a bullet hole in the floor. I think Varossa was trying to kills us, but Gunner got to him first. This dog is amazing."

Richards backed out of the area and returned to the living room. He sat down, pulled out his little tape recorder, pencil and paper. "Okay, let's start at the beginning."

The sun had fully risen by the time Richards finally finished questioning them and the coroner had rolled the bagged body out the front door. "This one will be for the textbooks. Of course, two murder charges will be filed against Varossa, as well as an attempted murder, kidnapping, et cetera, et cetera." He put away his things and stood up. He cast a glance at Jason. "How are you going to keep this woman out of trouble?"

"Guess I'll have to marry her."

Richards delivered a rare smile. "You don't need to show me to the door. I know the way out." A few seconds later, Richards called out. "Hey, your cat wants in."

"We don't own a cat," Jason responded as he unfolded himself from the sofa.

Gunner was lying on his back thoroughly enjoying himself as Dannah scratched his belly. When a large Siamese cat strolled into the living room with her head and tail held high, Gunner scrambled to upright himself. As the two animals faced off, Jason and Dannah held their breath, both fearing an all-out fight. The cat began to purr, rubbed against Gunner's leg, then jumped into the rocking chair and began to groom herself. It was impossible to determine who was more surprised—humans or canine.

Jason stared at the cat, then gave Dannah a stern look. "Is this one of your relatives?"

She shrugged. "Maybe. I guess we could name her 'Aunt Gova.'"

SHARLEEN JOHNSON RHINOCK

…has been writing for several years and has published novels in three different genres, including historical, cozy mystery and romantic suspense. After the death of their much-loved Norwich Terrier, Sharleen and her husband, Joseph Rhinock, have become cat people. They own two black and white domestic shorthairs, often called "Tuxedo" kitties.

Her interests are still gardening, genealogy, casino blackjack and every sort of craft known to humanity. She especially enjoys helping new writers learn the mysteries of the craft. Lately, she's been devoting a great deal of time and effort into healthy eating and healthy living.

Please visit her Facebook page and her website for the latest news.